DESTINED TO THE REAPER

The Shadow Realms

REGINE ABEL

CONTENTS

Could she give him her soul?

Determined to free her brother from the clutches of an evil necromancer, Kali enters into an improbable agreement with Pharos, an Angel of Death. Behind his cold and intimidating appearance, she discovers a kind, selfless, and protective male who fascinates her. She would blindly follow Pharos into the deepest pits of Hell. But the cost for his aid is Kali's soul, and that seems too steep a price.

For half a millennium, Pharos wasted away, enslaved by the necromancer who appropriated his powers to pursue reckless ambitions. Today, the stunning Blood Mage whose pure soul enthralled him turns out to be the key to his redemption. Kali is strong, dauntless, and loyal to her very core. The bride he awaited his entire life…

As the confrontation with their nemesis escalates, the possessiveness Kali awakens in Pharos further fuels his need to protect her. How can he do so when she denies him the one thing that will save her life?

DEDICATION

To those who do not let cruelty, hardships, and the seemingly endless unfairness of life cast them into the downward spiral of bitterness. Do not let anything or anyone dim your light, steal your joy, or crush your ability to hope. When you least expect it but need it the most, it is that very inner light that will guide you out of the darkness.

To those who understand the distinction between healthy ambition and reckless greed. If the pursuit of your dreams requires the destruction and trampling of others, then you need better goals.

To family. It is not the woman scorned you should fear, but a mother's wrath.

CHAPTER 1
PHAROS

A familiar rage simmered deep within me as Cornelius took malicious pleasure abusing yet another poor sod. The elder necromancer thrived on throwing his power around, crushing those weaker, and reminding them that they were beneath him and only lived by his mercy. In many ways, it was true. Worse still, he only wielded such tremendous control over life and death thanks to the powers I had unwittingly bestowed upon him.

Hermes, a petty trader way past his prime, shrank in on himself as Cornelius showered him with a plethora of insults. Bony, with withered skin heavily tanned by frequent exposure to the sun and the elements, the older male clutched the canvas fabric upon which sat the source of the necromancer's ire with both hands.

"Do you take me for a fool, you wretched scum?" Cornelius hissed. "Did you really think you could pass off this trash as a manticore bone?"

"It... it does come from a man... manticore," Hermes stuttered.

Even trapped as I was inside the necromancer's body, I could access all his senses. And right now, the acrid stench of the old man's terror permeated the room.

With a single flick of his hand, Cornelius invoked his Bone Magic to snap the man's wrist. Hermes shrieked, his knees buckling as he held his damaged arm pressed against his chest. If not for the dirty counter he partially leaned on for support, he would have collapsed onto the dust covered wooden floor of his shop.

Then again, calling this pigsty a shop was overly generous. The small rectangular room would qualify more as a storage area or warehouse. Boxes and crates haphazardly positioned alongside the walls, and a few more piled in the center contained the devil only knew what. Half of them were contraband, counterfeits, or cheap alternatives to premium reagents the various mages and dark art practitioners of the city required. Dust and cobwebs claimed ownership of the goods that had never found any takers. Why he hadn't gotten rid of them by now boggled my mind. But then, what else would one expect from a hoarder?

The shop possessed a single other room at the back that served as both Hermes's office and residence. A moldy brown curtain left wide open hid nothing of the just as disastrous space. A cot with a soiled mattress occupied the left corner of the back room. The gray blankets covered in yellowish stains had once boasted a pristine white color. The toilet and sink sat next to a small wood stove which he used both to cook and heat the room during chilly winter days. It expressed all one needed to know about the old trader's understanding of basic hygiene. As did the total absence of a bath or shower.

The old man's blubbering pleas utterly failed to mollify Cornelius. Why in the nine hells would he have assumed it might? My host—although jailer would be a more appropriate term—had no sense of compassion or empathy. To him, everything and everyone was merely another tool to help him achieve greater power.

"Lie to me again, and the pain you feel right now will be but a gentle tap in comparison to what I will do to you next," Cornelius warned in a dangerously low voice. "Where are the manticore bones I requested?"

Eyes bloodshot—likely due to an overindulgence in hard liquor—Hermes blinked away the tears trying to well in his eyes as he sniffed back the snot glistening at the edge of his veiny, bulbous nose.

"I swear I didn't try to trick you, Master Cornelius," Hermes said in a shaky voice. "I searched high and low for what you requested. The hunter from whom I acquired this swore it came from the offspring of a manticore."

"Sired on some random lesser other creature, you worthless toad!" Cornelius spat. "I need a pureblood, not some fucking mutt!"

"I'm sorry, Master. I thought it wouldn't matter…" Hermes said, his hand tightening beneath his damaged wrist where the skin had begun darkening as the broken bone pressed against it, as if attempting to pierce through. "I will set out again and find a pureblood this time."

"All Hallows is almost upon us, you wretch. I gave you strict instructions, and you yet again failed me. You have nine days to make this right."

"Nine days is impossible!" Hermes exclaimed with a crestfallen expression.

"Nine days!" Cornelius shouted. "And here's a little incentive."

Another wave of fury surged within me as the necromancer invoked my plague powers to initiate necrosis at the tip of the fingers of the same hand with a broken wrist. Hermes cried out as his nails darkened. The spell had been of low intensity, which made it even crueler.

"For every hour and every day you make me wait, the necrosis will spread," Cornelius said with pure malevolence.

"Deliver it in time, and I might consider reverting some of the damage. Fail me again, and we'll see how well you will take to a mechanical hand instead."

Ignoring the trader's begging and pleading, Cornelius stormed out of the shop, leaving the door wide open. The wave of fresh air that hit us did little to wipe away the lingering stench of old sweat, dirt, and rot from Hermes's place. It also did nothing to appease the fury raging inside me. Despite hiding those sentiments from my host, he knew exactly how his actions affected me, and he reveled in it. Even now, his entire foul being vibrated with smug cruelty. He loved reminding me that he owned me, that he could use my powers however he saw fit, and that my self-righteous indignation would only backfire against those I wished to protect.

I could count the extremely rare times I had used my plague powers against mortals. It was not something I enjoyed. For centuries, I dedicated my reaping abilities to easing the passage of the dying into the afterlife in the gentlest fashion possible, only reserving the most brutal approach to fiends and truly malicious people. To see my powers thus desecrated was an even greater torment than the loss of my freedom.

I immediately cast out those somber thoughts. Dwelling on the miserable fate that befell me would only send me further down the spiral of despair that constantly skirted at the edge of what was left of me.

As much as the pain Hermes would suffer over the next couple of weeks saddened me, I couldn't help but rejoice that Cornelius had not received what he had been hoping for. I didn't know what new evil plot he had in mind. The necromancer had been unusually secretive with me of late. Just like I could block my thoughts from him, he could block his from me. Most of the time, he took immense pleasure in making a display of informing me of his latest scheme for the mere pleasure of getting a rise out of me. That he didn't want me to know meant he was up to something dreadful that would have long-lasting and maybe even catastrophic effects on a large segment of the population.

Despite being his prisoner, I had some limited ways of thwarting or messing up his plans when they were too extreme. I didn't know what he wanted with a manticore's bones. Although long-lived and an adept magic user, I never dabbled in the arcane arts, let alone in the type of dark magic Cornelius loved. In the past 498 years as his coerced servant, I'd learned far more about it than I cared to. I only knew that bones and organs of those mythical creatures could be used for the type of rituals no one but the most powerful arcane users could hope to successfully accomplish and live to reap the rewards.

As was common, the countless passersby along the wide streets of the district immediately swerved away from us, giving Cornelius a wide berth. Saying people feared him would be quite the understatement. Everyone knew of his great wealth and the ruthlessness with which he leveraged it to bend others to his will. Much fewer knew of the darker dealings he was involved in. But all understood that steering clear of him and avoiding his notice was the safest way to go.

Over the years, the citizens of Willow Grove grew to embrace witches and peddlers of assorted services related to the occult. The arcane practitioners repelling the demonic hordes that had threatened the small town they used to be certainly played a large part in that. And yet, the locals still deluded them-selves into thinking that monsters only lurked in dark forests and cursed lands.

If only they knew how many demons, vampires, doppel-gangers, and countless otherworldly beings walked alongside them daily, they would lose their minds.

With All Hallowtide only a few days away, an even greater number of shadowy beings flocked to the city. As the citizens of

Willow Grove observed the ancient tradition of Souling and Guising, beings from the netherworld would be able to strut about in their true form. Not only would they do so without raising much suspicion, but they'd also likely earn tremendous praise instead for the realism of their costumes.

More and more cities and counties constrained the celebration to All Hallows Eve on October 31st. Some included All Saints Day—or All Hallows Day as many still called it—on November 1st. But we included All Souls Day on November 2nd.

For the children, it was a wonderful form of entertainment. Not only did they get to wear disguises, roam the streets after sunset, and be welcomed to come knock on the door of nobility and the wealthiest, but they also got to beg for food which was to be given unquestionably. For the poor, it was a chance at a full belly with something better than scraps or moldy leftovers. They could also beg for money instead without being sent away with a boot in the rear. In exchange for such bounty, they merely had to pray for the souls of the people they visited as well as those of their dead relatives, and to help ward off evil.

But adepts of the dark arts understood the true importance of those prayers. They genuinely helped ward off the increased presence of the foul beings hiding in plain sight during those three days. For that reason, the mages and sorcerers didn't object when the church started encouraging the people to give a tasty pastry called soul cakes to the visitors instead of leaving food and wine for the wandering spirits over that period. Contrary to old beliefs, such Pagan offerings didn't sate and send those spirits away but lured even more of them to the city.

A mesmerizing light ahead cast out all such wandering thoughts.

Conflicting emotions swirled within me at the sight of Kali Jenkins by our carriage. Like most necromancers, she tended to dress in dark colors. Where Cornelius loved black, Kali had a thing for dark shades of red, purple, and occasionally green. This time, a deep burgundy cinched dress flattered the delightful curves of her slender body, with a narrow waist that flared into a voluptuous rump begging to be grabbed, perky breasts perfect to fit a possessive palm, a long neck made to welcome thirsty fangs, an angelic face whose innocent appearance hid the hot vixen that lurked beneath, and plump lips made to swallow a man's thick c—

"Fuck you, Cornelius!" I hissed once I realized such foul and lecherous thoughts actually emanated from him.

I had many thoughts about Kali, some of them covetous, but never in such a disrespectful manner.

He chuckled maliciously, making the people nearby glance at him with an even more disturbed expression. Nobody knew of my existence, not even his apprentices. Only he could hear me, no matter how loudly I shouted. On rare occasions, if I or circumstances made him sufficiently angry, people could get a glimpse of my presence within him looking as if a demonic creature were trying to push out of him from under his skin.

Abusing Kali was but one of the many ways in which he enjoyed tormenting me. From the first time I'd laid eyes on her four years ago, I'd been enthralled by the beauty of her soul. In my wonder, I'd been too slow hiding my emotions. As a man whore, Cornelius would have naturally pursued her just to add another notch to his belt as she was an attractive woman. But knowing she had piqued my interest suddenly made her a challenge to conquer… and destroy.

In many ways, I felt responsible for the woes that now tortured her. If not for Cornelius's constant desire to hurt me, he would have quickly tired of the chase after Kali first turned him down. But the thought of defiling the one female to have prompted such a strong reaction from me in centuries was too good for him to pass up.

Even with the sorrow on her face, Kali looked stunning as she apologized to her brother—our coach driver. Every time I witnessed this, it further broke my heart. Jasper, her older fraternal twin, had begged Cornelius for an apprenticeship with him. Although his sister had tagged along, it had been more in the capacity of an advisor and not out of any personal desire to also become one of his pupils. Every year, hundreds of aspiring candidates came groveling for a position with one of the most powerful necromancers of our era, if not of the past few generations.

The moment the siblings stepped into his study, Cornelius knew he had no use for her brother, other than as a means to an end. His shock when she declined his invitation for them to join as a pair quickly shifted into an anger filled with malicious determination. No one refused him. He would not only humble her, but also make her suffer and rue every single day she denied him what he deemed rightfully his. And should she ever surrender—which to him was inevitable—he intended to make her pay a thousandfold for each moment she delayed.

And he did so by turning her brother into an undead servant. While Jasper would never have become a particularly powerful necromancer in his own right, had he not let excessive ambition blind him, he could have made a decent living from his profession and achieved respectable levels. If not for Cornelius's sick need for retaliation and obsession with punishing Kali, he would have simply rejected Jasper's request and sent him on his way.

Instead, Jasper was now standing in a decaying corpse, staring off in the distance while his sister spoke gently to him. His mind wasn't gone… not fully. He could still feel pain, sorrow, and regret. He could hear and comprehend most of the words she spoke to him. He simply couldn't respond.

To the rest of the world, Jasper looked like a dashing, elegantly dressed young man stoically awaiting the return of his employer by his carriage. The stern glances the crowd leveled on Kali confirmed they interpreted the scene as him staring away from the strange woman who wouldn't stop harassing him with her unwanted attentions.

While Kali's attire was the proper level of demure not to have her pegged as a sex worker, people probably assumed her to be a social climber attempting to use her womanly wiles to ensnare a handsome young man with a stable, well-paid position. As she only recently moved into the city, merely renting a small house near the Fey Woods, the locals didn't know of the blood bond that linked them.

Appearances could be so utterly deceiving, especially when helped by a glamour spell like the one that hid Jasper's true appearance or the fact that two skeletal horses were pulling that carriage.

"I will never give up on you, brother," Kali said in a pained voice. "I know you can't respond, but I also know that you hear me. Please don't despair. Just hang in there a little longer."

"My beautiful Kali," Cornelius said in a sickeningly purring tone. "How nice of you to come pay a visit to your brother. Or should I be so bold and assume it is my delightful presence you seek?"

By the way her body stiffened, and her head jerked around to look at us over her shoulder, Kali had been too focused on her twin to notice our approach.

The instant anger and disgust that flicked over her features— quickly hidden—gave me no small amount of pleasure. Too many females fell for Cornelius's mysterious charm. Tall and lithe, he had the pale skin and androgynous charm common to vampires, although he wasn't one himself. Piercing blue eyes with thick lashes peered out of his oval face framed by a curtain of long, black, wavy hair.

He quirked his lips in that obnoxious way he considered seductive as he tilted his head to the side to give her a slow once over. Feet slightly spread in a position he deemed manly, he rested both hands on top of the skull pommel of his walking stick in front of him. He didn't need it. His wide range of magic made sure to keep his body young and flawless. He just liked the style… not to mention the lethal blade hidden within, laced with deadly poison.

"Cornelius," Kali said in greeting with that delightfully throaty voice of hers.

She flicked her long, straight black hair over her shoulder as she turned to face him. It had been months since she last came to Willow Grove. I didn't know what she'd been up to during that time, but her power had undeniably grown. To my relief, I perceived no sliminess emanating from her aura, as was normally the case when someone quickly acquired new powers through morally questionable means.

Despite the politely neutral expression on her face, the hatred burning in her obsidian eyes couldn't be mistaken. Even though it wasn't aimed at me, it still stung to have her stare in my direction with such animosity. The darker shade her soul systematically took in his presence also saddened me. I felt bereft of its otherwise enticing light.

"It is normal for a sister to want to visit with her fraternal twin," she continued in a neutral tone. "But I also wanted to see you."

Cornelius immediately emitted a purring sound that whipped my anger and irrational possessiveness of the young woman into a frenzy. His delighted reaction revealed the fact that I had betrayed my emotions, which I quickly silenced.

"Ah! I knew you'd finally come to your senses and reciprocate my affections," he said in the most disgustingly suave fashion.

Once again, Kali clamped down on how repulsive she found him and waved a dismissive hand. "While your attentions flatter me, I am not looking for any type of relationship. All that matters to me is my brother and granting him peace. I want to discuss you releasing him."

He opened his eyes in an exaggerated display of shock and surprise. "Release him! Why would I let go of such a well-trained pet? You should be happy I've provided him with steady and reliable employment. In these tough economic times—"

"That's not employment, that's slavery!" Kali snapped, dropping any pretense of civility. "He is rotting on his feet! However he wronged you, it's been four years. He's suffered enough. He's been punished enough."

"No, my beauty. It is never enough," Cornelius said in a dangerously low voice. "Anyone who crosses me will feel my wrath. Mercy does not exist in my vocabulary."

"By the Gods, what the fuck do you want?! Surely there's something I can get you in exchange for his freedom?" Kali asked in a pleading voice laced with a mix of anger and despair.

I hated seeing her like this. I hated that my powers and my attraction to her had played a part in causing her this pain. And above all, I hated how helpless I was to fix any of it.

Cornelius took a step forward, invading her personal space. She immediately took a step back to restore the distance between them.

"You know what I want, Kali. Serve me in all ways, and I'll release him."

"Never!" she spat out. "He made that mistake, and see where that left him?"

"Jasper is weak," Cornelius said in a dismissive fashion. "Your power was always greater than his was or ever could be. I could make you legendary. Even now I can sense how much your powers have grown since our last encounter."

"I don't need power. I never craved it. All I want is for my brother to be free. All those who have served you met a very unpleasant fate. I will not be your next zombie," she replied angrily.

He shrugged. "Be loyal to me, and you'll have nothing to fear. Like you said so well yourself, you do not crave power.

They did, and their greed was their undoing. Serve me, and I'll show you things you never even thought possible."

"Fuck that!" she snarled.

"Oh, my darling, that's obviously part of the deal," he purred, stirring another wave of fury deep within me.

"The only way you'll ever have me will be my cold dead body," Kali hissed.

Cornelius snorted, both amused by my anger and her comment. "Are you threatening me with a good time, my dear? Dead or alive is all the same to me. Willing or not, you *will* serve me, Kali. And when I fuck that tight cunt of yours, I'll make you beg me for forgiveness for ever denying me."

"Fuck you, you twisted psycho!" Kali shouted before spitting on the ground.

It hadn't touched him, but I felt the cold anger rising within him to have been thus disrespected. My heart sank as I awaited what would follow. The air rippled around us as he summoned an illusion. No one walking past us along the street would see what truly was happening. To them, there would only be a carriage with Jasper standing at the ready while a mysterious young woman discussed with his employer.

"Jasper, your sister dropped something. We cannot allow the beautiful streets of our city to be sullied like this," Cornelius said in a sickly-sweet voice, his eyes locked with Kali's with a cruel glint as he spoke. "Be a good boy and lick it off."

Kali slapped a hand over her mouth, and tears welled in her eyes as she stared in horror as her brother—or what remained of him—got down on his knees to comply with the order. I could barely repress the cold fury threatening to overwhelm me. I wanted to lash at him, but it would only further infuriate him. In turn, he would find more disgusting ways of taking it out on her.

"I will kill you for this," Kali whispered, her voice burning with hatred.

"You're welcome to try, my love. I'll eagerly await your challenge," Cornelius said smugly.

After one final guilty look at her brother, who was now slowly getting back onto his feet, she stormed off, shattering the illusion.

I watched her walk away, feeling defeated.

CHAPTER 2
KALI

Angry tears pricked my eyes as I stomped my feet on the way to my horse. Guilt, rage, and a sense of renewed determination slapped aside the debilitating helplessness that always attempted to rear its head whenever I thought of Jasper's situation.

He'd been such a handsome man before he allowed his greed and thirst for power to be his downfall. As I got on my horse, I glanced at the necromancer's carriage traipsing past me. Many of the women nearby cast less-than-subtle appreciative glances at my brother, fooled by the glamour spell that hid the rotting corpse he had become beneath the pretty illusion.

I shifted my vision back to normal so that I, too, could enjoy one last look at him in his former glory. While Jasper was physically as light as I was dark, our personalities were the exact opposite. His shoulder length blonde locks gently swayed in the wind, exposing his fair skin, and striking blue eyes. Like Cornelius, my brother was lithe with a slightly androgynous beauty.

He'd shamelessly used seduction to get what he wanted from men and women alike. As my brother had been attracted to all genders, nothing was ever out of bounds or too outrageous for him, especially if it got him ahead.

As I began the long ride to the one person who might help me put an end to Cornelius, I once more berated myself for not having been firmer with my brother when he first entertained working for him. I'd always been too weak when it came to Jasper. Although he'd been the eldest, I'd been the mature one and the voice of reason. But his hunger for power superseded everything.

I deluded myself that he would soon realize what an abusive monster he had chosen as mentor. I knew men like Cornelius well. To them, people were just expendable tools, puppets to be used to further their ends. But instead of realizing his mistake and cutting his losses by leaving, Jasper attempted to take for himself what his master withheld from him.

He was so stupid, snooping around Cornelius's forbidden library, skimming off the top of his stash of reagents to perform his personal experiments and research, and sleeping with his concubines in the hopes of gathering juicy secrets he could leverage. What madness made him think Cornelius wouldn't notice or that he would simply let him get away with it with a mild reprimand?

Granted, not even I would have expected Cornelius to take things this far. But it had already been four years. It was now clear that he would never set Jasper free. That wretched necromancer was a sadist and a psychopath. I would derive intense pleasure in being an agent in his demise.

As I approached the wrought iron fences of Cliona Nox's domain, my pulse picked up the pace. By all accounts, the mysterious woman—informally known as the Weaver or the Hag—could be quite fickle as to who she granted her assistance. As you could not make an appointment with her, you had no choice but to show up and pray that she opened her gates.

My heart sank at the sight of what resembled a pair of stone imps leaping off the pillars framing the tall iron gates barring the way in. Their owlish eyes glowed red, lighting up their triangular faces framed by pointy bat ears. To my dismay, they appeared to grow, turning into full gargoyles as their stone skin took on a semi-leathery texture. With a blood-curdling roar, they gave chase to a man who had clearly been seeking an audience. Shrieking, the man rode off on his horse as bolts of fire cast by the creatures exploded behind him.

Although they missed, I didn't doubt for a moment that had the gargoyles truly sought to kill or harm him, it would have been a done deal at the first shot. I slowed down my horse as I closed the distance with the gate. While one of the creatures continued to 'encourage' the man to keep going, the other one circled back in my direction.

My breath caught in my throat, and I stopped my horse. Heart pounding, I debated whether to turn around and hightail it before it decided to burn me to cinders. However, the red glow of its eyes shifted into a pale yellowish hue, akin to the open flame of a candle. It flew around me before turning back towards the gate, then settling on top of the right pillar. Moments later, the second gargoyle gave up its chase and returned to its own pillar on the other side.

To my shock, as their bodies shrunk back to their original impish sizes, they both turned their heads to look at me. The same, non-threatening, pale yellow glow shone in their owlish orbs. Simultaneously, the tall, heavy doors parted open as if pushed by an invisible hand.

I swallowed hard and urged my horse to resume its advance, but this time at a slow walk. The deafening sound of my blood rushing in my ears failed to cover the loud pounding of my heart as I warily made my way through the still open gates. My head jerked left and right to look in turn at each of the guardians for any sign of discontent at my presence.

Halfway through the entrance, the gates started closing

behind me in a less-than-subtle fashion to tell me to get a move on. I didn't need to be told twice. Pushing my horse to half trot, I crossed the wide path delineated by a luscious forest made of the strangest trees and vegetation on each side, and which led to the house.

The humble shack that awaited me at the end of the two-hundred-meter packed dirt pathway took me by surprise. I didn't know what I had expected, but certainly not a simple thatched-roof cottage. It wasn't until I disembarked from my horse and attached it to the post outside that I realized this was some sort of glamour hiding the house's true appearance. That altering my vision to see past it revealed nothing testified to the insane power of the mage who had cast the spell to begin with.

I wondered why the Weaver would bother with such a thing. A part of me feared that it meant she had a thing for deception. Another wondered if it was a calculated move to avoid exposing any of her potential vulnerabilities by exposing what truly appealed to her. And then the last part didn't particularly give a shit. I was just grateful she agreed to receive me, especially seeing how the previous supplicant had all but been sent away with his butt on fire.

The dark wood of the worn-out door creaked open on its own with a drawn-out whine. My skin tingled as the potent magic of powerful wards glided over me as I entered the dwelling. I barely spared a look at the typical witch hut that greeted me with its plethora of scrolls, herbs, vials filled with various liquids probably best left alone, and other magical paraphernalia.

I only had eyes for the ageless woman sitting on a stool while spinning a glowing golden thread on a wheel. She was a few feet behind a large table and faced towards the right side of the house. Although fully aware of my presence, Cliona continued to spin in silence, making me wonder if I should speak first or clear my throat to claim her attention.

A gasp escaped me when a chair I hadn't noticed by the door

glided over the wooden floor to stop right in front of the table, where a guest chair would normally sit.

I emitted a small yelp upon hearing a loud clang behind me. I jerked my head around over my shoulder to realize it was merely the door closing. Embarrassed to be so jumpy, I cast a nervous glance at the Weaver. Finding her now sitting behind the table, her hands crossed on top of it and staring me straight in the eye nearly had me jumping out of my skin.

Although I didn't yelp again this time that she would have moved so quickly and soundlessly, I visibly recoiled and pressed a palm to my chest as if to keep my heart from leaping out.

"So jumpy, Kali," the Weaver said in a sensuously throaty voice laced with a hint of mockery. "How can you hope to defeat Cornelius if you are so easily frightened?"

"How do you know?!" I exclaimed, stunned.

My cheeks felt on the verge of bursting into flames from even more embarrassment at the less-than-impressed look she gave me. Rumors claimed that Cliona Nox was one of the Ancients, although nobody could prove it. After all, why would a goddess dwell among mortals and assist them with various plights that had to be meaningless to her?

A shiver ran down my spine as the round pupils of her purple eyes narrowed into a slit as her gaze flicked to the empty chair in front of the table before returning to me. I swallowed hard and gingerly closed the distance with the chair before settling down on it. Her pupils returned to their round shape which I took as a good sign. She tilted her head to the side while giving me an assessing look.

The long, delicate fingers of her right hand, tipped with vicious claws, absent-mindedly caressed the thick braid she'd bound her hair into. It was silver-white, but not the standard gray of an elderly person, and fell all the way down to her feet. It stood out nicely against her tanned skinned, the type of color one would acquire by spending a lifetime under the sun.

She seemed ageless, neither young nor old. But the power that emanated from her left me reeling. I didn't doubt it was only the tip of the iceberg.

"You haven't answered my question," she said at last, her face unreadable.

"I won't deny being a little unnerved," I said, proud that my voice came out steadier than I felt. "It's not every day that one gets to meet an Ancient, seconds after seeing a supplicant nearly getting roasted by your guardians."

An almost imperceptible smile quirked the corner of her voluptuous lips.

"There's nothing more insufferable than someone who won't accept that no means no the first time," she said dismissively.

I noticed how she did not argue my statement about her being one of the Ancients.

"Which makes me curious as to what earned me the honor of being granted an audience, especially since you know what my goal is," I said carefully.

"A bold one for sure, reckless even for most," she concurred, the intensity with which she held my gaze unnerving me. "The question is whether you're committed enough to your cause to see it through."

"He's been torturing my brother for years now," I hissed, the old anger squashing any nervousness I felt. "I want this bastard dead, and my brother freed. There's nothing I won't do to see this through."

"Nothing?" she asked with a dare in her voice as she raised a dubious eyebrow.

"Yes," I said firmly. "Whatever the cost, I want to take him down."

The Weaver snorted and gave me a slow once over. "You all say that but then balk and beat your chests when the time comes to pay."

I braced for what I had known might be the dealbreaker.

What did you offer a goddess in exchange for her assistance? From our humble beginnings, I had created a decent life for myself as a blood mage and necromancer. But one such as the Weaver would have no use for coins.

"I can see that," I said carefully. "So what would be your price to aid me in this endeavor?"

"Nothing," she deadpanned.

I recoiled. "WHAT?!"

A mysterious smile stretched her lips while her purple gaze took on a calculating edge. "You heard me correctly. The price for my assistance is nothing. I will grant it for free."

I frowned and narrowed my eyes at her. "Nothing is ever free, especially not when dealing with the arcane and the dark arts."

Her smile broadened, and a glimmer of approval sparked in her eyes.

"You are correct, young Kali. But *my* price is nothing. Where I'm concerned, your success will be reward enough for me."

"So there *is* a price?" I insisted, annoyed by her mind games.

"Of course, silly girl. There always is. But it is not one *I* request," she repeated in a noncommittal fashion.

This time, I loudly huffed with aggravation that she forced me to reword the question yet again in a way she would not be able to dance around the answer. Despite my annoyance, I was beginning to suspect it was deliberate on her part. When dealing with the occult, one had to be incredibly careful about not allowing loopholes. Was this her way of evaluating my ability to be thorough or how easily I could be played?

"So what is the price specifically?" I asked.

"Your soul," she said matter-of-factly.

I jumped to my feet, shock, anger, and disbelief soaring through me at such an outrageous demand.

"Sit down, you fool," the Weaver said with a bored expression.

"You can't—"

"Sit. Down," she repeated in a harsh tone, interrupting me.

The icy look in her eyes sent a chill down my spine. I swallowed hard and complied.

"Cornelius is protected," she continued in a conversational tone as if nothing had happened. "He's essentially immortal thanks to a Reaper."

"Nine hells," I whispered, horrified. "Why would they protect him?"

"I assure you that it is not willingly," Cliona said, her voice hardening again as did her gaze, but this time not aimed at me. "Pharos is his prisoner. Cornelius ensnared him and took him within himself so that he could benefit from all his powers. So long as he continues to hold the Reaper, you will be unable to defeat or kill him. Therefore, you must separate them."

I shifted uneasily in my seat, suddenly feeling overwhelmed by the enormity of the task before me. I had hoped for a spell, curse, or poison that would have taken care of him. But that would have been too easy. No wonder he remained unscathed over the decades despite the countless enemies who wanted nothing more than to end him.

"How could I accomplish that?" I asked in a subdued voice. "How do I separate them?"

"You must free Pharos. But you can only achieve that if he collaborates with you," she cautioned.

"How in the world am I supposed to accomplish that? If he's hosted within Cornelius, I'll never be able to speak with him," I said, my voice clearly expressing how ludicrous this sounded.

Cliona stared at me, unfazed. "You must summon him, like one would a demon or a spirit. You will have a narrow window to speak with him and convince him of your worth and dedication to this cause."

I licked my lips nervously and slowly nodded while digesting her words. "Okay, I can do that. But how do I summon him?"

"I will show you, if you are willing to pay the price required," she challenged.

My face immediately closed off. "Why does he need my soul in order for him to be separated from Cornelius? I'm trying to free my own brother from having his soul stolen by that son of a bitch, and your Reaper expects me to hand over mine in the process?"

"He needs a bond that supersedes the current one with Cornelius in order for him to escape," the Weaver explained.

"As in a new host?" I asked.

She nodded. "A temporary one until he can reintegrate his own body."

"Fair enough. But why do I have to give him my soul for that? Why can't I just host him?" I challenged.

"Because he is tethered. Your soul will create a stronger bond that will allow him to break free," she replied patiently.

I pinched my lips and realized I was subconsciously shaking my head. However desperate I was to find a way to free my brother, handing over my soul to a powerful being from the netherworld, a Grim Reaper at that, was where I drew the line.

"Surely there has to be another way that doesn't involve me giving away my soul?" I argued.

Cliona pursed her lips. Although she appeared to ponder the matter, at a visceral level, I believed she already knew the answer but was deliberately delaying speaking it either for dramatic effect or because she was wondering if I had what it took to see this through.

The thought she might kick me out nearly sent me into a panic. While I wasn't ready to pay such a hefty price, she was my last hope of saving Jasper. I'd spent the past four years looking for a way, none of which even remotely stood a chance.

"Maybe there is one," she said at last.

I perked up, hope swelling in my heart. "And what would that be?"

"You must carry a part of him within you."

"What do you mean?" I asked when her voice trailed off and she didn't expand. "Carry a part of him as a host or become possessed by him?"

"As a host," she replied.

I gritted my teeth with exasperation at the obnoxious way she forced me to drag every tidbit of information out of her in a slow drip, drip.

"Will that allow him to control me?"

"No."

"Will this be something permanent or only temporary?"

"Temporary. Pharos wants to be free. If you succeed, he will return to his own vessel, and there will be no more bond between the two of you," she said.

"Deal!" I exclaimed, although I bit back the urge to chastise her for not just telling me that from the start.

"Not with me, my dear," the Weaver said in a mocking tone. "It is he you need to make an agreement with. I can only tell you how to proceed in summoning him."

I narrowed my eyes at her. "For you to be willing to provide this aid free of charge, you must truly want to see Cornelius defeated. You are powerful, far more than I can ever hope to be. Why not take this matter into your own hands, especially since you already know how to perform the ritual?"

To my surprise, instead of the haughty expression I expected her to give me for implying one such as she would lower herself to perform such menial tasks, Cliona's face hardened with genuine frustration laced with anger.

"Believe me, child, if I could, I would have taken great pleasure in obliterating him in the most gruesome fashion," she said with such venom that a chill ran down my spine. "But we are all bound by rules. In my case, I may not interfere in the matters of mortals. I can nudge you in a certain direction, put down breadcrumbs, but not directly change the thread of Fate."

I nodded slowly. "Very well. How do I go about this?"

"You must go to a safe place of power, ideally a fairy ring. You chose an appropriate dwelling as there are a few suitable ones nearby with the right level of privacy. Make sure to set up wards to keep unwanted visitors from intruding. It is vital that you keep this secret. Cornelius may not know what is happening before it is too late, or he will shackle Pharos further," she explained.

"Understood," I said, feeling both nervous and thrilled.

She whipped out a piece of parchment and drew on it the strangest circle I had ever seen. It wasn't the usual summoning pentagram. It didn't even have a pentagram in it but an unusual series of swirls and lines around the edges of the circle, none of them crossing its center.

The Weaver got up and went to retrieve a medium-sized copper box and handed it to me. It contained a grainy substance that resembled salt, but I knew beyond the shadow of a doubt that it wasn't. Green strands in it, akin to tiny seeds, indicated the grains had been mixed with some kind of herbs I had never seen before.

For the next fifteen minutes, she painstakingly explained the process as well as the incantations I had to speak to summon the Reaper. Although she didn't say as much, based on the amount of 'not salt' contained in the box, I suspected I would have to perform the ritual more than once. No one gave away excess amounts of reagents for free.

To my shock, after she had me draw the circle with a quill on a piece of parchment, both the reference one she first gave me and the practice one I had drawn disintegrated and vanished.

"What the…?"

"This is the type of magic very few will ever learn or ever should," the Weaver said, a hint of a threat in her voice. "This knowledge is now seared into your mind. See that you never share it with anyone."

I didn't need her to add the 'or else' part of her statement.

"I won't," I replied in a subdued tone.

She gave me a stiff nod before relaxing her stance. "As I stated, Cornelius cannot know what is happening. Therefore, once you have drawn the circle and spoken the incantation, you must observe it for a response. If the edges glow orange or red, you must pause the summon."

"Why?" I asked, genuinely baffled.

"If Cornelius is awake, focused on Pharos, or wanting to use his powers, he will feel his absence if he's been summoned away. Should that happen, it will completely end all your chances of freeing him," she explained.

"I see. But how do I pause it? I've never done such a thing before."

"Speak this word of power, and then wait for the color to change back to a light blue. But be aware that the wait could be minutes or hours. There is also the slight possibility that he will not respond to your summon. This is not like invoking a demon with the intent of enslaving him. It is an invitation that can be declined or that he can walk away from whenever he sees fit."

"Damn," I muttered under my breath. It never once entered my mind that he might not answer the call. "But how does the circle know when the time is appropriate for him to answer?"

"The circle doesn't. The Reaper does."

"So he's the one changing the color?" I asked with sudden understanding.

She nodded. "It is his way of telling you to wait. Red means a long wait whereas orange indicates a shorter one."

A wave of relief flooded through me. It would still suck to be stuck to potentially be staring at a summoning circle for hours while waiting for him to finally show up, but at least I would know he intended to do so.

"But wait, what if he doesn't want to come at all?" I asked.

She smiled, the glimmer of approval in her purple eyes doing strange things to me. "Then the blue glow will fade like a switch getting turned off."

I raised an eyebrow to have her refer to the recent technology called electricity that had been spreading alongside all the steam operated machinery. She didn't have any of those modern tools and gadgets. For some reason, I had not expected her to know much about any of it. But then, I doubted anything in this world and beyond was actually a secret for her.

"Remember that you must convince *him* to trust *you*. You must be undaunted and steadfast in your determination. Pharos will put much on the line if he agrees to collaborate with you. Do not fail. There will be no second chances."

"I won't," I said, excitement bubbling within me.

The oddest expression fleeted over her timeless features. To my surprise, she didn't speak another word but simply turned her back on me. The stool she was sitting on silently glided back in front of the spinning wheel, and she began spinning more thread.

My confusion as to what to do next was quickly settled by the door opening behind me. Realizing I'd been properly dismissed, I rose to my feet and quietly walked out of her house. As the door closed behind me, I saw my chair sliding back to its original position by the entrance.

With the sun beginning to lower on the horizon, I raced back to the comfortable little house I had rented by the Fey Woods. As I had hoped, that intentional choice paid off. There was a reason the owner promoted it as the perfect getaway location for arcane practitioners. I knew exactly which fairy ring to use for the summoning. I secured my horse in the small stables. Despite my burning urge to head out right away, I forced myself to bide my time, have a light dinner, and even take a quick bath.

Cornelius was a night owl. He wouldn't be in bed for a while still. I didn't want to draw unnecessary attention by setting up the circle too early and then just sitting around waiting for the Reaper to answer my call. By the time the clock struck ten, I was on the verge of climbing the walls. Giving in to impatience, I began the short journey into the neighboring forest and down to the fairy ring located a stone's throw away from a small river.

Pausing to set up wards around a wide radius of my chosen location helped burn through some time, although nowhere near enough. It was barely a few minutes past eleven when I finished drawing the circle—whose design had truly been permanently seared into my mind.

A thrill coursed through me as I began to recite the incantation. The foreign words rolled off my tongue with an ease that genuinely took me aback. Granted, I was no novice when it came to the dark arts. But this ritual was in a language I had never heard before. I didn't doubt the Weaver played a part in this. I had not felt her casting any spells on me. And yet, she had somehow imprinted that design in my mind and those words on my tongue.

I squashed the sense of unease attempting to rear its head with questions as to what else she might have secretly done to me that might prove less favorable and focused on the task at hand.

As soon as I pronounced the last word, a whooshing sound resonated at my feet, akin to the sound made when throwing a match in front of an open gas burner. The dull gray color of the 'not salt' grains I had spread around to draw the circle began to glow as if lit from within. A wave of power radiated from it, like a wild animal ready to leap out.

Heart pounding with a mix of dread and excitement, I cast a protection spell on myself while waiting anxiously for my guest to appear.

But the white glow of the circle suddenly turned red. My jaw dropped, and my shoulders slumped. The relief I should have felt at this additional reprieve before facing the unknown that could totally change the course of my future never came. The depth of the disappointment that descended over me was nearly crushing.

Casting it aside, I spoke the word of power to pause the summon, as per the Weaver's instructions. The entire circle suddenly started pulsing at a terribly slow pace, although retaining its red glow.

Defeated, I settled down on the grass in front of the circle and began the long wait.

CHAPTER 3
PHAROS

A wave of disgust swelled through me as I stared at Alva, one of Cornelius's three apprentices. Standing next to the cells containing the live creatures of the necromancer's menagerie, she was hanging on to the bars, pushing out her ass, and shaking it in a lurid fashion. The menagerie varied from risen—zombie-like beings—to patchworked abominations, and captured mythical creatures held in metal cages reinforced by magic. The less vicious ones lined up the left wall of the room, while the most disturbing were held in an even broader dungeon accessible through a back door hidden by one of the front cells.

Further to the right, past the last cage, a series of deactivated constructs just stood or sat openly on the floor. In sharp contrast, the opposite side of the room was filled with artifacts, body parts, and various other powerful magical items displayed as trophies. Lethal traps and wards protected them from wandering hands.

Why Cornelius chose this setting for one of his recurring sexual escapades always boggled my mind.

Of the three apprentices, Alva was the one most aligned with the necromancer's twisted kinks. The only thing that topped her ruthlessness and cruelty was her thirst for power. By human standards, Alva qualified as a beautiful woman. With her long and curly, fiery red hair, brown eyes, and heart-shaped face, she drew many appreciative glances. I found her too skinny and overly pale. But it was her foul personality that made her even less attractive to me.

At twenty-eight, Piers, the second apprentice, was a solid eight years younger than Alva, although you would never guess she was well into her thirties. At 6'1, he towered over her by only a few inches. Just like Jasper, he was slender with an androgynous look to him. As with all his apprentices, Cornelius only chose attractive people as they were expected to warm his bed as part of their duties. Brown haired, blue eyed, and olive-skinned, he kept his hair trimmed short with sideburns. His ambition easily rivaled Alva's. Sadly for him, his respectable arcane powers held him back. Where Alva looked forward to engaging in the type of debauchery Cornelius enjoyed, he just went along with a certain level of indifference. It was but another task on his roster.

While Alva enjoyed sex with anything and anyone—person, monster, and even the undead—Piers technically was only drawn to women, although I increasingly suspected him of being asexual. That didn't stop him from bending over for Cornelius whenever he so demanded.

Removing his belt, Piers whipped it with non-negligible force against Alva's wiggling ass. While he had done so with a certain hint of malice, the wretched female only moaned, pushing her ass out further requesting more. Cornelius chuckled with approval before casting a sideways glance at Meri, his third and last apprentice. She responded with a stiff smile before starting to strip out of her clothes.

I couldn't decide if I felt more pity or disgust for her. She was the most powerful of the three but also the most spineless. She'd developed an unhealthy obsession for Cornelius. The foolish girl had convinced herself that she was head over heels in love with him. If not for her strong magic, she never would have secured a position with him as her mentor. Meri wasn't ugly, just not his type. Short, average-looking, and on the plump side, she didn't check any of the boxes that appealed to him, aside from her undivided loyalty and non-negligible talent that he could exploit.

She hated all those group sex activities he imposed on them at least once a week. Stupidly, she complied to please him and in the hopes he would eventually develop some affection for her and maybe even grant her the 'privilege' often bestowed upon Alva to share his bed on certain nights. You'd think after three years, she would have finally gotten a clue that it would never happen. And yet she kept hoping.

I couldn't fathom how anyone would think debasing themselves like that could get someone to love and respect you. The worst part of it all was that Cornelius enjoyed her pain and humiliation. He cruelly kept dangling the promise of a potential closer bond between them only to get her to consent to increasingly degrading scenarios. He'd never even fucked her once. The only thing he'd ever given her of himself was the honor of swallowing his cock. Otherwise, he would have Piers have his way with her, especially anal, as he knew she hated it with a passion.

But today would be even worse for her.

As soon as she was done stripping, Cornelius gestured with his head at the constructs. Despite her best efforts, Meri failed to hide her crestfallen expression. It wasn't the first time he had forced her to pleasure some otherworldly being. But those constructs were the worst for her. They were mindless, soulless creations built out of miscellaneous body parts stemming from random living creatures—human or otherwise—and in some cases including mechanical parts. They felt nothing and only came to life under a magical spell.

Heedless of Alva's moans as Piers continued to whip her,

Meri made her way to one of the biggest construct, who began to stir in response to Cornelius's compulsion. The women would take turns getting plowed by that abomination. While Alva would enjoy it, Meri would fight back tears through it. What killed me about it was that she could say no and knew it too. But she dreaded even more the thought of giving him any reason to cull her out altogether from their little entertainment. Even though he never touched her the way she dreamt of, watching him rutting over Alva or even Piers gave her the illusion she was part of it all.

"I don't need to witness this bullshit," I mentally hissed at him.

Cornelius chuckled, his malice seeping into our psychic connection. He knew how much his parties disgusted me. He made them drag on even long after his endless appetites were sated. At first, I thought it was to further torture his apprentices and me. It took me too long to realize he was also charging one of the many talismans he wore—this specific one made of the blood, bones, and hair of a succubus. It greedily fed on sexual energy, serving as a magic amplifier that came in handy when he fought or attempted to subdue elder demons.

"You're such a prude, Pharos. After a few centuries of abstinence, I would have expected you to be grateful for an opportunity to enjoy the pleasures of the flesh through me," he telepathically spoke back to me in a mocking tone.

"Nothing you can ever do will ever provide me any form of pleasure, except my freedom," I snapped.

"You wound me!" he retorted tauntingly. *"After all this time, you and I should be more than friends, brothers even. I can never let you go. Relax, and learn to enjoy what delights life has to offer."*

"What you call delights are just foul and abhorrent debaucheries. You're welcome to indulge in them without me."

He chuckled some more. We already had that conversation a

million times before. Although pointless, rehashing my griev-ances provided some distraction from the events taking place around us until he tired of me and finally allowed me to fade into the background. Obviously, I wasn't entirely gone. But it compared to entering some form of hibernation sheltering me from seeing, hearing, or feeling anything, and especially not the sliminess of his soul caging me.

Sadly, he rarely released me until things were in full swing, forcing me to sit through far too much of his twisted games.

The sound of his mental voice poking more fun at me faded in the background when a sudden energy tugged at me. I stiff-ened, startled by what I initially thought to be some kind of psychic attack against Cornelius. Despite being hosted by him, I wasn't tied to his nervous system and therefore couldn't share whatever physical pain he might endure. Granted, some of it could seep through our psychic link, and he even occasionally tried to unload some of it onto me to make his suffering more manageable on the rare occasions an opponent succeeded in getting a hit on him. But I possessed my own powers to block him and even to resist some of his attempts at coercing me into doing certain things.

It then dawned on me that it wasn't an attack but a summons. What I initially assumed to be a tug was in fact the steady pull of a portal. It even began swirling before my mind's eye.

What in the nine hells is this? Who could possibly call upon me this way?

I immediately clamped down on my emotions so that Cornelius wouldn't catch on. With the portal's pull growing in intensity, he would soon detect it. I could not allow it. Only someone who knew my sacred name could perform this summons. Was my freedom finally within reach?

In my eagerness to find out, I almost jumped through the portal only to rein myself in at the last minute. This could be a trap leading me into an even more dreadful fate than the one I currently endured. And even assuming no enemy awaited on the other side, Cornelius would feel me leaving if I wasn't discreet, and he would reel me back in before reinforcing my cage to prevent any chance of future escape.

I needed to handle this smartly.

With much reluctance I sent out a discreet magic tap through the portal telling the summoner to pause it until the time was right. I could only hope they would understand the message and not take it as a rejection. In half a millennium of captivity, this was the first doorway to open for me. I couldn't bear the thought of another five hundred years of this if the summoner gave up and permanently closed the portal.

As a million thoughts swirled through my mind, I suddenly felt Cornelius probing my consciousness. I clamped down on my emotions and refocused on him. As I had missed whatever nonsense he'd been spewing, my lack of snarky response had raised his suspicions.

I shifted my attention to Meri, allowing the disgust I felt to fill me, drowning out my emotions about the portal. The pathetic female was now on all fours, teeth clenched while the massive construct pounded into her from behind. He had the bull legs, tail, and knotted cock of the lesser demon Cornelius had kept after killing him. His torso belonged to a human male who had failed to pay his debt on time. The head had been chopped off a troll, although the eyes belonged to a wolf shifter. And the arms came from a demonic ape.

Next to them, Alva was on her knees, bobbing in front of Piers's groin, her ass, legs, and lower back red with angry welts where he'd belted her.

"You go enjoy your pets. I am done with this farce. You're welcome to try and force me to stay, but I am not," I said with all the contempt I could muster.

Visibly satisfied that my strange tuning out had been prompted by how sickening these little parties were to me, the suspicious edges of his prodding faded, and Cornelius snorted. The controlling and cruel parts of him wanted to coerce me into staying to assert his dominance. To my relief, he decided to let go this time.

Watching Piers fucking Alva's face was getting him hard. Even though she was the one stirring his fire, he would be plowing Piers first, just to spite him.

As he began unbuckling his belt, I faded into the background.

Despite my burning urge to rush to the portal, I bided my time, fading deeper and deeper until my host would barely even be able to notice my presence. Once he fully got into the action, he would no longer pay me any mind. Considering the amount of alcohol and drugs they had brought into the room, this would last at least three or four hours. Afterwards, they would rehydrate and pass out in bed. Technically, I would have until the wee hours of the morning before I had to return.

I spent the next eternity hoping and praying that the summoner wouldn't leave out of impatience. By the time I felt confident enough to send another tap through the portal, a little over forty minutes had elapsed since it first opened. The swiftness with which they fully reopened it had my spirit soaring. Whoever it was wanted to see me as eagerly as I wanted to get out.

Nevertheless, reining myself in, I carefully followed through the swirling tunnel that appeared before my mind's eye. Moving too swiftly, even in this deeply faded state, would tug at the tether still binding me to Cornelius.

A cool evening breeze, fresh air, and the discreet singing of running water in the distance struck me before the world fully formed around me. My shock at finding myself in the middle of the Fey Woods paled in comparison at discovering the identity of the summoner.

"By the Gods! It worked!" the woman exclaimed.

"Kali?!" I breathed out, flabbergasted.

A shiver coursed through me upon hearing my own voice, even though it had a disembodied edge to it. I had not heard myself like that in five centuries.

She recoiled, her eyes widening as surprise took over her excitement, before giving way to wariness.

"How do you know my…?"

Her voice trailed off, and she blinked as if struck by a sudden understanding. I nevertheless answered her not-fully-formed question.

"I bore witness to your encounters with Cornelius," I replied, my voice harsh. "You doubted your ability to succeed, and yet you summoned me. What is this? How did you learn this ancient ritual?"

She licked her lips nervously and visibly fought the urge to squirm.

"The Weaver taught me," she answered quickly. "I asked her for help defeating Cornelius to free my brother. She said I had to free you first before he could be vulnerable enough for me to kill him."

It was my turn to recoil. A million thoughts swirled in my head, although shock, hope, and confusion warred within me in equal measure. Why would the Weaver intercede now? Why send Kali of all people?

Sure, she was a decently powerful mage. However, I highly doubted she was fierce enough to see this through, especially considering the risks and sacrifices it entailed.

"You foolish girl! You do not have the power to kill Cornelius," I snarled.

"Without your powers, he—"

"Even without me to leech from, he will remain more powerful than you can ever hope to be," I interrupted. "You are too weak to challenge him."

A mulish expression laced with anger settled on her face.

"The Weaver thinks I can do it! *I* think I can do it! There's nothing I wouldn't do to free my brother!"

"The only thing you will do is die!" I snapped.

"You don't know that," she said, crossing her arms on her chest and lifting her chin defiantly. "Whatever happens to me, what do you care? For me to even attempt to defeat him—or for him to kill me—you need to be freed first. So what do you have to lose?"

"Everything!"

She blinked, confused by my response. I advanced to the edge of the circle containing me. It was odd having a body again, even though this one was nothing more than a shadowy representation of my soul. To her, I would look like a white Wraith.

"Did the Weaver tell you what the task entails to free me?" I asked in a stern voice.

"She said I need to host you back into your body," Kali replied, sounding a little uncertain.

"Do you even know where my body is?"

She frowned at the taunting edge in my tone. I flinched inwardly upon recognizing it as one Cornelius often used against people he was preparing to berate. It shamed me that his foul influence should so taint my own behavior. In a way, it had to be expected after spending five hundred years as his prisoner.

Kali shook her head, her stubborn—borderline arrogant—stance loosening into one of repressed wariness.

"It is located in one of the sacrificial chambers at the bottom of Hemdell Crypt," I said in an icy tone.

Right on cue, she shuddered. Her arms crossed over her chest slid down a few inches to hug her waist instead. It had been a subconscious gesture, but highly revealing, nonetheless. The anger such a reaction stirred within me battled with the disappointment I felt and something else I couldn't quite put into words.

"See? If that makes you shudder—as it should—you are

nowhere near ready for such a mission. If you fail, the chances that Cornelius will notice are extremely high. And once he does, he will shackle me in such a way that there will never be any hope of me ever escaping."

"It's not like you have any now," she snapped, visibly stung by my chastising tone.

Her comment struck a nerve. A low hiss emanated from me as I moved even closer to the very edge of the circle in a threatening fashion.

"Tread carefully, little girl," I growled.

She pinched her lips and lowered her eyes. As aggravated as I felt by her insolent remark, I couldn't help but find her boldness attractive. There was strength behind her delicate appearance. Clearly, she had been bullied in the past and learned to stand her ground. More importantly, she'd grown wise enough to know when to strategically retreat.

"Look, I don't have a death wish. I need your collaboration to make Cornelius mortal again so that I can free my brother," Kali said in a reasonable tone with a slightly pleading edge. "You need someone like me to free you from the prison he trapped you in. We can help each other. I would be a fool not to be disturbed at the thought of entering the belly of Hemdell's Crypt. You would have had better grounds to be concerned if I had been dismissive of the danger it entails. But that does not deter me. I can do it."

"And how do you expect to pull that off?" I couldn't help but ask tauntingly.

"By recreating this circle near your body inside the crypt, no? If I go during the day, most of the foul creatures will be dormant," she said in a hopeful tone.

"That will not work," I said with a dismissive gesture of my hand. "While going during the day is a wise approach, creating the circle near my body will not suffice. I need you to become a conduit for me."

By the way she stiffened, I immediately suspected the Weaver had hinted as to what the cost would be for her to help me. Kali was visibly not keen on it. Had she come here to waste my time?

"And how do I do that?" she asked, her voice tense.

"By giving me your soul," I replied, matter-of-factly.

"That's absolutely out of the question," Kali replied with a finality that made it clear there would be no further debate on the matter.

A wave of anger surged through me. While I understood her reluctance to make such a sacrifice, her flat-out refusal would have felt like less of a slap in the face had it been a surprise for her. But she came here already knowing what I would say. What in the nine hells kind of game was she playing? Why would she give me hope only to crush it right away?

"Then go away and stop wasting my time!" I hissed.

I angrily turned my back on her ready to let my consciousness seek the path back to Cornelius. But that dreadful prospect chilled me. As furious as I felt about Kali leading me on, for the first time in centuries, I was enjoying a semblance of freedom. It would be a couple more hours before I truly needed to go back. Why waste such an opportunity when it likely wouldn't return for decades if not centuries?

"Wait!" Kali shouted, panicked.

I peered at her over my shoulder. Despite my rigid stance, deep down, my misplaced pride was grateful for her providing me with a way to save face as I lingered here.

"Please, let's discuss this rationally," she said in a reasonable tone rife with tension. "If you only need to return to your body, why do you require my soul?"

I slowly turned back to face her and approached the edge of the circle again. She looked quite small before my shadowy form. Her head barely reached the middle of my chest. Technically, I could scale myself down, but it would require energy I did not want to waste. Oddly, seeing her looking so delicate in comparison stirred within me a pleasant protectiveness. Considering I needed her to perform a dangerous part of this mission to free me, that she should prompt such a reaction from me should be terrifying instead of agreeable.

"What is the point?" I asked in a slightly haughty tone. "It is clear you will not consent. What would discussing the matter accomplish?"

"You are asking for an insane price to help you," she retorted stiffly. "I think it's only fair and highly reasonable for me to understand why in the world you would ask that, and how the fuck it's relevant to the task needed."

I pursed my lips as I weighed her words. Of course, it was indeed a reasonable request. Only a bumbling idiot would consent to such a thing without challenging it. I didn't know why I was acting in this obnoxious fashion so contrary to my normally charming disposition. I wanted to believe it was merely to drag things out longer without being too obvious about my reluctance to reintegrate my cage.

"You giving me your soul creates one of the most powerful bonds possible between two beings," I explained at last in a far gentler tone. "That bond will supersede the one currently leashing me to Cornelius. It will allow me to easily transfer from his vessel through you and into my own body. Without it, the moment I attempt to reintegrate my body, the tether will pull me back to him."

Kali frowned. She lowered her gaze to the ground as she reflected intensely on my words before glancing back up at me. "Assuming I agree and give you my soul, would that be a temporary thing? Would you pledge to fully return it to me, no tricks and no strings attached?"

As soon as I began shaking my head, anger and an air of betrayal settled on her stunning features.

"No, Kali, I would not return it to you," I replied in a calm voice. "Before you get angry, know that it is not out of greed but merely because it is impossible. Once given, a soul cannot be taken back or returned."

"That's a lie!" she snapped. "Demons do it all the time. You sign a contract in blood, and should you fulfill the conditions set therein within the agreed upon deadline, then it will be returned to you."

I smiled. "You are correct as far as how those contracts work. However, their soul is not given *yet*, which is the operative word. It is the equivalent of putting a lien on it. Should you fail to fulfill your commitment, then you forfeit your soul's ownership, which then becomes the permanent property of the demon to do with as they please. In our specific situation, a lien would not work. I do not seek to take possession of your soul. I simply must to create the necessary bond."

Her shoulders slouched, and my chest constricted at the air of defeat marring her face. Once again, a wave of protectiveness surged within me.

From the first time I had laid eyes on her, she had stirred a potent possessiveness and hunger in me that never abated over the years, only growing stronger. In many ways, stating that I didn't seek to take possession of her soul was in fact a lie. I craved it with a fierceness that defied logic. Even now, its shimmering colors mesmerized me. Now that I was free of the limitations of Cornelius's human vessel, I could finally hear the haunting melody of her soul. It was like the blissful sigh of the wind in response to the gentle caress of the rays of the sun at its zenith. It had a sensuous and yet crystalline quality to it that I could listen to forever.

"I'm sorry," Kali said at last, putting an end to my wandering thoughts. "I cannot do that. That's too steep a price. I'm not fighting this hard to free my brother only to become a slave myself."

"You would not be a slave," I objected, feeling a little stung that she would think me capable of such a thing.

Granted, it was a fair assumption, especially under the circumstances. But I still felt offended by it.

"Says you," she countered with a challenge in her voice. "I don't know you. The Gods only can say how all those centuries trapped in the twisted fuck that is Cornelius has affected you. The bottom line is that my soul would no longer be mine for as long as I live, and probably even beyond. It will give you an insane power over me, and I'll be helpless to do anything about it. Tell me I'm wrong."

I bowed my head in concession. "You are correct in each of your statements. Unfortunately, I have nothing else to offer you of my pure intentions other than my word and a pledge."

She shook her head, but I doubted it was conscious. Her brow still creased, she continued to think furiously.

"This is not a bridge I'm willing to cross. But the Weaver said there might be another way that does not involve me giving you my soul. She talked about becoming your host," Kali said in a hopeful voice.

My face instantly closed off. Beyond the fact that I genuinely wanted her soul with an almost rabid hunger, I really didn't like the other option because of all the ways it could go wrong.

"There may be another way," I admitted with much reluctance. "But it is a lot riskier. And truth be told, I highly doubt you would consent to that one either."

Her brow shot up with undisguised curiosity with a sliver of wariness. "Riskier, how? And why would I have an issue with it?"

"It would require for me to give you a part of my soul instead. Once that happens, the part of me that remains within Cornelius will be weaker. He might notice my thinner presence. But more importantly, should he require the use of my greater powers, they will clearly lack the potency they should normally have. If he suspects what is happening, not only will he shut it down, but he will be able to trace the link back to you as he reclaims the part of me you will be carrying. And then, he will come after you with a vengeance."

She once again shuddered, realizing that there would be no easy conclusion to this plan.

"But what if I go first to the crypt and you give that part of you to me right before we transfer you to your body? That way, even if Cornelius notices, he will never have enough time to react and shackle you again," Kali suggested tentatively.

Her shoulders slouched again when I shook my head. "That would not work. Or rather, it would only work if you already hosted at least a quarter of my soul, but ideally a third. But hosting in that fashion requires multiple sessions with only a small fraction transferred each time to avoid detection because I am tethered. What you suggest is what we would have done had you given me your soul. Then, you would have gone straight to my body and the transfer would have been almost instantaneous."

"Damn," Kali muttered under her breath. "How many sessions would it require for me to host enough of you for this?"

"At least three sessions, but more than likely five," I said in a slightly taunting voice.

A part of me was enjoying this, knowing how she would lose her mind once I went into details as to what it entailed. The other part was steadily hoping she would consent to it, not only for a chance to regain my freedom, but also to fulfill one of the many desires she awakened in me from the first time we crossed paths.

She flipped her long black hair over her shoulder even as she narrowed her eyes at me. "Okay. So we do those three to five sessions for me to become your host. But what happens after I transfer you into your body? Will I be totally free of you?"

"Yes," I said truthfully, although feeling a little rejected by her eagerness not to have any lingering ties with me.

"You will have no power whatsoever over me when this is over?" she insisted.

"None," I replied in the same factual tone.

"And while I'm hosting you?"

I rolled my eyes, starting to feel a little annoyed. My reaction was unfair as thorough inquiries were of the utmost importance before entering into such an agreement. But the irrational part of me just wanted her to trust me and believe that I would protect her, even from myself.

"With this approach, I will have no power or control over you before, during, or after the task is complete. While you host me, I will not have any way—or desire for that matter—to cause you any harm or affect your ability to control your own body, mind, or actions. This, I pledge."

This time, her shoulder slump didn't express discouragement but relief as her face lit up with excitement.

"Perfect. This I can do. So how do we go about it?"

I stared at her, a myriad of thoughts flying through my mind as I pondered how to drop the news on her. My initial intent of easing her into it was squashed by my mouth running away with a will of its own.

"Strip, step inside the circle, and lay down on your back," I deadpanned.

"WHAT?!" Kali shouted, taking an involuntary step back.

"You heard me," I said in a cold voice.

"But… but why?" Kali asked with obvious denial.

"You know why. The transfer is performed physically through mating."

"But you're not physical!" she exclaimed, waving at me in an obvious fashion.

"Inside this circle, I am partially tangible. Through mating, I will transfer to you part of my ethereal essence, a bit more with each session until the bond is strong enough."

"I am absolutely not okay with that," Kali said in a similar definitive tone as the one she used when she refused to give me her soul.

"Then we are done here," I said in a harsh tone.

She stared at me in disbelief. "You can't be serious! Surely there's another way?"

"There is none. You can either give me your soul or lie with me to receive my essence. The decision is yours. But choose quickly and wisely."

"But you could kill me!" Kali exclaimed as if it was self-evident. "This circle is my only protection."

That took me aback. Although that well-founded fear should have been obvious, my mind had instead instantly assumed it was revulsion at the thought of lying with me that triggered such a negative response from her. As justified as that reaction would be, it still soothed me to know that was not the main reason for that resounding rejection.

I tilted my head to the side and raised an amused eyebrow.

"Technically, you're not wrong. By entering the circle, you do expose yourself to my potential wrath or madness. But how would that benefit me? I'm trapped in a prison that I cannot escape on my own. You're the first hope I've encountered in the past five hundred years. Why the fuck would I jeopardize my one opportunity?"

"You're asking a hell of a lot," Kali said, sounding a little distraught.

"I am not asking from you anymore than I am asking of myself," I countered. "What you fail to realize is that I am taking as many, if not even more risks than you are. Do not forget that giving you a part of me is a great threat to my welfare. A single mistake on your part could end me. We're both taking risks. The question is how much are you willing to take?"

Kali heaved a sigh and rubbed her temples, looking overwhelmed.

"I need time to think. This is not what I expected."

"There is no time," I countered. "If you cannot commit to this course of action now, you will have to wait another week before we can initiate the process should you decide to go through with it."

Kali stiffened and gave me a confused look. "Why one week? Why not tomorrow or the day after?"

"Because establishing the first bond takes longer. Tonight is the perfect opportunity as Cornelius will be occupied for at least the next couple of hours without expecting or seeking my presence. After tonight, I will only be able to come to you when he sleeps. Initiating the first bond at that time is too risky. There is a non-negligible chance that he will feel it. The only next safe time will be in a week when he performs another one of his little orgies that carry on through half the night."

She stared at me in silence for a long time. Judging by the shimmering colors of her soul, like a multi-colored halo around her head, too many conflicting thoughts and emotions were raging through her. To my shock, she simply turned her back on me and walked away. A sharp pain slashed through me as I stood there, numb, watching her leaving. Shock, betrayal, and a deep sense of defeat crashed over me.

I turned away to look at the clear water of the river a short distance away gleaming under the soft glow of the moonlight. None of this made sense. The Weaver wouldn't have sent Kali to me if she didn't genuinely believe she could see this through. Fate wouldn't have chosen for the one female to have stirred me in generations to be the first to contact me after years of despair only for this to go nowhere.

She just needs more time to come to terms with this.

I desperately clung to that thought. A part of me wanted to call out to her and beg her to come back. But this was too dire a mission to be embarked on half-heartedly. She needed to be fully committed. I had waited five hundred years, what was another week?

What if she doesn't summon me ever again?

The sound of a soft voice in the distance startled me out of my grim thoughts. I jerked my head around to see Kali casting a cone of silence spell above one of the wards she set about ten meters away from the fairy ring she chose to build the summoning circle in. A wispy light flew off from the ward to the next one, then the third, and onward through the eight wards that formed a perfect circular perimeter around us.

Stunned, I watched her quietly walk back towards me, the oddest mix of determination and wariness fighting for dominance on her beautiful face. She stopped in front of the circle and locked eyes with me.

"Pledge that you will not do me any harm, physically, mentally, or otherwise if I enter the circle," she said in a firm tone.

"I pledge it," I replied, trying to clamp down on the hope returning vigorously.

"Swear that from this moment forward, once I enter the circle, while I'm inside it, and even after I leave it, your interactions with me will be devoid of any malicious intent towards me and remain constrained to the sole purpose of transferring a part of your soul to me so that we can free you from Cornelius."

I opened my mouth to respond but then hesitated. Taking that oath was not an issue. But as much as I respected her reasonable need to protect herself against potential foul play, it bothered me to no end that she didn't trust me. My reaction was irrational, yet I needed her to know beyond any doubt that whatever went down between us, she would always be safe with me.

CHAPTER 4
KALI

I frowned, the suspicion that had begun to abate surging back with a vengeance within me as I stared at the ghost-like form of the Reaper when he failed to answer right away.

"You do realize that magic circles serve different purposes, correct?" he asked in a mysterious tone.

That took me aback. Why this sudden change of topic when I demanded the final pledge that would ensure my safety once I stepped inside? Had he been trying to fool me all along?

"You haven't answered my request," I replied in a stern voice.

"I promise to answer in a moment," he said with a dismissive gesture, his disembodied voice beautifully haunting. "But please indulge me by answering mine first."

My frown deepened, unsure what the purpose of this all could be. Of course magic circles served various purposes. The main use was to form a protective barrier between the caster and whatever entity they summoned. But they could also be used to contain energy or form a sacred space as part of a given ritual.

"Yes, I am aware of it," I conceded, my voice making it clear I failed to see the point of this question. "They are mostly used as a containment field during summons or to form a magic well for a ritual."

He nodded, the glow in his eyes intensifying as he moved even closer to the edge of the circle, the flowy skirt-like lower half of his body brushing against its very limit. All my senses went into high alert. I didn't know what was about to happen, but my flight instinct was frantically rearing its head.

"This circle is neither. This is a portal, not a containment field. If what you fear is that I will harm you the moment you cross into the circle, then you are severely mistaken as to its protective capacities."

My heart skipped a beat as my sense of unease grew another notch.

"What does that mean?" I whispered.

Pharos didn't answer right away. Instead, he glanced to our right before pointing at a tall tree about eighteen meters away. One of its branches dangled at an odd angle after somehow getting snapped.

"You see this broken limb?" he asked.

I nodded, tension knotting my back. Seconds later, I gasped, and my skin erupted in goosebumps as a powerful wave of Death Magic shot out of the circle in the direction of the tree. Half a beat later, the branch didn't just fall off but turned into ashes carried away like a dust cloud by the soft evening breeze, all lingering life force or energy sucked out of it.

Impossible!!

Summons couldn't cast spells beyond the barrier of the magical circle confining them. My heart sank at the realization that he could also slay me right where I stood with no chance of escape. Horrified, I jerked my head back towards him, only to find him staring at me with a vicious expression.

Moving so fast it looked like a blur, Pharos reached out to me over the magical line, grabbed my neck, then yanked me inside the circle. He glided back a few steps as he did so, taking us to its center. I collided against his chest, my scream of terror dying in my throat as my entire body froze, paralyzed.

Flesh Magic...

This couldn't be happening! It *shouldn't* be happening. I attempted to cast a disruption spell only to find myself unable to tap into any of my magic.

"Calm, Kali," the Reaper said in a commanding voice. "If my purpose had been to kill or harm you, I would have done so a long time ago. Portals offer no protections to the summoner and aren't constraining for the summoned entity. Never forget that, should you ever attempt this again with another being."

To my shock, his arms holding me tightly against him released me, and the paralysis keeping me locked in place lifted. I couldn't scramble out of the circle fast enough. So much in fact, that I stumbled back and would have fallen hard on my ass if not for his kinetic magic propping me back up.

One hand pressed to my chest, I gaped at him, too stunned to speak a word or otherwise react. The mocking smile that stretched the partially defined features of his wraith form made me snap out of my traumatized daze. My cheeks heated with embarrassment upon realizing that storming back out of the circle had been prompted by the lingering illusion that remaining outside would keep me safe.

"Now to answer your previous request, Kali Jenkins, I swear not to harm you from this moment forward, during whatever interactions we will have inside the circle, or after you have left it. I hold no malicious intent towards you and seek a mutually beneficial collaboration with you to be freed of Cornelius. Does that response satisfy you?"

Despite the sense of relief that washed over me, I couldn't help still glaring at him for that little stunt. I gave him a stiff nod while muttering my annoyance as my heart continued to try to settle back in my chest from the scare he just gave me.

"Yes, it does. But you didn't have to make your point in such a flamboyant fashion," I grumbled.

Instead of the mocking snort I expected, Pharos took on a serious expression. "Yes, I did. Time is of the essence. You and I are about to make great sacrifices that could cost both of us the ultimate price. If we are going through with this, trust—or rather the lack thereof—will be our undoing. I am not the entity you should fear. You need to know beyond any doubt that no harm will ever come to you from me, not because I can't, but because I choose not to."

I almost argued that this could be just a trick to get me to lower my guard before he stabbed me in the back when I least expected it. But I kept my peace. If even disembodied he's so easily nullified my magic, I could only imagine how much more powerful he could be. Reapers possessed many powers, including elemental manipulation and illusion. He could easily make me do what he wanted while fooling me into thinking those were my choices.

"Why do you stay inside it then?" I asked with genuine curiosity. "If it doesn't constrain you, couldn't you simply go to your body?"

He shook his head. "The magic of the portal keeps this form whole. The moment I step out, I start losing some of my integrity. The only way to maintain it is by expanding magical energy. The farther away, the greater the strain. If I go too far without the power to maintain myself, I will eventually get sucked back through the portal into the vessel that was hosting me before the call. But long before that happened, Cornelius would feel the strain tugging at the tether and know something is amiss."

Without another word, I gave him another stiff nod and began to strip out of my clothes.

I still had mixed feelings about this whole situation. While sex was often used as part of certain rituals, I dabbled in the type of magic that didn't require such practices. Many dark arts practitioners actually sought it out not only because sex with occult creatures was usually off the charts, but it tended to enhance the human partaking in it—assuming their otherworldly partner wasn't evil aligned.

I wasn't prudish and didn't have moral qualms about what would soon take place between us. I'd simply never been the type to share my body with anyone that I didn't intend to form a committed relationship with. Right or wrong, I fell squarely into the category of people who couldn't help but form an emotional bond with the person they became intimate with.

The intensity with which he observed me as I finished removing my clothes and setting them in a neat little pile next to me was beyond unnerving. When he first suggested this coupling, it struck me as ludicrous since he didn't possess a corporeal vessel. With traditional summons, the entity entered the circle with its true body, not just its consciousness. And yet, this portal had somehow made his soul tangible.

The feel of his body, when I crashed into him, came back to the fore. It had been firm and yet soft. Spongy wouldn't qualify as an appropriate descriptor. Maybe pillowy? But more importantly, an unexpected warmth radiated from it, and it lacked the horrible stench of death and decay that I dreaded.

My stomach fluttered with a feeling I couldn't quite describe as I stepped back inside the circle. It was the oddest mix of fear, anticipation, and curiosity. Now that my distrust of him continued to steadily wane, my mind could finally focus on appreciating the strange being before me.

Pharos had something elegant and noble about him—not words I ever expected to associate with a type of wraith. He was extremely tall, nearly seven feet, although I suspected that his long skirt made of white smoke, and the fact that he slightly hovered over the ground played a significant part in this. His body wasn't exactly covered in a white robe. It was just the white smoke or glowing aura around it that created such an illusion. The features on his face were too undefined to be able to say what he actually looked like. It was as if a sculptor created the basic shape of a face with the eyes, nose, and mouth, but didn't complete the work. The generic mannequins some fashion stores used to display their garments would be an apt comparison.

Moving slowly, as one would with a frightened animal, the Reaper carefully drew me against him. A shiver coursed through me in reaction to the sharp contrast of the cool evening air and the unusual warmth of his ethereal body. To my shock, he leaned forward and pressed his lips to mine.

As I normally never indulged in these types of activities with otherworldly beings, I hadn't really known what to expect. Foreplay had certainly not featured on the list. For a reason I couldn't explain, I instinctively sensed that he was trying to ease me into it, as if he knew of my inexperience with one such as he.

That messed with my head.

The part of me grateful for that consideration also acknowledged it meant things could drag on longer than I might want or prefer. However, how much time this took largely depended on my ability to let go and open myself to the process.

The more tense I remained, the tougher the psychic barriers erected by my subconscious would be, effectively acting like a repellent. There was a reason consent was so important in many rituals. Granted, in most cases of possession or dark magic, the victim or sacrificed couldn't have been a less willing participant. However, there were multiple ways to break down someone's resistance, pain, doubt, and fear being chief among them.

Where religious people often used their faith as their shield, making them waver on even a single aspect of their belief often sufficed for a demon to create the breach necessary to get in. And once fear kicked in, whatever defenses they possessed crumbled at an exponential rate. Similarly, pleasure—especially when all-encompassing—drove the person receiving it to either open themselves wider to receive even more, or it overwhelmed them so much they lost themselves to it, leaving them ripe for the reaping.

That thought should have frightened me. But the unexpected flame of desire sparked low in my belly as Pharos's hands started roaming gently over my naked body. Tilting his head to the side, he deepened the kiss in a gentle but dominant fashion. Once again, relief washed over me in the absence of foul taste or smell. It was too subtle for me to pinpoint it exactly, but aniseed popped to mind.

The texture of his tongue against mine also messed with my head. It was smooth, silky, almost creamy in its softness. Where his body was hot, his tongue felt cool. I wouldn't call it cold, despite the slight tingling it triggered without falling into numbing territory. Simultaneously, his hands on my body, and mine on his sent me down a spiral of sensory exploration like I'd never experienced before.

It took me too long to realize that his touch was more than just physical. The tingling that seemed to seep deep into me, down to my bones, was some form of spiritual response. Considering he was the embodiment of a soul, it utterly made sense. But it was the way my body was responding to him that retained my attention.

I was more than turned on. Within the handful of first caresses, my nipples hardened, my breasts felt heavy, and a dull throbbing manifested itself between my thighs. When his palms glided over the curve of my behind, I instinctively found myself pressing my pelvis against his. I wanted him to hold me more tightly, to be entirely surrounded by his ethereal essence.

It made no sense, considering that only moments ago, I'd been ready to run for the hills, horrified at the thought of coupling with a being like him. And yet, something inside me completely flipped around the moment he kissed me, as if a switch had been turned on.

He felt right.

For a split second, I wondered if he was using one of his potent magical abilities to trigger this response from me. While undeniable power swirled around him, engulfing us, none of it was targeted directly at me. For a reason of its own, my body wanted him in a way that transcended basic lust.

I quickly cast out the thought that having been celibate for a while could explain this reaction. Curiosity at mating for the first time with a spirit also didn't feel like the justification for it. As a necromancer with respectable skills in Soul Magic, it was the unexpected beauty of his soul that ensnared me.

It sang with the most delightful melody to my ears even as it vibrated all around me. Standing outside the circle, I had not perceived it, likely because I'd been too frazzled by everything else to pay attention. But now that I was wrapped in his embrace, he was all that I could feel, and I couldn't seem to get enough.

Stop overthinking. Why not enjoy the moment instead of treating it like a chore?

Before I could even acknowledge the wisdom of that intrusive thought, Pharos's hand slipping between my thighs from around my behind made me gasp against his lips. His fingers boldly rubbed against my slit before dipping inside me. He moved them in and out of me a few times, then his middle finger settled on my clitoris. He flicked it a couple of times, drawing a moan from me, followed by a yelp when the ground dropped from under me.

I felt myself falling backward. However, instead of crashing onto my back, I glided down like a feather twirling in a slow descent. I realized then that Pharos was lowering us onto the grass-covered ground inside the circle. With his fingers still moving in and out of me at a gradually increasing pace, he broke the kiss to brush his lips along the sides of my neck, and down to my breasts. He lingered there for a few moments, each lick of his otherworldly tongue on the hardened bud of my nipple sending a lightning bolt of pleasure directly into my loins.

With a will of their own, my hands settled on his head, all but vanishing in the white smoke that surrounded the more solid part of his ethereal body. It wanted to feel like hair, but it was too intangible to give me any real grip.

As I parted my legs to make room for him to settle between them, it suddenly struck me that I had not felt his shaft—limp or otherwise—when I had pressed my pelvis against his earlier. Did he even have a cock in this form?

His lips gliding down my body to take over where his thumb had left off had me crying out as a bolt of pleasure hit me so hard I nearly climaxed. My back arched as his mouth latched onto my clitoris. I never expected him to go down on me, but all rational thought fled as the tingling sensation I had felt on my lips when he kissed me now acted like electric sparks all over my engorged little nub. Each one struck me as a micro-orgasm building into an even bigger one ready to send me over the edge.

And then it did.

My spine seized as I cried out. A wave of searing heat shot through me from my core outward. My body shook from spasms of bliss as Pharos continued to devour me. However, even in my daze, I realized the burning sensation inside me—strange but pleasant—wasn't a physiological response to extreme pleasure but a foreign presence seeping into me.

Pharos was sharing a part of himself with me while ecstasy had me fully open to him. Even as he kept me flying high with his expert tongue and hand, I fleetingly felt cheated that he could accomplish it while going down on me instead of by riding me. This should be a relief.

And yet…

As I began to come back down to reality, instead of pulling away from me and calling it done, Pharos climbed on top of me and claimed my lips in a possessive kiss that had another bolt of lust surging through me. I didn't understand my responses to this stranger. I didn't even try to question it. Spreading my legs for him to settle more comfortably, I caressed the odd texture of his back as his tongue plundered my mouth, and his hands kneaded and explored me with a growing urgency and possessiveness.

Where he'd been eerily quiet through our encounter so far, the Reaper started emitting a low growl that resonated straight in my clit. Moisture pooled between my thighs, and my inner walls contracted with anticipation when I finally felt something hardening around his pelvic area. I couldn't tell if he had extruded or if he could somehow summon it. In truth, I didn't care.

The ache to be filled was quickly growing almost too painful to bear. As if sensing my need—or simply giving in to his own—Pharos pushed himself inside me almost brutally. He swallowed my shocked gasp in a voracious kiss. I couldn't even begin to describe what that initial penetration felt like. It burned and yet didn't quite hurt. My body resisted even as it yielded. It was as if that strange hardness wrapped in the even stranger pillowy outer texture of his body had initially shrunk itself only to expand a split second after he was fully sheathed.

Pharos immediately setting a frantic pace wiped out any possibility for me to ponder the matter further. His otherworldly cock was wrecking me. With each thrust, he grew ever-so-slightly thicker, filling me to bursting. Unusual protrusions along his length provided additional sensations against my inner walls that just fanned the flame of the inferno raging in my loins.

In no time, I was writhing beneath him, his thick cock pummeling my sweet spot with a deadly accuracy that soon had me seeing stars. I threw my head back and cried out, once more swept away by ecstasy. To my shock, the burning feel of the reaper's hand closed around my neck, in an almost savage choke. He didn't constrict my airways but forced my head back down.

Without slowing the unbridled way in which he pounded into

me, he crushed my lips with his, reclaiming them angrily. Another wave of searing heat flooded my body, this time through my mouth, down my throat, and spreading outward in my chest as he breathed more of himself via that otherworldly kiss.

I was drowning in too many overwhelming sensations, from the insane heat of his body around me, his essence within me, his hands and mouth claiming me, and his cock fucking me senseless. I didn't fight or question any of it and gave myself over to my lover.

Before I could even recover from that second devastating orgasm, Pharos suddenly pulled away. A powerful shiver coursed through me at the abrupt loss of his heat with the sharp contrast of the cool evening air over my feverish skin. A startled cry escaped me when the clearing spun around, and I found myself belly down onto the soft grass. The Reaper yanked my hips up and rammed himself into me in one powerful thrust that had me shouting again.

He immediately started pounding into me hard and fast, setting an almost punishing pace as if he had lost all control. It should have frightened me. But the pleasure pain of his brutal possession had liquid flames coursing through my veins as my inner walls greedily contracted around his length, wanting more of his savage passion.

I attempted to push up on my arms to get on all fours so that I could rock back and meet him thrust for thrust. To my shock, Pharos's hand closed around my nape and pinned me down to the ground, my left cheek pressed against the grass as he continued his intense sensual assault on my more than willing body.

Over the endless string of moans pouring out of me as another peak of ecstasy began building inside me, Pharos's low growls mixed with rumbling moans took on a deeper, darker edge that almost sounded like they were emanating from an elder beast escaped from the deepest levels of the underworld.

As with every other irrational response the Reaper stirred within me, this threatening sound prompted a mix of fear and lustful excitement. I attempted to turn my head to look at him over my shoulder. But Pharos tightened his grip around my nape, and a threatening growl made it clear I was to remain still. As if to reinforce the warning, a prickling sensation in my left butt cheek hinted at claws sinking into me. Despite the strength of the sting, I couldn't say for sure whether he had broken skin.

I didn't care.

I was burning from the inside out, my mind feeling on the verge of fracturing as waves upon waves of pleasure crashed into me. Just as I was preparing to give myself over once again to bliss, a dark shadow spread over me. Pinned as I was, I couldn't get a good look, but it seemed to show a large pair of wings spreading on each side of the Reaper's shadow cast by the soft light of the moon. The shadow also appeared to grow, confirmed moments later by his hand on my nape, his cock inside me, and his pelvis banging into me feeling as if they were significantly expanding.

A blinding light exploding before my eyes wiped out any thought from my mind. A savage cry tore my throat as I tumbled down a bottomless vortex of ecstasy. My skin felt on the verge of combusting as a powerful beam of energy blasted through me. I vaguely heard a feral roar in the distance. A part of me realized Pharos had surrendered to his own climax, and that the overwhelming power threatening to burn me to cinders from within was his essence filling me. But I couldn't think or otherwise react. For a split second, I wondered if I would die. It was too much and yet an insane little voice whispered that it wasn't enough.

Another scream of pleasure-pain escaped me, then the tingling deep inside spread outward, growing in intensity until I felt myself falling out of my body. Then darkness engulfed me.

I didn't know how long I was out. When I regained

consciousness, I stared at myself in shock to find me fully dressed, cradled in Pharos's arms. He had returned to his normal size, no wings visible. But his eyes glowed with an insane intensity as he stared at me.

On instinct, I pulled away from him and scrambled back a couple of steps, still sitting on the ground. The Reaper didn't attempt to pull me back. He merely tilted his head to the side and gave me a 'Are you serious?' look that had my cheeks burning with embarrassment.

"Good, you are conscious again," he said in a conversational tone. "I must go back before Cornelius suspects anything. As soon as I am gone, destroy this circle. We cannot risk anyone stumbling on it once your wards wear off."

"Okay," I said in a subdued voice, unsure how I felt about his matter-of-factly behavior moments after fucking me to an inch of my life.

But what did you expect? Snuggles and words of love?

He kind of snuggled me while I was unconscious. Was his distant behavior a response to the instinctive way I'd scrambled away from him upon regaining consciousness? It hadn't been personal. I'd merely been startled.

He rose to his 'feet' prompting me to do the same.

"Stay away from Cornelius and his minions until I am free. You carry a part of me inside you now," he warned in a serious tone. "If any of them come close enough to you, they will sense it, and all will be lost. Do you understand?"

"Yes," I said, feeling inexplicably unnerved.

"Good. In that case, until tomorrow, my bride."

My bride?!

I stiffened and gave him a baffled look. Before I could ask him what he meant by that, Pharos grabbed me by the nape and crushed my lips in a painful kiss. With a will of its own, my body melted against his, a spark of lust igniting low in my belly, despite the soreness lingering between my thighs.

To my chagrin, he ended it as quickly as it started, then nipped my bottom lip hard enough for it to sting, but not to break skin. I gasped, my right hand flying to my lips to cover the spot he had bitten, only to see him vanish in a puff of white smoke as he crossed back through the portal.

I stood there dumbfounded, alone in the clearing. Too many conflicting emotions swirled through me. What did he mean by *his bride*? Had he screwed me in more ways than one? The power of his essence flowing through my body was undeniable. However, I didn't feel anything else that could indicate potential foul play.

He pledged not to harm me in any way before, during, or after our encounter.

Although that thought appeased some of the worry trying to rear its head, at a visceral level, and in a way I couldn't explain, I didn't believe he would wrong me. Nothing about my reaction to the Reaper made any sense. Even now, I felt utterly bereft and cold, in a way that went beyond just the loss of his unusual heat surrounding me.

It's his soul. You love the feel of it around you.

And I did. It was mesmerizing in a way I couldn't explain. But then, Reapers were considered demigods. Could that be the reason for my response to him?

Heaving a sigh, I set down on the task of removing the circle and then disabling the wards I had set up around the area. There was no point dwelling on why I felt the way I did around this strange being. I was just grateful it turned out the way it did instead of being an excruciating nightmare.

Anyway, I was committed. Cornelius would pay for what he had done to far too many people.

CHAPTER 5
PHAROS

My soul paced restlessly in the slimy cage that was Cornelius's vessel. As repulsive as it had felt over the centuries of captivity, it now made me beyond nauseous. Thanks to Kali, the recent taste of freedom I enjoyed, and the intoxicating sweetness of her soul only exacerbated the foulness of my host.

I visited my bride three times already. A couple more visits should suffice to allow for a smooth transfer into my own vessel. With All Hallows quickly approaching, the timing could not have been more perfect. Over those three days, the veil between the mortal world and the Shadow Realms significantly thinned. If we performed the ritual then, it would be easier for the shriveled husk of my body to fully regenerate. Plenty of wandering souls would abound for me to feed on, not to mention the fiendish creatures that haunted the crypt where my vessel lay in stasis.

That thought immediately unnerved me.

Once back in my body, I would be nearly unkillable, even in my weakened state. The same could not be said of my female. She did not grasp just how deadly the crypt was for a human, even one with the respectable arcane powers she possessed. I had to convince her to give me her soul. It was the only way to guarantee she would survive the journey there.

The powerful longing—not to say rabid hunger—that struck me at the thought of owning her soul left me reeling. I ached to possess all of her… but consensually. I needed her to want to belong to me. It didn't make much sense. Granted, she possessed one of the most beautiful souls I'd ever seen or touched. If I had a physical body right now, just remembering how she felt wrapped around me would have wrested a moan out of me.

Blast it to Hell! I was obsessed with her.

And tonight, I will have her again…

I felt hot and cold all at once at that prospect. I hated this ethereal form that kept me from getting the full experience of mating with her. And yet, the pleasure she gave me far exceeded anything I ever felt before. How much greater would it be in my true body? How much more intense could our coupling be? Would she even allow it, once I was back to my old self?

Kali genuinely seemed to enjoy sex with me, despite her initial outrage and reluctance when I brought it up. After that first time, she appeared eager when I visited her the second and third times. While her orgasms had been undeniable—I'd made certain of it—I couldn't say if she would have welcomed my attentions again if not to ensure the success of her mission to destroy Cornelius.

She probably would not.

That thought stung. In fact, it cut me deep. Once I was back in my own vessel, Kali would have no more use for me. She would have what she wanted: me out and Cornelius vulnerable. A deep anger fueled by a potent sense of loss reared its head as I tried to make peace with the fact that my time with her was quickly coming to an end. Was I truly falling hard for her, or was it just an instinctive reaction to finally experiencing pleasure, hope, and gratitude after centuries of despair?

"Why are you so damn restless?" Cornelius mentally hissed at me.

I clamped down on the instant panic his sudden intrusion stirred within me. I needed to do a better job of reining myself in not to tip him off. Since Kali first called me, I had been alternating through bouts of euphoria and depression. Such extremes were bound to draw his attention to me, which was the last thing I wanted.

I reverted to my best defense and diversion tactics: snark.

"Why do you think?" I telepathically replied with contempt. *"I'm bored with your pathetic projects. I'm tired of constantly being exposed to that decomposing stench you enjoy wallowing in. That trash you call a construct will not work."*

"Then tell me how to fix it," he hissed aloud, drawing Meri's attention.

He waved his hand dismissively to tell her never mind while emitting an angry grunt. Confused, she nonetheless kept her peace and resumed sewing the partially decayed limb of whatever strange creature it had been harvested from onto Cornelius's latest project.

I chuckled with disbelief laced with disdain. *"Like fuck I will. The only entertainment I still get to enjoy is seeing you fail repeatedly,"* I said maliciously. *"The Gods know you've been doing a lot of that lately. By the way, how is Ronika faring these days?"*

"Silence!" he snapped, remembering this time to do it mentally.

Naturally, I ignored his command and further poked at the wound, distracting him from his original inquiry into my unusual behavior.

"It must sting to have been so soundly defeated by a little human. She succeeded in less than a month where you pathetically failed for decades. Not only did she thwart your efforts of appropriating her lands, but she also claimed the Wraith for

herself, and acquired an insane amount of new powers you could only dream of."

"*I said silence!*" he shouted angrily.

With his huge ego, narcissism, an endless sense of entitlement, he couldn't bear the slightest hint of ridicule. He was so incredibly thin-skinned, he was easily manipulated once you knew which buttons to push.

"*I still remember that tantrum you threw after she publicly humiliated you,*" I continued mercilessly. "*And then, you had to give up the Wraith's tail! You're so pathetic. And now you can't even raise a lousy construct.*"

Cornelius slammed his fist on the operating table upon which he was assembling the latest construct. Meri yelped and took a couple of wary steps back in fear.

"*Ronika didn't beat me!*" Cornelius mentally snapped, ignoring his apprentice. "*She cheated and somehow sold her soul. You better than anyone can see that she's no longer mortal!*"

"*She cheated!*" I echoed in a mocking fashion with a whiny tone. "*That's always the go-to excuse of sore losers. She didn't cheat, she outsmarted you. And even as undead as she now is, you don't have the power to control her. For all your boasting, you truly are a lousy necromancer.*"

Cornelius fisted his hands as he leaned on the operating table, staring angrily ahead without seeing. Meri was still keeping her distance, the look on her face clearly indicating she was considering bolting out of there—which would be a wise decision.

"*A lousy necromancer that beat you, didn't I?*" he snarled. "*So what does that make you?*"

If I had a body, I would have shrugged. Unlike him, these types of jabs didn't affect me.

"*You didn't beat me, but I'll concede that you tricked me. In a fair fight, I would obliterate you. Keeping me trapped here doesn't make me entirely helpless or under your control. You like to play with rot? Here, I'm feeling generous today,"* I said in a malevolent tone.

Invoking my death aura, I caused the various body parts he and Meri had been stitching together to start rotting and decaying. In seconds, heavy necrosis spread throughout the limbs, making them darken and the stitches fall out.

"STOP!" Cornelius shouted aloud.

"It's not me!" Meri exclaimed, panicked. "I didn't—"

"GET OUT!" the necromancer yelled at her before mentally ordering me to stop again.

She didn't have to be told twice and bolted out of the room, nearly stumbling in her haste.

I burst out laughing and expanded my aura, damaging even more of the precious organs he had painstakingly acquired over the past few weeks. Cornelius ran out of the laboratory to limit the damage. Some of those organs or body parts were insanely rare and exotic. Replacing them would be extremely costly and time-consuming.

Even as he ran up the stairs, Cornelius tried to push me down into the psychic void that I usually faded into when wishing to isolate myself from his foulness. Normally, I happily sought its refuge. But today, I resisted both to spite him and to help enable the plan that had sparked in my mind a few moments ago.

"Stand down, you wretch!" Cornelius hissed as he once again tried to cast me down.

"That's not very nice, Necromancer. I'm not feeling the love," I said tauntingly. *"But I won't impose my presence where it is not wanted. Be warned that if I leave, you will not see me again for a long time."*

"Just go!" Cornelius snapped.

"Gladly!" I replied with a mocking laughter.

This could not have played out better. I faded happily, thrilled that he so easily took the bait. In truth, I couldn't have lasted at this little game much longer. Personally using my magic instead of him channeling it through his own power quickly drained me. Since I'd given so much of myself to Kali already, I tired even faster. I needed to tread carefully not to tip my hand.

But right now, all that mattered to me was that I would soon see my bride again.

Thanks to the bond now established with her hosting parts of me, I would normally simply send her a psychic nudge that would indicate it was time for her to run to the fairy ring and draw the portal. This time I went directly to her.

It was a bit of a reckless move, but it would still be hours before she would even attempt to open the portal. Beyond the fact that I couldn't contain my impatience to see her again, I didn't want to waste any time with her. We had a few matters to discuss, as well as prepare our incursion into the crypt.

Using the thin link connecting us, I teleported my consciousness to her. It always felt like falling through a void before the world materialized again around me. Most mortals wouldn't see my ethereal form as I appeared in what looked like Kali's necromancer workshop. People with psychic abilities might get a glimpse of a ghostly silhouette, while those who dabbled in the arcane would feel a sudden surge of otherworldly energy before they altered their vision to see what had triggered that reaction.

Leaning over a large counter, Kali was waving her hand in front of a shallow cut in her palm and drawing out little drops of blood. They hovered in front of her. With another gesture, she stretched them into needle like darts, then congealed them so they would be preserved and ready to use at a whim. She'd been halfway through the process when she felt me arrive.

Her head jerked up, her face taking on an alarmed expression as she immediately raised her hands in a defensive stance ready to cast an offensive spell on the intruder.

She froze when she saw me. Shock gave way to disbelief and confusion as she altered her vision to see me more clearly.

"Pharos?! What…? How are you here?!" she exclaimed.

"We're bonded," I replied dismissively, feeling the intense strain of that excessive use of power. "Cast the circle. This is draining me too quickly."

To my relief, Kali didn't hesitate and burst into action. The swiftness with which she created the portal after only drawing it a few times over the recent days impressed me. As soon as she finished, I glided in, an intense sense of relief washing over me as its stabilizing power took over for me. Instead of the pale apparition I had been, I solidified again at no cost to me.

"Blood Magic?" I asked with curiosity while gesturing with my chin at the pouch filled with blood darts on the counter.

She glanced at it over her shoulder before looking back at me. "Yes. I specialize in Blood and Bone Magic."

I raised an eyebrow. "Not Soul or Flesh Magic? Necromancers usually focus on those two first."

She shrugged. "I don't want to make zombies or steal someone else's freedom by enslaving their souls."

I gave her an indulgent smile. "You can use those types of magic for far more than creating zombies. Combined with Blood or Bone Magic, they can grant you far greater powers and allow you to cast extremely useful spells."

"I know but…"

"But?" I insisted when her voice trailed off.

"I am learning the basics of Flesh Magic," she conceded reluctantly. "But I really don't want anything to have to do with Soul Magic. I've seen the way most of those who practice it start abusing it. As time goes by, they stop seeing those to whom those souls belonged to as people. They only see them as tools to enhance their own power. I've seen the devastation it has caused."

"Then you will always be weak," I said sternly. "Soul Magic would be of great help to you in the crypt."

She shrugged again, her beautiful face taking on a defensive expression. "I am preparing for our mission in the crypt. I've read everything available about it."

I burst out laughing. She scrunched her face, stung by my instinctive reaction. I didn't mean to embarrass or mock her, but she was being truly delusional about what trials awaited her… awaited us.

"Kali, going in will be easy. Coming back out will be a completely different story. Whatever you may be reading about Hemdell can never prepare you enough for what you will face," I cautioned in a reasonable tone.

"Okay, but I will have you on the way out," she said in a self-evident tone. "Between our joint forces—"

"I cannot help you," I said in a tone that brooked no argument.

She recoiled, shock and a hint of betrayal sparkling in her obsidian eyes. "Why not? Why wouldn't you want to help me after I've freed you?"

"It has nothing to do with what I want," I countered. "Beings like me are bound by many rules. As a Reaper, I cannot simply go around killing creatures and people who happened to be inconvenient. I can only kill or harm when the target poses a direct threat."

"And they will do exactly that!" Kali exclaimed, visibly baffled that it wasn't obvious to me.

"They will threaten *you*, not *me*," I corrected in a gentle tone. "Very few creatures, even the mindless ones, mess with Death. They give us a wide berth. Once I walk again, even in a weakened state after so many centuries of stasis, they will know they cannot stand against me. But they will come after you. A threat to you isn't one to me. Intervening would impact Fate's plans for you. We are not allowed to tamper with the Wheel or the Thread of Life."

She stared at me in disbelief. "So you're just going to stand by and watch me possibly get overwhelmed and die?"

"I will not be able to help you, Kali. And I do mean *not able*. Intervening will cause me debilitating pain that will make me unable to actually assist you. It is not by choice. There is one way around it, but you will not consent."

Right on cue, Kali's face closed off, and she crossed her arms over her chest in a disgruntled fashion.

"Let me guess. You will help me if I give you my soul," she ground through her teeth.

"Yes," I replied in a factual fashion.

"That's too steep a price. As you said yourself, I'll never consent to it."

"I don't want you to die, Kali," I said in a suddenly pleading tone as I moved forward to the edge of the circle.

"Then don't reap me!" she exclaimed.

I shook my head with an apologetic expression. "If your body dies, and I don't reap you, your soul will linger and start to decay."

"Decay?!" she echoed, baffled. "Wouldn't I automatically go into limbo until a Reaper comes for me?"

I shook my head again. "You need one of us to get you into Erebus to begin with. It is but the entrance hall to the various areas of the afterlife a soul can be taken to, based on its unique circumstances. You need a Reaper to crossover. And then the Ferryman will take you to your final destination. If you are not reaped, you will linger in the mortal plane and decay."

"Like the wandering souls?" she asked with a shudder.

I nodded. "Most of the souls that haunt the crypt and other similar damned places belong to those who were prevented from crossing over by a curse, or who foolishly refused to be escorted. Then you have those who doomed themselves by committing heinous enough acts to be punished by being left behind, but not necessarily enough to be thrown into the darkest pits of Hell and eternal damnation. For them, decaying is a greater mercy."

She swallowed hard, her wheels spinning as she reflected on

the matter. "All right. But I have not led a bad life. If you don't reap me, wouldn't another Reaper come for me?"

I hesitated, suddenly feeling embarrassed, then shook my head. "No other would come for you as you are marked."

"Marked? What does that even mean? Did Cornelius—?"

"No," I interrupted, shifting uneasily as I carefully chose my words. "None would come because I have claimed you. Your soul is mine to reap."

"What?! You've taken my soul?!"

"No!" I exclaimed, raising both my palms in an appeasing gesture. "Your soul is entirely yours. Neither I nor anyone else have any claim on it but you. I only get to be the one who will escort you to the other side when your time comes."

Although all tension bled out of her shoulders, she continued to stare at me with confusion and a hint of suspicion.

"Okay, but why?"

"Because I like your soul," I admitted sheepishly, feeling insanely self-conscious.

Her jaw dropped, and her eyes widened. Although stunned, Kali also seemed flattered. That reaction prompted my mouth to just run away.

"I like the way it feels around me, its mesmerizing shimmer, its enthralling melody so soothing and comforting, and its divine taste."

"Its taste?!"

As I was speaking, Kali had been gradually softening, her peach skin taking on a rosier tinge in response to those flattering comments. But that last one had her instantly horrified and wary.

I smiled, both amused and embarrassed to make this revelation. "Reapers can feed in several ways. Draining the lifeforce of a fallen's remains or lesser souls are common methods. But we normally feed off the energy emanating from people's souls. The stronger the emotions, the more energy they generate."

"Like a succubus?!"

I hesitated. "Partially. Feeding from emotions does not drain the target, contrary to the way a succubus does it. As you will recall, I pledged not to harm you in any way. The energy that you produce is the sweetest thing I have ever tasted. It is quite addictive. It's a good thing too, as it helps give me enough energy to fool Cornelius in not noticing that my soul is thinner from sharing parts of it with you."

"I see," Kali said, rubbing her nape uneasily.

She didn't quite know how she felt about it all. I couldn't blame her. And yet, my stupid mouth ran away with me again.

"Give me your soul, Kali," I said in a pressing tone. "Not only will I protect you, but I will make you long-lived."

She opened her mouth with a frown upon hearing the first sentence, likely to shut me down in no uncertain term. However, my second comment piqued her curiosity.

"Long-lived? Not immortal?"

I smiled and shook my head. "Only the Gods and the Ancients are immortal."

"What about you?"

My smile broadened. "As I am neither a God nor an Ancient, I am indeed mortal, but long-lived. Other Reapers and I *can* be killed. It is just extremely hard. My body regenerates fully in little time, even if it was completely burnt or destroyed beyond recognition. I could do the same for you."

Her eyes widened ever-so-slightly at that. It was a little underhanded to dangle such a carrot before her. Who in their right mind wouldn't want such an ability? It struck me how shameless I was willing to become if it convinced her to give me her soul. The need to own her was driving me insane.

"But you would own my soul permanently," Kali said at last. "So as enticing as this all is, it remains a hard pass for me."

"If you die in the crypt—and you *will*—all of this will have been in vain. Cornelius will win," I snapped.

She lifted her chin defiantly. "I had a reasonable life, and I should therefore have a decent afterlife. At least, you will be free. As much as I would love to kill Cornelius myself, I take comfort in knowing that you will see that he is properly punished for what he did to you."

I pinched my lips, unable to argue with her logic, but not yet willing to drop it, despite knowing she was still not ready to cave in on this… if ever.

"And what of your brother?" I challenged, another wave of guilt surging through me at this low blow—honest though it was. "Even if I kill Cornelius after you have passed, it will not free your brother. Jasper's soul is decaying. Soon, he will be a mindless ghoul. Someone needs to perform a ritual to free him."

"And you can't do it?!" she exclaimed.

I shook my head with an apologetic look. "I cannot interfere in the lives of mortals other than to reap them. You will have done all of this in vain if you do not survive the crypt, unless you find someone else to take care of your brother once you're gone."

"Is this some kind of trick to force my hand into giving you what you want?" Kali asked, narrowing her eyes at me. "I mean, if I give you my soul, and you become my owner, won't it also preclude me from intervening in the lives of mortals?"

"No, silly woman. I will own your soul, but you will still be human with all the same rights and none of my restrictions. I will simply make you long-lived and near immortal."

"So you won't stop me from doing anything I want but that you may disagree with?" Kali insisted.

"Why would I? If I disagree, I will try to reason with you. But if you insist, then it is your choice to make. I am not your master."

"But you could be, if you so choose," she countered.

"If I so choose, yes, I could be," I said with a shrug.

She gaped at me as if I were a creature that should not exist.

"Wow! You could have lied instead of admitting to my worst fears!" Kali exclaimed.

I frowned. "Is that what you would want? For me to lie to you, ply you with pretty untruths to wrest what I want from you through deception?"

She pinched her lips and gave me a 'Don't be silly' look. "Of course not. But you didn't have to be so blunt about it."

"There will always be nothing but honesty between us, however unpleasant the truth may be," I said in an imperious tone.

"Fine. But this soul giving business is still a no go for me. I'll figure out another way to get out of the crypt in one piece," she said stubbornly.

I clenched my teeth. As much as I understood her reluctance, it still felt like a personal affront and rejection.

"You will be my bride, Kali. And you will freely give me your soul," I said in a slightly menacing tone.

"I am not your bride," she said with the same mulish expression she always took every time she rejected my claim.

That pissed me off.

Flicking my hand, I invoked the kinetic powers of Flesh Magic to draw her to me. Kali gasped as she glided into the circle and all but collided with me. Despite her surprise, she didn't resist or try to fight me off when I leaned down and crushed her lips in a brutal kiss.

I all but tore off the dark, short sleeved dress she'd been wearing. I could feel her displeasure upon hearing the ripping sound of the fabric. Yet, her tongue battled with mine with the same furious passion. There was no tenderness or gentle foreplay in our coupling. It was raw, brutal, filled with frustration, mutual anger, fear, and desperation.

As I pounded into her, surrounded by the mesmerizing beauty of her aura, shining even brighter from the tempest of conflicting emotions warring inside her, I gorged on its potent and intoxicating energy.

As she writhed beneath me, her inner walls contracting around my cock, I once more cursed that wretched ethereal form that cheated me out of the full contact I craved with my female. I would be damned before I allowed her light to go out because of her stubbornness. Whatever the cost, she would give her soul to me.

Kali was mine.

CHAPTER 6
PHAROS

One day. One entire fucking day of travel to reach the wretched Ashire Wilds. Of all the ways to ruin my plans, Cornelius couldn't have done a better job. On top of riding a carriage for hours into the next town, we'd spent over twelve hours on a boat before getting on yet another carriage. And still, we hadn't reached our destination.

This had not been in the cards at all. But of course, one of Cornelius's countless contacts reached out to him about a manticore sighting in that untamed region. This couldn't have happened at a worse moment. With Hermes's failure to acquire the bones and organs he wanted, the necromancer wouldn't miss this opportunity of securing it for himself.

I had no idea what he intended to do with it. While Cornelius had kept secrets from me over the centuries, he had never been so thoroughly tight-lipped about a project. I knew him enough to guess it was something I would find so abhorrent I might try to sabotage it. I hadn't worried about it knowing that either I would find an opportunity to do just that at some point, or he would be clever and devious enough to ensure I couldn't meddle with it.

Either way, trying to guess what it entailed would have merely been a waste of time.

One of my principal worries lay in the fact that we were miles away from home… from my bride. Much too far for me to warn her of my absence, and especially much too far for me to attempt to teleport to her using our bond. Not only did I doubt I possessed enough power to project myself across such a great distance, but there would be no way I could achieve such a feat without Cornelius noticing.

The second source of concern—and in this instance the main one—was the fact that for such a hunt, Cornelius would undoubtedly make extensive use of my powers. The mostly quiet schedule he originally had focused on pursuing further experiments at home with new spells and constructs, would have allowed me to complete the process of partial transfer without drawing too much attention to myself. But the hunt was a different matter altogether.

Not for the first time, I berated myself for the foolish impatience that prompted me to teleport to Kali last night instead of waiting for her to open the portal. On top of burning a great deal of energy, I had further weakened myself by sharing more of my soul with her. Feeding off her energy didn't come remotely close to replenishing what I had lost.

During an epic battle, I would fizzle out quickly. Then, Cornelius would know something was amiss.

The whole journey through the field of tall grass that would eventually lead us to the rocky outcropping in the distance where the manticore was rumored to reside, I prayed that the creature would see us coming and escape. Beyond the fact that I feared exposure, I truly didn't want one of those too-rare mythical beings getting destroyed over some dreadful and selfish scheme the necromancer had concocted.

Sadly, the spying ravens the necromancer sent scouting ahead found their target. Through their eyes, Cornelius surveyed the area and set the plan to capture or kill the creature.

We made slow progress towards the rocky area where the manticore had carved its nest. Alva—who was adept at Terror and Dread Magic—summoned a few nightmares to terrorize the wildlife roaming the tall grass of the valley leading up to the manticore's lair. They were mindless, shadowy figures that would track down anything with a heartbeat and inflict superficial wounds to terrify and torment their prey. As they fed from their terror, Alva would siphon part of that energy to boost her own magic.

At the height of their fright, Cornelius would use my Death Aura to instantly slay the creatures. On bigger beasts—especially mammals—he would first cast a low-level necrosis on them to increase their pain and distress, further amplifying the benefits Alva gained from her Dread Magic. As dozens of creatures died, Meri raised their skeletons and set them to follow.

It cut me to the core to have my powers thus desecrated, used for gratuitous and violent murders. Before being captured, I never used my divine gifts in such an unconscionable way. I could count on one hand the number of times I had used necrosis. In all other cases, I kept my death aura either to protect myself and others or in an act of mercy like to grant peace to those only moments from dying in the slow agony of a plague, drowning, or suffocating.

As was his wont, Cornelius exclusively drew on my powers to perform these tasks. Finding less and less creatures to build his undead army, he kept expanding the radius of my death aura, which drained me exponentially. He always used my powers first to save his for the ultimate battle. In his narcissism, he wanted to give himself the illusion that he held all the credit for the final victory.

This time, that shameless tactic played in my favor. By the

time he deemed his army large enough, I was running on fumes. A short while longer and I would have been completely depleted.

While Alva and Meri had been riding on their Dread Horses so that they could scout the nearby areas for prey, Cornelius had remained inside the comfort of our carriage driven by Jasper. With the manticore's lair but a short distance ahead, he finally disembarked and mounted his own Dread Horse, which had been attached to the carriage.

After ordering Jasper to stay there, he led the way with at least two hundred risen creatures of various sizes in tow.

A loud screech greeted our approach as we closed in the distance with the dark rock formation that seemed to rise out of nowhere in the middle of the valley. Judging by the powerful aura that emanated from that general direction, I could feel the presence of some sort of magic well. It would explain why the creature would have selected this area to settle in. That arcane surge could also have been the cause of the terrain swelling upward into that small rocky hill, like a lava eruption would have done to form a volcano.

A shower of darts raining down a few meters in front of us stopped us dead in our tracks. With a flapping sound, the manticore came to hover a short distance ahead. Intelligent blue eyes peered at us from his human face. Judging by the size of his lion's body, the length of his scorpion tail, and the span of his bat wings, I judged him to be about five-years-old, which would equate to around thirty years for a human.

He menacingly waved his tail covered in the same venomous spines that had fallen before us. The manticore could shoot them like a porcupine's quills to paralyze or kill his victims. Despite having shot at least two dozen of them, new spines were already growing back to replace the ones he just used.

"Who dares trespass on my domain?" he shouted with a booming voice.

"My name is Cornelius Cromwell. My apprentices and I traveled a long way to come make you an offer you simply cannot refuse."

The manticore's eyes widened, and his lips parted, revealing three rows of sharp teeth.

"What could a mere human possibly have to offer me that I might desire?"

"The honor of serving me, of course," Cornelius said with obnoxious smugness. "I will make you more powerful than you can ever dream of."

The manticore barked a laugh at such a preposterous statement. Even at his young age, he constituted a significant enough threat to warrant the necromancer coming with his two most powerful apprentices and an army of undead. But even that was no guarantee of success… at least not without me. It infuriated me that my presence was the reason for Cornelius's cockiness.

But what infuriated me more were the mind games my captor was currently playing with the cub. When dealing with the arcane, one had to be extremely careful about the wording of an agreement. Cornelius wasn't lying when he promised to make him more powerful than he could ever imagine. What he failed to mention was that to achieve that goal, he would turn him into some kind of abomination and rob him of his free will and maybe even of his sanity.

"I serve no one, human. But *you* will serve *me*. I was about to head out to hunt for a snack. How kind of you to deliver yourself to me," the manticore said in a sickly-sweet voice.

"You misunderstand me, manticore. I wasn't asking your opinion on the matter. As per my initial statement, I'm here to make you an offer that you *simply cannot refuse*," Cornelius reiterated, this time putting an emphasis on the last three words. "You are young, inexperienced, and clearly clueless. You boast about owning a domain and yet have set up no defenses for it. Word of your presence here is already spreading far and wide.

Others will come to hunt and kill you. Serve me and you will get to experience the type of future you never could have imagined."

Indeed. One of misery, suffering, and hopelessness.

"Let those others come," the manticore hissed. "Like you, they will die by my hands, and I shall feast on your bones."

And he undoubtedly would if he could kill Cornelius. Under different circumstances, he would have had a fifty percent chance of success, despite being outnumbered. But by having me tethered to him, the necromancer essentially made himself immortal.

It was his turn to laugh at the manticore. "You wish you could. But I cannot die. The same cannot be said of you, little cub. So here's your choice. You can serve me willingly, or I can make you. Dead or alive, you're coming home with me as my servant."

The anger that descended over the rather handsome features of the manticore echoed the rage his words stirred within me.

"This conversation is over. Now, you die!"

With this, the manticore whipped his tail forward, firing at least twenty of the spines lining it at us. Alva instantly flicked her hands forward well shouting a word of power. A red haze flashed before us just as the darts crashed against the protective shield she had raised with her Blood Magic.

"As you wish!" Cornelius said with malicious glee.

He deliberately made that offer in a fashion obnoxious enough to force the confrontation. The necromancer didn't just like winning, he loved physically and mentally destroying his opponents in the process. Such petty and cruel tactics only revealed what a small and weak man he truly was that he required crushing others to validate his sense of self-worth.

An excruciating pain shot through me. Despite not having a physical vessel, I felt as if my spine had been torn right off my back when Cornelius invoked my Soul Magic to sever the manticore's soul from his body, making it easier to control and manipulate the creature.

Such a spell required an insane amount of power. No mortal could achieve it on their own. Even I would struggle to do it, especially on such a high-ranking mage as was a manticore. For a Reaper, only the use of our scythe made such a task easy. It didn't kill the target, only broke the bond that kept them bound to their mortal vessel.

That manticore's disbelieving laugh only confirmed what I already knew. The spell had failed in a spectacular fashion. At my full power, my ability channeled through Cornelius's own impressive skills should have at least partially damaged that link. It barely even made a scratch.

"You foolish human! Did you really think you could bind me like that?" the manticore mocked.

Below the shocked anger that erupted inside the necromancer, I felt the first seed of suspicion taking root. As we had faced far more powerful enemies in the past where he had used a similar tactic, Cornelius instantly knew that this time something was wrong. As much as I loved to interfere with his plans, I could not refuse him the use of my magical abilities. Therefore, this could only mean that something had tampered with my powers.

But the manticore firing another volley of spines at us as he simultaneously breathed down fire had the necromancer rolling out of the path of the inferno and poisoned needles. This time, he was the one to simultaneously cast a blood shield to absorb what he couldn't have avoided.

Without waiting for his command, Meri set forth her skeletal army. The confusion on the manticore's face as he flew in circles around us while showering us with flames and darts only confirmed his lack of battle experience. Obviously, it seemed illogical to send walking skeletons towards him when he was flying well out of range from their potential attacks. Despite its tremendous heat, the fire he breathed didn't destroy the bones. It only melted the flesh and remaining tendons off them.

Exactly what Meri wanted.

While Cornelius continued to block the manticore's attacks with Blood Magic, Alva created diversions with her nightmares. They didn't frighten the creature but put him on the defensive, hindering his ability to attack Cornelius. His reddish-brown fur covered a leather skin so thick the sharp claws of the nightmares barely scraped him on the rare occasions they managed to get a swipe in.

On top of their powerful magic, dragon fire, and lethal poison, manticores were also extremely fast both in their attacks and in their flight. It made hitting them with a spell, arrow, or any targeted weapon extremely difficult. You had to try and anticipate where they would be in time and space and fire at that location, hoping you wouldn't miss—which you usually did.

While Alva was genuinely attempting to strike him—and failing miserably—Cornelius was deliberately shooting his blood arrows wide in between casting protective shields. It was a deliberate strategy to lull the manticore into believing he was dealing with inferior opponents and therefore lower his guard. It also provided Meri with the time needed to set up her trap as her undead army took position in a half-circle around the area the creature was flying in as it rained fire and poisoned darts on us.

Sorrow and anger warred within me in equal measure as Meri used her Bone Magic to make her undead minions take a prone position on the ground, arms and legs tucked below them —for those who possessed such limbs—and their backs rounded towards the sky. Invoking her powerful bone manipulation skills, she began reshaping the bones of their backs, turning them into spikes pointing upward.

Once again revealing his inexperience and cluelessness, the manticore failed to see the trap rapidly closing around him. In a reckless display of bravado, the foolish cub dove down breathing a steady stream of fire at the risen creatures, burning what flesh remained on their bones, shattering a few of them with a brutal swipe of his wing, and even picking one up in a fly by. As he soared back into the skies he made a show of biting a thick limb from his catch, effortlessly crushing the bones between the three vicious rows of teeth in his unnaturally large mouth in his otherwise handsome human face.

Seizing this moment of distraction, Cornelius siphoned a large chunk of the magic reserves Alva gathered earlier from the creatures she terrorized and combined it with my Soul Magic abilities to attempt once again to sever the manticore's link to his body. Alva faltered from the sudden loss a split second before the effects of his greed struck me as well.

This time, the same excruciating sharp pain tore me asunder, and I felt myself going faint as a strange tingling similar to a person about to lose consciousness spread through me. The world darkened around me. As I had no eyes of my own, I saw and experienced the environment through all of Cornelius's senses. That the strain on me had been so violent to temporarily separate that connection terrified me.

"Why the fuck are you so weak?!" Cornelius mentally hissed when the attack miserably failed again.

Feeling dazed, I didn't know by what sorcery I managed to gather my thoughts enough to blurt out what I hoped he would deem a plausible enough explanation.

"You're attacking a manticore, not some weak human. He's near his magic well and wisely keeps flying along strong ley lines. You wasted a lot of my energy by casting my death aura over a ridiculously wide radius," I explained. *"The three of you will tire before he does. You cannot take his soul."*

"But YOU could!" Cornelius countered before rolling out of the way of another volley of poisoned darts.

"His life thread is not severed yet," I argued. *"There is still a*

chance he will survive this encounter. Therefore, no, I cannot harvest his soul for you—not that I would have."

"Fine, have it your way. I don't need him alive. It would have been nice, but all I truly need are his bones for my little project. I'll be sure to remember how you made things harder once it's completed," Cornelius mentally replied in an ominous fashion. *"For now, let's use one of your favorite abilities."*

The malicious way he laughed upon speaking those last words chilled me. While I genuinely could not have helped him kill the manticore before Fate deemed his time had come, shame filled me for once again making the situation worse for someone in the necromancer's crosshairs. After all this time, I knew better than to allow my stupid mouth to provoke him, considering how thin skinned he was. He always needed to put me back in my place by hurting others in my name and doing so with my powers.

Despite how drained I'd become, I still possessed enough power for Cornelius to use my death aura in a targeted fashion. By channeling it through his own magic and aiming at a specific target instead of using it over a wide radius, it required a lot less fuel to have a potent impact. In this instance, the death strike he used against the manticore acted on him like a savage blow.

The cub faltered, his flight pattern becoming erratic as he drunkenly tried to recover. Alva's nightmares swooped in, clawing him from all sides. With a series of powerful blows and through savagely whipping his tail, the manticore fought the weaker creatures back. Just when it looked like he would prevail, Cornelius hit him again with a second death strike. This time, the cub emitted a pained roar and blood trickled from the corner of his mouth.

Simultaneously, Meri set off her trap.

With a single vocal command, the prone skeletons she had lined in the half circle around the manticore's domain burst into action.

The sharpened bones she had reshaped on their backs shot into the air with the power of a crossbow bolt. Still destabilized by the debilitating pain of the death strike, he failed to dodge the incoming bone spikes. Despite his valiant efforts, several of them found their mark. He shrieked as a few of them embedded themselves in his sides, legs, and left shoulder. A couple more tore through his bat wings.

Enraged, the manticore did what it should have done from the start and dashed towards Cornelius. In his lack of experience and the arrogance of youth, he made a show of his power, threatening and taunting instead of going for the kill. By dragging out the fight for entertainment, he had given the enemy the upper hand.

Having expected that reaction, Cornelius threw half a dozen blood darts at the charging creature. I couldn't tell whether they reached their target or not as the manticore breathed a long and steady stream of fire at us. For a split second, I thought he had succeeded in breaking through my host's blood shield until the flames hit the invisible wall before us. It didn't stop us from feeling the intense heat.

My spirit soared when the shield began to falter under the sustained fiery assault and as the manticore closed in on us. Between the fire and force of the impact, the shield would collapse, and the beast would be able to tear Cornelius limb from limb. Granted, my regeneration powers would keep him from dying, but it would not spare him from the intense agony of having his body torn to shreds. As I wouldn't share in that pain, I prayed for that moment to come.

It didn't.

I heard the heart-wrenching scream of the young manticore half a beat before I saw multiple volleys of bone spikes tearing through the sky. The wall of fire faded just as a loud thud resonated barely a couple of meters in front of us.

Grievously wounded with at least two dozen spikes protruding from his body at different angles, the cub had crashed onto the ground and was scrambling to get back on his paws. Like vultures, Meri and Alva closed in on the creature, hands waving as binding incantations flowed freely out of their mouths.

A cruel chuckle escaped the necromancer as he smugly strolled towards his fallen opponent. With an impressive determination laced with desperation, the manticore attempted to flee. Even with his severe injuries, he still managed to fly away at an impressive speed while clumsily yanking some of the bone spikes out of his body. However, his escape was short-lived. With a powerful spell combining Flesh and Bone Magic, Cornelius took over control of the manticore's wings, paralyzing them.

The poor creature went into a freefall, crashing heavily once again. It knocked the wind out of him. His painful groans mixed with his wet and whistling breathing, hinting at pierced lungs.

He never had a chance to get back up.

His attempt at flicking his tail, both to fire his poisoned spines at his tormentors and to attempt to sting them with the sharp needle at the tip, was quickly thwarted. Pulling on the skull pommel of his walking stick, Cornelius revealed the vicious blade hidden within. With one swift swipe, he used it as a sword to chop off the tail.

Working swiftly and efficiently, Meri and Alva shackled the cub to the ground. Where Alva merely used her Blood Magic to weave arcane threads around his limbs, Meri revealed the darker side that lurked deep within the lovesick naive girl she usually portrayed herself to be.

Without blinking, she yanked two of the bone spikes embedded in his side then coldly stabbed them in his front paws. With a swift incantation, she once more used bone manipulation for the bones to reshape themselves into some form of grappling hook that nailed his limbs to the ground. Oblivious to his agonized screams, she repeated the process with his back paws.

Refusing to accept what was now clearly inevitable, the

manticore tried to escape again—even at the risk of tearing his limbs off—with a vain attempt at flapping his wings again. Sadly for him, Cornelius was maintaining his paralysis on them. Not wanting to continue to expend that energy, the necromancer subjected those magnificent wings to the same dreadful fate his tail had met.

"You should have served me, you fool," Cornelius said tauntingly as he circled around the mangled creature to stand by his head. "Now, you're going to die, slowly and painfully. And I'm going to enjoy hearing your agony during every second of it. You see my pretty little Alva over there?" Cornelius asked, gesturing with his head at his apprentice. "She's extremely adept at Flesh and Blood Magic. Her specialty is harvesting organs while keeping the host alive so that they retain even more of their magic properties. And you, my little friend, are a treasure trove of magic ripe for the reaping."

He gestured for Alva to proceed. The eagerness with which she retrieved the necessary paraphernalia from the saddle of her horse was beyond repulsive. She was as cruel as her Master. Meri, her face devoid of emotion, began drawing a few runes on the manticore's body while muttering some incantations both to stifle his own magic and to keep him alive well-beyond what nature intended once Alva got to work on him.

Cornelius chuckled with shameless cruelty upon hearing me mentally cursing him. I wanted to spare the cub from the prolonged agony they were about to subject him to. But his life thread still had too long remaining on it for me to intervene. And weakened as I was, the powers I could use would only add to the torture he would endure. If I still had a body, I could have at least ended his pain, if not his life.

As Alva started slicing his chest open, the manticore didn't scream, but locked eyes with Cornelius. To my shock, I realized he wasn't looking at the necromancer, but directly at me.

"Release me, Reaper!" he shouted in a pained voice. "Grant me peace!"

Cornelius burst out laughing, mocking both him and me. Despite his prior request to rip out the manticore's soul for him, my host knew better the limitations that constrained me. However, the baffled look Alva and Meri cast in turn towards their master and their victim reiterated the fact that Cornelius was doing an excellent job of fooling them into believing the tremendous powers he possessed actually came from him instead of the demigod he had enslaved.

They had no idea I lurked within him.

Annoyed by their inquisitive looks, he snapped at them to resume their task. The next five minutes devolved into a gruesome spectacle of pure evil as they painstakingly started removing the least vital organs from the creature, taking their sweet time to wrap them in spells as they placed them in the special containers Alva had brought so that they wouldn't decay or lose the potent magic that emanated from them.

To add insult to injury, Cornelius used my regeneration powers to help sustain the cub who was quickly failing from the sadistic abuse inflicted upon him. Too focused on my guilt and sorrow, further compounded by the heart-wrenching sound of his screams, I didn't hear this subtle but unmistakable ripping sound of the brief tearing of the Veil from a traveler teleporting through it.

And then I felt the beloved familiar energy.

Haroth!!

"Reaper! You're much too early!" Cornelius snarled upon seeing the impressive silhouette of my brother standing two meters ahead.

The two apprentices once more started, looking in confusion at the empty space where their master was looking. Meri was the first to realize what was happening and altered her vision to be able to see the Reaper. Alva followed suit moments later. As regular mortals, their necromantic powers were the only thing that allowed them to get some sort of glimpse. But to them, he would merely look like a vague, robed figure. Thanks to me, Cornelius would see my brother in his full glory.

A powerful ache, sense of loss, and longing crushed me as I took in his dark robe and gleaming scythe. The familiar sound of his chains clanking as he closed the distance with us further exacerbated the sharp pain of all that had been taken from me. Below his hood, his eyes glowed red—testifying to his fury and illuminating the sharp angles of his skeletal face.

It hurt even more that part of his rage was actually aimed at me.

Obviously, Haroth understood that I had not chosen this fate, and that I couldn't help how my powers were being abused. That didn't lessen his resentment. By allowing myself to be captured, I had caused endless suffering that never should have existed as Cornelius never would have had the power required to inflict it to begin with.

And yet, beneath that anger, my brother felt a great deal of pity for me.

"My apprentices and I plan to play with him for a while longer. I'm sure you can find plenty of other dying souls to keep you occupied for an hour or so. We should be done by then," Cornelius said with an arrogance that made me want to tear him to shreds.

"I think not," Haroth replied with a voice cold enough to freeze an erupting volcano.

"His thread has not ended!" the necromancer hissed with disbelief.

"It is close enough. Unlike Pharos, I am a Grim, not an Angel of Death. As I am not bound by the same constraints, I say he's done."

"NO!" Cornelius shouted.

But it was too late. With a swift swipe of his scythe, Haroth killed the manticore. At a glance, it looked as if he had attempted to behead him. While the two girls only saw a blur, Cornelius and I clearly saw the blade sever the soul's link to the body before yanking it out.

It was a luminous glow that spread through the few bone knots at the base of the scythe. Like many Grims, Haroth carried the souls of the fallen in that fashion as he did not care to interact with them during their journey to the other side. I literally walked them, their souls retaining the ethereal silhouette of the physical person they had been before their passing as I ease them into their new journey ahead.

Yielding once more to his volatile temper, Cornelius foolishly took a threatening step towards my brother. "You fucking—!"

"Do not threaten or insult me, human. Then again, maybe you should carry on and give me a good reason to put you out of your misery," Haroth said, waving his scythe in a less-than-subtle fashion.

Cornelius laughed while looking at the Reaper with an incredulous expression. "Seriously?! I can't die, you idiot!"

My brother tilted his head to the side, the bones of his skeletal face shifting to reveal a terrifying toothy grin. He normally had a very pleasant smile, but this time, he was deliberately using one of his Grim appearances for a more dramatic effect.

"You want to bet? I'd be happy to teach you the error of your ways."

"You wouldn't dare!" Cornelius said, this time, a hint of worry seeping into his voice.

He almost added that Haroth wouldn't want to risk killing his own brother, but he caught himself at the last minute before casting an annoyed glance at the women. He angrily gestured for them to move away and grant him privacy.

"Why are you sending away your females?" Haroth asked

loud enough so that they would hear him. "Are you afraid they will find out the secret of your power? That they will learn you truly are a weak necromancer leeching off the Reaper you have ensnared?"

The women gasped, their heads jerking between their master and the Reaper.

"Leave!" Cornelius shouted at his apprentices, his face twisted with fury.

They didn't have to be told twice. They all but ran back to their Dread Horses that patiently waited a good fifty meters away.

"But to answer your unspoken question," Haroth continued mockingly, "yes, I would kill my brother. Considering the foul way in which you are using him," he added waving at the mangled remains of the manticore, "killing you both would be me showing him mercy. So you go ahead and threaten me again, Necromancer. And then you'll find out whether I can or would kill you both."

Seething with rage, Cornelius clenched his teeth but wisely kept silent. Like the manticore had done earlier, Haroth locked eyes with my host, but he was looking directly at me. An odd thrill coursed through me when his consciousness brushed against mine. But the brief wave of joy that contact brought me quickly turned into dread when my brother frowned. I didn't need him to speak to know he had realized what was happening with me.

Please don't give me away!

I couldn't speak with him, only pray that he wouldn't drop any hint that might further raise Cornelius's suspicions.

To my utter relief, my brother turned on his heel without another word. The air blurred around him, and the discrete ripping sound resonated half a beat before he vanished.

With an endless series of the foulest curses I had ever heard, Cornelius ordered the women to come back and swiftly complete the task. With the manticore dead, the necromancer was forced to expand even more of my regeneration abilities to maintain as much of the magic properties of the creature's organs. By the time the gruesome task was completed, I was utterly drained.

And Cornelius knew it.

At this point, there was no denying that he suspected something was amiss. I could only pray that he didn't understand yet what it was and what to do about it. Kali needed to transfer me into my own vessel in all haste.

To my dismay, instead of embarking right away on the long journey back home, Cornelius spent the next day plundering the manticore's lair and studying his magic well. The worst part of it all was that the great distance once again prevented me from warning Kali of my current predicament. I would have given anything to be able to contact her. Considering my current state, I couldn't have given her more of myself, but feeding from her would have greatly improved my situation.

My only blessing through it all was that Cornelius didn't draw on my magic during the remainder of our stay here nor when we finally set back on the way home on the third day. This proved the most terrifying and distressing seventy-two hours of the past few centuries.

Cornelius had now completely blocked his thoughts from me. That he would totally keep me in the dark confirmed that he was either on to me or up to something terrible. Whatever he was planning, I had no doubt he would set it in motion the moment we got home.

As I faded in the background, begging for my energy to replenish quickly, I prayed to all the Gods and powers that be that Kali didn't give up on me thinking I had reneged on our agreement.

CHAPTER 7
KALI

For the twentieth time—which felt more like a thousand—I glanced at my watch. I'd been sitting in the clearing by the circle for at least four hours now. I didn't understand what could be holding him up so late. He hadn't attempted to respond to the summons, not even to give it the 'pause' signal. As I feared leaving it active for too long a stretch to avoid alerting Cornelius, I paused its call. Once every twenty minutes or so, I would reactivate it only for a few seconds as a nudge.

Despite his annoyance with me last night that I wouldn't give him my soul, I didn't believe for one second Pharos would back out of this. Not this far in, and especially not with this being his one true hope of regaining his freedom. In the end, even if I keeled over while attempting to exit the crypt for not caving in to his request, it wouldn't change the beneficial outcome for him. Pharos would be free.

Plus I still felt his essence inside me.

Although I couldn't tap into his Reaper powers, I had noticed a significant boost to my magic abilities since the first time we mated. After last night, it had gone up another notch. As it would make no sense for Pharos to give me a part of himself and then just bounce, I could only assume something was interfering with his ability to come back to me.

I didn't want to give in to panic and assume the worst. And yet, my mind kept wondering if Cornelius had discovered our plans and further shackled Pharos. The complete silence significantly fueled that fear. Did his little stunt of teleporting to me last night expose him? Had his presence inside the necromancer faded so much it revealed the plot?

By the fifth hour, I gave up and returned to my house, feeling defeated and extremely concerned. I made my way to bed, jumping at every sound, every sensation, imagining it was a sign from Pharos.

While I initially embarked on this crazy mission for the sake of my brother, I couldn't deny the genuine worry constricting my heart for Pharos. Sure, he'd proven to be a fantastic lover. But it went deeper than that. I actually cared about him. There was something about being in his mere presence that lifted my spirit. While a man acting possessive towards me usually had my hackles up in a blink, I irrationally liked it coming from Pharos, even though I pushed back when he did. His almost obsessive need to own my soul, the way he described its beauty and how it affected him, and especially how his voice dropped an octave whenever he called me his bride did wondrous things to me. A part of me genuinely liked the idea of being claimed by him.

I was developing quite a crush for Pharos.

It didn't make sense to the extent that we'd had very few conversations that hadn't focused on our mission. I knew next to nothing about him, not even how Cornelius managed to trap him to begin with. From what brief interactions we've had, Pharos seemed honest and honorable. Although assertive, he never gave me the impression of being bossy. No matter how much he disliked my decisions—and clearly expressed his opinion to that effect—he ultimately respected my choices and didn't try to bully or shame me for them.

I liked that a lot.

Can I see myself pursuing a relationship with him when this is all said and done?

That thought gave me pause. Right now, I couldn't be certain if the way he was acting with me was a true reflection of his personality. I was his ticket to freedom. How did I know he wasn't keeping a potential darker side in check until he got what he wanted? What would he be like in his normal everyday life? What did he even look like in the flesh?

Does he even have flesh?

Once again, I was struck by how clueless I was about him. I'd never seen a Reaper in person before. From all that I had read about them, mortals usually only saw them in their full glory at the time of death. The few exceptions were high-level sorcerers, and especially necromancers. But even then, those with arcane powers rarely could see them fully, only the hooded figure, often faceless, wielding a scythe. By most accounts, only a skeleton lurked beneath that usually black robe. Was that Pharos's case?

Is that a problem for me?

While I considered myself more of a Bone and Blood Witch than a necromancer, The idea of fucking a skeleton held zero appeal. If he turned out to be some kind of a shade or wraith, that would already be a lot less distressing. After all, his current form could be labeled as such to a certain extent. And I couldn't get enough of intimate moments with him that way.

The flame of shame sparked low in my gut mixed with the one of my blossoming arousal. Pharos was ruining me for any other man. He'd been fiercely passionate and blissfully voracious in each of our encounters. But that had not stopped him from being intently attentive to my pleasure. Granted, making me climax served his main purpose of making me loosen enough to be more receptive to hosting parts of him. It also provided him with the emotional and sexual energy that helped replenish his reserves of power.

However, I'd been surrounded by his soul as he made love to me. A soul could not lie. The attraction—not to say affection—he was feeling for me couldn't be denied.

That thought, more than anything else, answered all my previous questions. I loved the feel of his soul as much as he loved mine. Regardless of what his body turned out to be—skeleton, wraith, or anything else in between—I wanted to keep exploring whatever this was between us.

If he was willing, I wanted to pursue a relationship with him and see where it took us.

But why didn't he contact me tonight?

I heaved an aggravated sigh as the same pointless questions about what might have kept him away replayed in my head. It was already close to four in the morning. Despite the late hour, sleep eluded me. I tossed and turned for hours, dozing in and out, each time awakening with a start, wondering if it was in response to a poke from Pharos… which it hadn't been.

Morning found me a complete wreck and still no news from him. I spent the entire day beside myself, counting each minute as they stretched endlessly until nightfall. In a terrifying repeat of last evening, I waited in vain in the clearing without even the slightest hint of Pharos attempting to contact me. I returned home devastated and feeling utterly helpless.

I couldn't do anything except wait for him to reach out to me. But what if he couldn't? I wanted to believe the situation wasn't as dire as my paranoia kept claiming it was. That night proved even more fitful than the previous. I woke up exhausted, stressed, and even angry. As much as I repeated to myself that Pharos wasn't staying away of his own free will, the nasty voice at the back of my head wouldn't stop repeating that I'd been played.

The plan had been for me to go to the crypt either today or tomorrow. Last night would have established whether I was hosting enough of him to allow for a quick transfer before Cornelius could intervene.

Even if I'd been so bold to go ahead regardless, two separate issues kept me from proceeding. First, I had no clue about his body's specific location inside the crypt. Second, I couldn't make the journey into the bowels of this accursed place without being certain Pharos could go through the ritual as soon as I reached my destination. If exiting would prove as dire as he claimed, it would be foolish for me to throw away that attempt without confirmation that he would be there.

In spite of my growing sense of the futility of it all, I got back to work preparing for the mission. As I had done over the past few days, I spent the next few hours further studying every-thing I could get my hands on regarding the crypt and its inhabitants.

When I once more failed to hear from him by mid-afternoon, I gave up on this happening today. No one in their right mind would venture into that place at night. While daytime was extremely dangerous, nighttime was essentially suicidal. My goal had been to head out first thing in the morning, a plan I had intended to discuss with him last night.

As the sun began to set on the horizon without even the slightest poke or nudge from Pharos, I weighed my options. Tomorrow would be October thirty-first: All Hallows. Pharos heavily hinted that it would be an excellent day for the ritual as the Veil between the mortal plane and the Shadow Realms would be thinner. Death Magic would be significantly enhanced over the three days of All Hallowtide, reaching its peak on November second.

Based on our prior conversations, Pharos wanted to have his ultimate confrontation with Cornelius on that last day: All Saints Day. None of this would be possible unless we proceeded with our plan in the next 24 to 48 hours.

Struck by a sudden inspiration, I decided to stir the pot by writing a note to Cornelius pretending I was open to offering him some form of payment in exchange for my brother's liberation. As he was always on the lookout for rare artifacts or reagents, surely there was something he wanted that I might be able to acquire for him. Obviously, he would soundly reject that offer. The wretched male wanted to break and humiliate me. The more I resisted his demands, the more determined and rabid he became in his sick need to put me back in my place and teach me never to challenge my betters.

However, he wouldn't be able to read it without Pharos also seeing it. I hoped it would be enough of a nudge to get him to let me know somehow what was going on. Worst case scenario, it would make Cornelius reveal that he was on to us so that I could take the appropriate measures to protect myself.

As I couldn't come anywhere near Cornelius or his minions for fear they would detect Pharos's essence inside me, I sent the note by a raven, not holding my breath regarding a quick follow up. Knowing that foul necromancer, he would delay his response out of sheer cruelty, thinking I was desperately waiting with bated breath. Except, I didn't give a shit about hearing from him. Getting a sign—any sign—from Pharos was all I cared about.

To my shock, I received a response less than an hour later. Heart pounding, I retrieved the note bound to the leg of the raven before greedily reading it. I barely noticed their bird taking flight to return home.

My jaw dropped, and then an intense wave of relief washed over me as I read the note. Written by one of the servants, it indicated that Cornelius was out of town for a few days and would return in the morning or the day after next. As disappointed as I felt about that impromptu trip derailing our plans, the depth of happiness swelling through me at the knowledge that Pharos was safe and that circumstances beyond his control were the only reasons for his silence left me reeling.

I really cared about him.

Considering the horrible nights I'd spent over the past two days, I decided to turn in early. To my shame, now that all tension and worry about his welfare had been lifted, I caught myself fantasizing about the Reaper. How could I have gotten so addicted to him in such a short time? Sure, I'd been celibate for a while. Considering how mind-blowing sex was with him, any red-blooded woman would be craving him as much as I was. A nagging small voice at the back of my head hinted that my inability to just have casual sex without becoming emotionally involved explained my reaction to him. But at a visceral level, I knew this was different. Something special was happening between us.

No sooner did I get under the blankets than my hand found its way between my thighs. Try as I may, with my fingers rubbing my clit, and my left hand fondling my breast, I vainly tried to rekindle some of the intense sensations Pharos systematically stirred in me. While I succeeded in finding some kind of release, it so thoroughly paled in comparison to the devastating orgasms my lover gave me that I found myself feeling even more frustrated and achy than before I touched myself.

Exhausted, I let sleep claim me with the secret hope my dreams would provide me with a more satisfactory experience of naughty dalliances with my Reaper than my hand had.

And did I ever sleep!

However, none of it was of a raunchy nature. It did prominently feature Pharos. But he didn't speak a single word. In my dream, I was startled awake by him standing at the foot of my bed. Pharos waved for me to follow. As I was sitting up in my bed, the room blurred, and I found myself standing in my nightgown outside the entrance of the crypt in the middle of the Hemdell graveyard. He pointed at the sun above us. Judging by its position, it was at its zenith. Pharos then pointed at the crypt, and a purple thread appeared to shoot out of his index finger then flowed in its direction.

Before I could question him, the Reaper started gliding towards the entrance. I lifted my foot to shadow him only for our environment to blur again. This time, we were inside the building once my surroundings stabilized.

While it had been no bigger than a large mausoleum, the crypt served as a doorway into an immense underground lair. Multiple staircases took us through nine various levels, as if in a twisted attempt to replicate those of Hell. The purple thread continued to mark the way, stretching ahead each time Pharos pointed the direction to follow. Jumping from one specific location to the next with that same blur, my companion led me through the crypt. Each time, he would silently gesture at the way to go. It would be quite the journey through a stairs maze, hidden passages among walls pockmarked with arched alcoves that undoubtedly hid foul creatures, a flooded area with dark water beneath which some massive fiendish creature lurked, and finally a large chamber with a sacrificial altar. A desiccated body, that I could only presume was his, lay atop it.

Pharos indicated a spot by the head of the altar. With his fingertip, he drew a circle as if to mark where I was to draw the portal.

And then we were back in my room. He cupped my face with both hands and leaned in to kiss me. He vanished half a beat after our lips touched.

I woke up with a start. The brightness of the room indicated it was already morning. One glance at my watch confirmed it was just a few minutes past eight. However, the vivid memory of it all convinced me that this had not been a dream, but an actual visit from Pharos to give me the instructions I lacked. Despite how undefined the facial features of his wraith-like form were, undeniable tension had oozed out of him.

Pharos was scared.

Whatever happened during that trip, I believed Cornelius had either begun to suspect foul play, or he had discovered the whole thing. Either way, we needed to act. To my relief, I felt properly rested.

After a quick analysis of my vision, I concluded that Pharos wanted me to go to the crypt today at noon. The question was whether that time should be when I reach the altar or when I started my descent inside that forsaken place. After debating it for a moment, I decided that he meant for me to begin the journey at noon. After all, he showed me the sun at its zenith right before entering the crypt.

I silenced the negative voice at the back of my head trying to crush me with wave upon wave of doubt. When it came to taking a stance on serious matters, I became the queen of second guessing. I had committed to a course of action and would see it through. If I allowed myself to dwell on it, I would soon become paralyzed by uncertainty. And now was not the time for this.

If we didn't see this through today, all would be lost. I could feel it in my bones.

I quickly dressed and chowed down a more substantial breakfast than what I normally ate. Not only would I need the energy, but I couldn't risk growing weak and hungry halfway through a potential battle. If my suspicions were right, we would be in there for a while.

I packed everything I needed for the mission and cast a series of protective spells and wards on myself. Considering the type of abominations I was likely to encounter in the crypt, those protections wouldn't do much. However, even the slightest help would be welcome.

My chest constricted as I placed an envelope with a note for the owner of the house I'd been renting and enough money to cover the remaining half of my lease in case I did not return. The mere fact that this was a possibility twisted my insides. As I got on my horse to head towards the crypt, my mind returned to Pharos.

He honestly believed I wouldn't be able to make it out of

there alive unless I gave him my soul. That thought constantly tormented me. I wasn't ready to die. But I also wasn't ready to surrender the most fundamental part of my being to anyone else, not even him. To me, it felt like another form of death, but one where I no longer even have any control over my destiny. If my time had come, I wanted to be whole when I crossed over.

I just prayed things wouldn't become as dire as he predicted.

The forty-minute ride to the Duskwallow burial ground inside which the Hemdell crypt was located flew by much too fast. Having arrived a little over half an hour before noon, I took my sweet time attaching my horse in a safe place far enough from the graveyard. There was sufficient grass all around for it to graze if needed. I cast a spell on its lead to have it loosen on its own should my mount feel threatened, or should I not return within six hours. I fed it a couple of apples, patted it farewell, then made my way towards the burial grounds.

Tall, rusty iron fence gates stood open at the entrance. It always struck me as a little ridiculous for them to be there as no fence closed off the perimeter of the sprawling graveyard. According to legends, there had once been a beautiful fence surrounding the place. But conflicting, if not flat-out contradictory tales tried to explain what had happened to them.

Today, they would have been useless.

Invisible magic walls kept the foul creatures that lurked here contained within this cursed place. It wasn't foolproof, to the extent that certain otherworldly beings were able to wander beyond its perimeter. Although also fiendish and malevolent, they fell into a different category. As I understood it, the protective wall only worked on mindless and feral creatures. Those who would never be deemed intelligent or even sentient, like wights, zombies, and nightmares.

My skin tingled from the powerful magic as soon as I passed through the open gates. The air immediately shifted, taking on the unpleasant scent of rot, mold, and decay that would greet you upon entering an abandoned house. The further in I got and the stronger the stench became. It had the putrid and festering edge of stagnant water. The entire place oozed with dark energy, but it was still mostly dormant. Not for the first time, I silently thanked the powers that be that my mission wasn't time constrained. I didn't even want to imagine how dreadful this place would be in the evening, had I been forced to come after nightfall.

The deceptive peacefulness of my surroundings, and the eerie silence made the beating of my own heart sound like thundering drums in my ears. My skin felt sticky and slimy, as if an evil mist filled the air. The way it clung to me felt like it was attempting to seep in and corrupt me like everything else here.

The graveyard was divided into various sections. At the entrance, countless mostly damaged or destroyed tombstones marked the burial location of hundreds of people, most of them peasants, servants, and commoners. The deeper into Duskwallow you got, and the taller, fancier, and more impressive the tombstones became, reflecting the higher status of those they had been erected for. But even that didn't spare them from being defaced or destroyed.

The beginning of the wealthy dead folks' section was heralded by a path made of dark stones lined with a series of pillars on each side. My stomach churned as I glanced at the feminine busts sitting on top of them. They had a Grecian look to them, probably in honor of some priestess or deities to watch over the dead. But their faces held none of the grace and beauty they initially possessed. They had the faces of pure evil. As I walked past them, their dead eyes followed me, and their plump and sensuous lips parted in an unnaturally wide smile filled with needle teeth.

Despite the wickedness emanating from them, I didn't hear any calls for an attack and didn't perceive any attempts to do so from them. It was as if they were just gleefully anticipating this shit show that was about to take place. A shudder coursed through me, and I cast down my burning desire to tuck my tail between my legs and run out of here.

As respectably powerful as my arcane abilities were, it was becoming painfully obvious that I might be biting off way more than I could chew.

A swift glance around me revealed the presence of random bones and partial skeletal remains scattered here and there. Some protruded from the ground at various angles. I couldn't say if whatever it belonged to had tried to emerge from the ground or had been stabbed into it. Either way, I expanded my bone magic survey abilities to perform a surface scan of them.

As suspected, most of them had little to no magic or life force remaining. Others had already sucked them dry or mostly used them up. While I would not be able to draw any magic from them if needed, I would still be able to manipulate them to turn them into constructs or bone Knights. They would be quite weak, but they made for a useful distraction, not to mention that there was strength in numbers. If a single one could be easily dispatched, sent as a swarm, they could overwhelm an enemy.

Comforted by that thought, I closed the distance with a building in the center of the 'fanciest' section of the graveyard. It had previously been an elegant and exquisitely adorned mausoleum. The once pale beige stones, decorated with sculpted figures and bas-relief carvings, looked almost burnt from the dark patches covering them. It was too dark and too slick to be dirt accumulated over the centuries. It reminded me of black blood. No vines or other wild growths could be found anywhere on or near it. Even the most parasitic forms of life knew to steer clear of this wretched place. No light reflected on its surface either.

I glanced at the sky to find the sun right overhead as I stood at the exact spot I had been in the dream-vision Pharos walked me through last night. A look at my watch indicated it was still a few minutes to noon.

For a brief instant, I considered waiting for both needles to be exactly on twelve before deciding to move forward. If Pharos had wanted me to enter specifically at noon on the dot, I believed he would have made sure to spell it out for me. Every second spent here increased the chance that I would face unpleasant company. I wouldn't dally any longer than necessary.

As soon as I reached for the handle of one of the two heavy metal doors, they silently parted open before me. The stench of evil slapped me like a physical entity. I fought back a gag reflex. It wasn't that the smell was so horrid. In fact, it was quite mild in comparison to some of the things I had been exposed to during my necromancer training. The first things that came to mind were a mix of rot, sulfur, and over ripe fruits. But it was the intense malice weaved into it that made my stomach churn. It was so intense I could almost taste it.

Steeling myself, I stepped inside to head towards the staircase. The moment I entered, something tugged at my chest, as if attempting to pull me forward. It took me aback at first, and then I realized that it felt like a slight psychic nudge from Pharos.

It was too different from the rare occasions he had done this before to be emanating from him. But I suspected it might be his body inside feeling part of his soul nearby and clamoring for it. As freaked out as I felt about venturing into the belly of the beast, the apparent confirmation that his body lay somewhere inside gave me a renewed sense of purpose and determination.

The first staircase felt suffocating with its low ceiling and narrow walls that made it impossible to see what awaited me on the landing below. That no torches or other sources of light illuminated it made the confined space even more claustrophobic. I considered casting a light spell but decided against it. It wasn't a long way to go before reaching the bottom, which clearly was properly lit.

My jaw dropped as I got off the last step. The room I entered proved to be even bigger than in my memory from the vision. It was vaguely rectangular, with five landings located at different heights in the space and connected by a variety of staircases leading to other levels and semi-hidden passages. At a glance, the lowest landing was located at least twenty meters below my current position.

All around me, alcoves covered the walls, some tall enough to act like a doorway, others the perfect size to fit one of the many caskets on display, and smaller ones serving as deep shelves on which a plethora of bones and skulls had been haphazardly piled on. However, what initially resembled thick, blood-covered cobwebs covered far too many of those alcoves. But on further inspection, they seemed to be fleshy membranes woven into spider-like webs.

As I walked past a row of caskets, I realized that quite a few lay open. Those that weren't empty displayed obvious signs of having been desecrated in one outrageous form or another. I averted my eyes, not allowing my fertile imagination to recreate the horrors that had taken place here.

The eerie silence of the place was only disturbed by the echoing sound of my footsteps going down the second set of stairs, the crunch of dirt and small pebbles beneath my boots, and the occasional odd sound impossible to define. And I wouldn't even speak of the creepy sighs that could simply be the result of the wind passing through random openings.

Following the path Pharos had indicated in the vision, I walked across the second landing to find the secret passage hidden by an optical illusion of the stone walls. This one, too, proved insanely claustrophobic. Barely two meters wide, it stretched over at least ten times that distance. On each side, carved directly into the walls, four stacked recessed shelves overflowed with human skulls. Judging by the extreme size differences, a few clearly belonged to young children.

Only three torches at about a six-meter interval each illuminated the enclosed space. The purple flames of the magical fire projected dancing shadows that freaked me out even more, creating the illusion that the skulls were moving.

I almost heaved a sigh of relief once I finally reached the other side. It turned out to be another large open area similar to the first one I entered previously. However, this one had the massive pool of water at the bottom from last night's dream. Since I could see the top of a few alcoves now underwater, I could only assume this pool had not been intended but resulted after some kind of flood. The pool had the green tinge of unclean water filled with algae. Despite the thick, chalky film that hid what lurked below, the water stirred, hinting at the presence of something swimming in its noxious depths.

It was the first living being I'd perceived so far.

Using my Blood Magic, I stretched my senses to assess it. The wretched thing was gigantic. It overflowed with arcane power, the type likely to overwhelm me in a confrontation. I quickly withdrew when a slithering sensation creeped over my psychic mind. The creature was aware of my presence and was assessing me as well.

Intent on avoiding it, I walked closer to the walls, while still maintaining a safe distance. I didn't doubt something might jump at me from behind the fleshy membranes that covered them.

However, my feeling of unease cranked up another notch as I felt for the first time evil closing in from behind. A dark entity was stalking me. I didn't feel the threat of an imminent attack. It was biding its time, waiting for the strategic moment to strike, likely once I was trapped in an area that would make it difficult for me to escape.

A spark at the edge of my vision startled me. I barely held back a yelp and pressed my palm to my chest at the sight of a weak purple glow ahead. For a split second, I feared it was some kind of shade or nightmare taking form before me. I altered my vision to help me better see ethereal or ectoplasmic presences. To my shock, it turned out to be the purple thread from my dream. It appeared to be shooting out from my chest and spreading all the way along the path leading to the room where Pharos would be lying.

The sense of the evil presence closing in spurred me on. I hastened my steps although not as much as I would have liked. If the thing stalking me had strong predatory instincts, running or loudly broadcasting my fear might trigger it to go on the attack. If I had to battle before summoning Pharos, I didn't want it to be in such an open space with far too many potential enemies to join the fray.

Thankfully, I didn't have another narrow passage with bone shelves to cross. I didn't doubt my stalker would have lunged at me had he been tailing me in that previous passage. After what felt like an eternity, three more staircases, two additional land-ings, and one large open corridor, I finally reached two humon-gous doors that I did not recall seeing in my dream. If not for the purple thread now shining brightly before me and vanishing behind the doors, not to mention the extremely strong pull that tugged at my chest to move forward, I might have wondered if I had made a wrong turn.

Another glance over my shoulder didn't reveal any presence. All I could see were countless skeletal remains and bones scat-tered around the edges of the large room. It was empty of any furniture. But tall arches on each of the walls were adorned by tinted glass windows, each one depicting some horrible human sacrifice performed by monsters and demonic creatures.

Although they were shaped like windows and even seemed illuminated from behind like from daylight, they couldn't be real windows. We were far too deep underground for this.

Dismissing them from my mind, I closed the distance with the immense doors. To my relief, they too opened with a will of their own. I had dreaded they would require some sort of complex puzzle solving or ritual to be granted access.

But all such musings also flew right out of my mind as I took in the spectacle before me. The large circular room was indeed the sacrificial chamber Pharos had shown me. A small bridge led to a central island in the middle of which his body rested atop a rectangular altar. All around the island a thick pool of blood almost appeared to simmer as the occasional large bubble of air popped at its surface. Inside it, I spotted several fleshy chunks of gore and bones.

On either side of the pool, another large platform lined the left and right walls. Like in the stairs maze, they were pock-marked with more alcoves over three levels, All of them covered in those fleshy web membranes.

But it was the terrifying statue on the back wall staring down at Pharos's inert form that claimed all my attention. I immediately recognized her for what she was: a Keres. Those demonic creatures—usually females—were the spirits of violent death and doom. While they couldn't kill anyone themselves, they got creative in inciting others or facilitating them to perform the deed so that they could feed on the dead and dying. They had a particular predilection for blood, which explained the pool at her feet.

She looked partially embedded into the roughly carved rock wall at the back. Her hands were extended forward, her sharp claws pointing upwards as if in a summoning gesture. Her head, slightly bowed, hid nothing of her terrifying face, humanoid in structure, but framed by two dozen snake-like hair. But it wasn't Medusa's mane. Instead of snakeheads, humanoid skulls with bulging eyes tipped the snake-like tendrils of her hair. She looked emaciated, the tanned and almost mummified texture of her skin stretching tightly over her bones.

Despite her petrified appearance, the reddish beige hue of her complexion made it clear she wasn't a nightmarish sculpture adorning the place. She might appear dormant, but my gut told me the Keres was keenly aware of my presence in her chamber. Once again, I quieted down my urge to hightail it from here. The knowledge that she could not personally attack me went a long way into helping me keep my cool. Even in her apparent stasis, the power radiating from her had me nearly petrified.

Clamping down on my curiosity to get a closer look at Pharos, I circled around the island to place a few wards by the outer edges of the pool and near the alcoves on the walls. Beyond the fleshy webs, I detected lifeforms hiding behind them. They felt undead to me. However, I could also feel that they possessed flesh and blood. For this reason, I set down a series of blood darts aiming at the alcoves. If whatever lurked within came out, I could shoot them with the darts. Once it started coursing through them, I could use my Blood Magic on them to bend them to my will.

As I walked in front of the entrance doors to circle back to the other side of the room, I sensed my stalker nearby. It had stopped its approach. My gut said it feared entering this room far more than it ached to harm me. As I placed more wards and blood darts on the right side, I kept stealing furtive glances at the Keres. Although she had not moved, I knew with unshakable certainty that she was intently observing me.

And she was mad.

My task completed at last, I crossed the short bridge onto the circular island. This time, I feasted my eyes over his body. Although also desiccated, his mummified appearance was nowhere near as gruesomely sunken in as the demonic female on the wall. To my shock, I noticed wing bones on each side of his body.

Could he be an Angel of Death and not a Reaper?

I knew there was a distinction between them, with one having more restrictions than the other. If memory served, the Angels reaped the souls of the righteous, while the reapers indiscriminately took both good and bad people to the afterlife on top of acting as executioners whenever they so wished.

There would be time to dwell on that further once we were both safely out of here.

Despite his disturbing appearance, I felt no repulsion or disgust. Granted, as a necromancer, I was used to skeletons, decay, and rot. But this felt different. Obviously, I wasn't attracted by his mummified appearance, but I found myself eager and curious to see what he would look like once his regeneration kicked in. At least, I was relieved to notice skin over most of his body including most of his face, and especially his mouth. It would have bothered me had he possessed a fully skeletal face.

Yeah, I had a thing for kissing.

Still, judging by the way his skin receded around parts of his rib cage and around his eyes, I suspected that in his normal form, Pharos naturally had some exposed bones. I couldn't see anything below his waist as he was wearing some ornate boots, pants, a skirt, a hood, and pauldrons on his shoulders.

But as much as I wanted to continue studying him, the clock was ticking. However, something felt off. An insane amount of Death Magic was swirling around his unconscious form. It took me a moment to realize what was distressing me about it. It was flowing from Pharos, into the statue.

By the Gods, she's leeching him!

Was that how Cornelius managed to enslave Pharos? Did he make a deal with the Keres so that he would get his soul, and she would get his body? With his formidable regeneration powers, he would effectively be an endless source of fuel for her to feed on. From the beginning, I struggled to figure out how a mere mortal could have ensnared a demigod. This could explain it.

As I couldn't see any rune, glyph, or other magic conduit allowing the transfer, I took a closer look at his body, and only then did I notice some claw-like bone spikes embedded into his skin.

Crestfallen, I stared at the claws, uncertain what to do. Should I remove them first before summoning Pharos? How long would that even take? Would it trigger the demon? But if I summoned him first, would that leeching negatively affect him? Would it delay the transfer so long that Cornelius would realize something bad was happening?

Too many questions without answers exponentially exacerbated my anxiety. The Keres' ominous presence and the anger I steadily sense growing inside her made it even harder for me to think.

"Fuck it!" I muttered in annoyance under my breath.

Having made my decision, I stood at the position Pharos showed me in the vision at the head of the altar and began drawing the summoning circle. My heart nearly leapt out of my chest when the demon turned her head to look at me with a malevolent expression as she bared her dagger teeth. Heart pounding, I reminded myself that she couldn't attack anyone. Forcing myself to focus, I hastily completed my task, praying that my wards would hold, and above all that Pharos would answer the call.

CHAPTER 8
PHAROS

The journey home proved endless. We arrived in Willow Grove a little after midnight. The entire ride from the docks back to the city, I keenly looked for the call of Kali's circle. Considering I hadn't responded to it for two nights in a row—assuming she drew them—it made sense that she should have given up on the third night, especially at this late hour.

We'd been too far away for me to even perceive the previous calls. Unlike the standard summoning circles, the portal rings needed to be located within a far shorter radius of the person being invoked. I wanted to believe that Kali had not lost all faith in me and was merely waiting for me to come to her again or at least give her some sort of sign.

As soon as we arrived home, the servants handed a pile of documents to Cornelius, many of which involved strange deliveries to one of his mansions located in a couple of cities over from here. It surprised me. Cornelius had no love for that accursed place. And yet, it held foremost importance for him. From what little I'd been able to glean from his mind, he intended to use it for a major project.

The Glocker Manor had been the theater of one of the most

gruesome slaughters in the State's history. The previous owner, Friedrich Glocker, was obsessed with the insane thought that he could bring back his deceased beloved, Melina Hartwick. To achieve this goal, he lured and slaughtered countless young women who shared even the slightest physical resemblance with his old flame. In his madness, he'd convinced himself that he could reassemble her, piece by piece, and summon her soul back from the afterlife.

Not only was that impossible, but Melina would have never wanted to return to him. She never reciprocated his feelings and made it abundantly clear every time he tried to woo her. That day, in his rage at being rejected yet again, he grabbed her by the shoulders and violently shook the young woman to make her hear reason. Thinking he would strike her, she fought him off, which only triggered him further. Things escalated to the point he ended up striking and choking her. It was only once she stopped fighting that Friedrich realized he had smothered her.

That tragedy sent him over the edge. Thanks to his wealth and influence, he managed to avoid facing justice. But his riches and prosperous businesses dwindled as he became consumed by his demented undertaking. His efforts caused more pain and misery, both to his innocent victims and to himself. After multiple attempts at summoning Melina's soul, Friedrich only succeeded in summoning a Liderc.

Although they shared many similarities with their distant cousins—the succubi and incubi—Lidercs were even more fiendish. They took on the appearance and personality of a deceased beloved of their target. Every day, every night, they would come to their lover, feeding them the illusion that they were reunited at long last while sucking their lifeforce dry. Their victims would wither away in an illusion of bliss until their stark reality hit them too late.

In many ways, it had been too kind an end for Friedrich, considering the nearly two hundred desecrated corpses they found on his land after his passing. The only justice in all of it was how the fake Melina made him squirm, frequently reminding him of how he had wronged her, and making him beg for any sliver of attention she bestowed upon him even as she leeched the very life out of him.

What does Cornelius want with such a place?

But those wandering thoughts flew right out of my mind when the servant showed him the note Kali had sent. My initial reaction upon seeing it was panic. She must have given up on me to be willing to consider negotiating with that slime again. Then, even as Cornelius chuckled with a smugness laced with malice, I realized the message hadn't been meant for him, but for me. She wanted me to give her a sign, and I intended to do just that as soon as Cornelius went to bed.

Thankfully, exhausted by the long journey home, he only dealt with the most urgent matters among the notes he had received. Most of it came down to him sending messages to various people he would see in the morning. It gave me the perfect glimpse into when he would be too busy and far from home to be able to counter my escape attempts.

And there was no way around that escape taking place tomorrow.

Although Cornelius still hadn't said or hinted at anything, his suspicions had not abated. He kept his thoughts hidden more than ever from me. Through the journey back, and even once back here at home, I discreetly siphoned any life force I could within range without being so greedy my actions would be detected. It was more like skimming on the surface of everything and anyone, even down to the plants and shrubbery in the vicinity.

As soon as my host finally went to bed, I visited Kali in her dreams. It was the safest and least costly way to contact her. The only thing making it possible was the bond we shared through the parts of my soul now residing within her. I could only pray that she wouldn't dismiss it as just a dream. I couldn't speak for fear it would leak out to Cornelius. I also couldn't linger for the same reason.

To my chagrin, I couldn't even lean in to the far-too-brief kiss I gave her before leaving. The powerful emotion it stirred within me was frightening. The depth of affection I felt for her was far too dangerous. Cornelius would feel it.

That she might come to harm at his hands because of me was a devastating thought.

Morning came far too late. Contrary to his habit, the necromancer slept in much later than usual. Seeing him reschedule one of his early meetings made me feel faint. For a terrifying moment, I feared he would stay home. I could have wept with relief when he finally headed out a few minutes shy of eleven thirty on his way to an alchemist at the other end of town.

That couldn't have been more perfect.

Time trickled endlessly while they intensely debated some preparation he wanted her to make for him. The alterations to the standard formula were throwing the alchemist for a loop. That Cornelius made it a point to hide some of the ways he intended to use the concoction only increased the complexity for her. Rather than distressing her, the challenge it posed thrilled the woman. That suited me just fine. The longer he remained here, the more focused he was on their little project, the less aware he would be of my imminent departure.

Assuming Kali comes through for me.

As Cornelius didn't mind me fading during times such as these, I dropped to the background as far as reasonably possible without raising his suspicions. Over the years, I'd discovered that he resented having to expose some of his secrets to me. Finding out he preferred when I faded while he debated things such as what was taking place now ended up playing in my favor. As I never had any interest in the dark arts, it had been no hardship to ignore what he was up to.

They were still deep in their discussion—which looked like it would last for at least another couple of hours—when that blessed call finally arrived. It took every ounce of my willpower not to rush through the portal the moment it opened. Being already greatly faded, it took me a lot less time to discreetly cross over.

A joy too great to bear swelled through me at finding myself inside the crypt.

"Pharos!" Kali exclaimed as soon as I appeared inside the circle. "You came!"

The happiness and relief she felt turned me upside down. The shimmering lights of her soul radiated with the strength of a thousand suns, their beauty and warmth heating me to my core. I wanted to pull her into my arms, let her magnificent aura wrap all around me, and lose myself in it. But the slimy air rife with evil, the distant tug of Cornelius's tether, and the pull of my own vessel nearby claiming me forced me to focus on the task at hand.

As I feared, our bond was still too weak. The necromancer would feel my departure unless we took far longer than we could afford for a slower trickle.

"Of course," I said, the emotion I felt audible in my voice. "I feared you wouldn't understand my message. But we have little time. Cornelius suspects something. I don't know how much, but we must hurry."

"Okay," Kali said, her voice tense but her face determined. She pointed at the side of my inert body. "There's a problem. See these claws, I believe they're leeching you. Should I remove them from you first or can it wait until after we've transferred you?"

I flinched upon seeing my body. I'd been so enthralled by the radiance of Kali's soul that I'd barely spared myself a glance. This wasn't how my bride should have seen me for the first time.

The Keres leeching me had turned my body into a shriveled, desiccated husk.

"Yes and no," I said, distraught by that extra hurdle. "Her claws must be removed before I transfer into my body, but your own magic is too weak to fight her. You will need to use mine. Time is of the essence. I will fully give myself to you. As soon as that happens, Cornelius will know and will try to reel me back to him. Focus on removing those shackles, then transfer me."

"How?" Kali asked, her tension growing another notch.

"Kiss my body's lips. I will handle the rest."

Of all the thoughts that could have crossed my mind in this dire situation, it shamed me that it was relief that she didn't seem repulsed by the prospect of kissing my shriveled body that dominated.

"Be ready for attacks," I continued before glancing over my shoulder at Grizelle.

Her mouth stretched into an evil smile. "Going somewhere, Pharos?" she asked in her dreadful voice that sounded like nails on glass.

"It is time for me to leave your hall," I said in a snarky voice. "You're a bit too greedy in your *hospitality*."

She burst out laughing, the sound insanely creepy. "You wound me, my precious. But your feast I cannot afford to lose. So I must insist you remain."

"That is not going to happen," I snapped.

"We shall see," she replied, her voice taking a cruel and menacing edge.

Still partially embedded in the wall, Grizelle waved her hands, and the fleshy membranes covering the alcoves on the walls surrounding the outer edges of the island began to open.

"Stand down, Grizelle, or I will kill all of your minions," I hissed.

"You shall do no such thing, Reaper!" she retorted maliciously. "You are bound by the covenant. You cannot interfere with what is about to happen to your little pet."

"I can intervene when I'm threatened," I countered.

She huffed angrily. "My minions know better than to attack the likes of you. It is the human they will feast on."

"The human is the host ensuring my rebirth. Killing her is a direct attack against me. I'm allowed self-defense. Stand down or face the consequences," I warned.

It was a technicality, but it would give us the breathing room to complete the ritual. If Kali had to fight back the swarms Grizelle would unleash upon her while trying to free me of the claws shackling me, we might never finish in time to thwart any attempts Cornelius might make to prevent it.

"Very well, Reaper. Be reborn," she spat angrily. "But then, I shall feast on the wretch who took you from me."

The deep pain that menace stirred within me echoed the fear that flashed over Kali's beautiful face. A wave of despair washed over me as more fleshy membranes opened. My mind raced as I tried to think of ways I could assist my female once I wasn't officially able to protect her anymore as my survival would no longer depend on her. But I kept coming up short.

"Give me your soul, Kali," I pleaded one last time. "It will make the transfer even faster, and both of us will be safer for it. Cornelius is on to us. We have too little time!"

"Then let's not waste it in pointless discussions," Kali replied, her face closing off before taking on a mulish expression. "Give yourself to me. I will unshackle you, and then kiss you to initiate the transfer."

Feeling both heartbroken and defeated, I nodded stiffly while ignoring Grizelle's triumphant chuckle behind us. I didn't want to lose Kali, but it was now clearly inevitable. Even her life thread showed the likelihood of her survival to be next to nil. A feeble path where she made it out alive, but I wasn't foolish enough to cling to it.

"As you wish. Step inside the circle," I said, my heart aching. "I will kiss you. As soon as I do, it will initiate the process. Do not let anything distract you. Remember that Cornelius will try to reel me back in. Between that and unshackling me, you will have a lot to juggle. If you gave me—"

"I said no," she snapped angrily. "The matter is settled."

Without another word, she stepped inside the circle. I gazed at her with infinite sadness. Despite her annoyance, a glimmer of guilt and uncertainty shone in the depths of her obsidian eyes. It gave me a sliver of hope that she might still be swayed once things became truly desperate. Cupping her cheeks with both hands, I leaned forward and pressed my lips to hers.

I felt her shock as my energy flowed into her. Unlike the times I'd shared part of myself with her through coupling, this method was more brutal, like trying to force feed someone through a funnel. People instinctively attempted to resist that invasion, which was one of the reasons we avoided such a method. But despite her surprise, Kali embraced all of me. My bride didn't just embrace me, she drew me in with the tenderness and fervor of a lover.

My ethereal presence faded, absorbed into her. Nine hells, how I loved the feel of her around me! It was like being cradled by the Gods themselves. I vaguely wished she had been the one inside me instead. Still, that didn't stop me from reveling in the perfection that she was. Even my magic blended harmoniously with hers whereas it often clashed with Cornelius.

But now, my body was clamoring for me with renewed intensity.

As soon as Kali stepped out of the circle to begin removing the claws digging into my body, I felt the tug from Cornelius. Although he wasn't actively pulling at me yet, the necromancer now knew something was amiss. Depending on how distracted he remained with the alchemist, it might take him a few minutes to fully investigate what was happening.

That answer came swiftly enough.

A wave of shock, disbelief, and burning rage flooded the link still tethering me to the necromancer. As unnerving as this felt, I couldn't help but love the potent panic beneath it all. Without me, Cornelius would become half the sorcerer he currently was —maybe less. Even if he furiously rode back home, it would take him at least thirty to forty minutes to arrive. He would then need to set up a circle to perform a recall and binding ritual. It wasn't much, but more than enough to complete the transfer. By then, it would be too late for him to shackle me again.

Coming directly to the crypt offered an even less promising outcome as he was currently no less than an hour and a half away from the burial grounds. And once here, it would take him an extra twenty to thirty minutes to reach this altar.

My biggest worry was for Kali. By now, Cornelius would have felt her through our connection. While his priority would be to bind me again, if only out of spite, he would attempt to retaliate against her. I could only hope that he wouldn't be able to send some kind of abomination to punish her and further ensure that she did not make it out of here alive.

However, a pained hiss from Grizelle reclaimed my attention. I hated that I could no longer see the room but through Kali's eyes. She was frantically removing the ten hooks embedded in my flesh—each one corresponding to one of the claws at the tip of Grizelle's fingers. My bride cast a nervous glance towards the Keres only to see her extruding from the wall, her face contorted in a terrifying grimace.

Kali froze, her flight instincts surging fiercely as she struggled to resist them.

"Focus," I mentally spoke to my female, startling her. *"Grizelle will not harm you. A Keres cannot kill without cause, only in self-defense."*

"I'm attacking her!" she countered in a hushed voice, not knowing how to speak telepathically to me.

"No, you're merely removing her claws that are hurting me. You're protecting me. Use my magic to cause necrosis to the tips of her claws," I ordered.

I didn't know how well Kali would be able to use my powers. But to my shock, it appeared to come to her naturally. However, she blasted a far more potent necrotic aura than she intended. It wasn't surprising. Having me inside her multiplied my bride's powers tenfold.

Grizelle shouted in pain and made a gesture with both hands, as if to yank them back. Simultaneously, the hooks shackling me to the altar and draining my natural regeneration abilities retracted from me.

"You will regret this, human!" Grizelle shouted.

Kali gasped as the eyeballs inside the skulls adorning the tips of Grizelle's thick locks shot out of their sockets on spindly spider legs. They scattered along the walls, scurrying towards the open alcoves. Simultaneously, the dreadful silhouettes of countless Skarachs crawled out of their somber lairs.

The nightmarish creatures had the upper torso of a skeleton with eight long limbs that allowed them to either walk on two legs with six arms to attack their target or walk on all eight limbs like a spider. What made them creepier was the fact that they leaned backwards to walk like a spider, with their chest facing up. As their heads could pivot by three hundred and sixty degrees, it didn't impede their ability to see, whichever position they were in. Their skeletal faces didn't have a nose, only an oversized mouth above which a dozen small red-eyes without pupils peered around, and a set of horns. But it was the bigger gaping hole in the center of the smaller eyes that was the most terrifying.

Each of the scurrying eyes from Grizelle's hair ran up to a Skarach and embedded themselves in that gaping hole, becoming one of the Keres's puppets.

"Focus, Kali!" I mentally shouted at her as my body, now freed from the claws leeching it, started regenerating.

My voice snapped her out of her horrified daze. Without hesitation, my bride leaned forward and pressed her lips to those of my body.

CHAPTER 9
KALI

Nothing could have prepared me for the insane surge of energy that rushed into me when Pharos gave himself over. My entire body overflowed with Death Magic. I could see and feel things I never even imagined existed. Like walking at the very edge between the mortal and esoteric world, right on the thin line of the Veil.

Beyond the fleshy membranes, the luminous outlines of the abominations that lurked behind them now stood out clearly to me. I could even see the slight pulse of their heartbeats, and the purplish thread of varying length around them. For a reason I couldn't explain, I instinctively knew it to be their life thread. Otherworldly whispers filled my ears, the voices of dark forces calling out to each other, warning them of the presence of the intruder that I was… of prey to be devoured. Even in the pool of blood, twisted blobs of energy indicated more creatures ready to surge forth.

I also realized I could drain all their life force with a mere flick of my hand. Despite the powerful temptation it stirred within me, I instinctively knew that I would never be able to contain all that energy. I would burst, destroyed by that excess of greed. So many sorcerers met their ultimate demise in comparable situations, too hungry to harness and exert power that was never meant to be theirs.

It took me barely seconds after Pharos gave himself over to me for all these thoughts to fire off in my mind. However, two forceful external tugs snapped me back to the dreadful reality of the moment. Although I had never touched minds with Cornelius, I instantly recognized his presence. Shock and anger emanated from him, like a slimy hand clinging to Pharos and trying to pull him back. And Pharos's own body was also savagely clamoring for his return.

The instinctive jealous rage that swelled through me in response to those two tugs left me reeling. I didn't want to give him up. Every cell of my being was screaming that he was mine to keep. For the first time in my life, I felt whole. The divine light of the Gods themselves filled every fiber of my being. Granted, the insane power holding him gave me would be addictive to any sorcerer in their right mind. But it was the beauty and purity of his soul that enthralled me. We were one, vibrating in perfect harmony.

We were meant to be together.

But even as those thoughts swirled inside me, I shut them down and began to remove the claws in Pharos's body. I nearly wet myself when the Keres began to detach from the wall she was partially embedded in. Even with his powers boosting mine, I didn't know that I could go head-to-head against a demon such as Grizelle. When Pharos asked me to use his necrosis on her claws leeching him, I wondered if he'd lost his mind. This would be a direct attack against her, overriding her offensive restrictions. And what if I burned the entire place down by invoking abilities I had no experience with?

But I intrinsically trusted Pharos.

Swallowing down the bile of fear trying to choke me, I expanded those foreign powers as weakly as possible to test the potency of their output. The ease and oddly instinctive way it came to me boggled my mind.

That my trust in him served us right was all that mattered.

No sooner did I use his necrosis than Grizelle screeched and retracted her claws. I didn't get a chance to marvel at the fact that Pharos's body immediately began to regenerate, as the Keres went on the offensive.

"You will regret this, human!" Grizelle shouted.

I felt faint as the eyes inside Grizelle's skull hair exited their orbits to race along the walls towards the alcoves. I stood transfixed as the walking eyes settled inside the cyclops-like empty orbs of the Skarachs. Once more, I barely repressed the urge to use the Reaper's powers, which bubbled inside me like a barely contained tempest. It was too great for me to handle, especially in my current state of terror.

A second later, my wards went off, launching some of my blood darts at the first Skarachs surging forward.

"Focus, Kali!"

If not for Pharos's voice shouting inside my head, I might have remained frozen in a complete panic. I clamped down on the possessive rage that reared its head again. A horrible voice at the back of my mind was whispering for me to keep him, to run out of this wretched place, and blast his Death Magic at anything that would come at me. Even if I brought down this entire tomb, I believed his regeneration powers would keep me alive. But I would never do such a thing to anyone, least of all him.

Casting out such dreadful temptation, I leaned down and pressed my lips to his.

Although I knew it was only Pharos leaving me to reenter his own vessel, it felt as if my very soul was being torn right out of my body. His own voraciously dragged him out of me. To my shock, even as I felt torn asunder, I perceived the brief but powerful maelstrom of emotions coursing through Pharos before our link was severed. Pain at being torn out, bliss at finally reconnecting with his body, but also a tremendous sense of loss at parting from me.

It turned me upside down to realize he had felt as keenly as I did how perfectly aligned our souls were.

Simultaneously, Cornelius's outrage and disbelief stabbed through our connection before it snapped, permanently severed.

I straightened at the blood curdling screeches emanating from the Skarachs swarming out of the alcoves. They flattened themselves against the invisible wall created by my wards. A few of them were thrown back by its repulsion. Opening their mouths impossibly wide, they spit some stringy phlegm that I recognize as the fleshy substance that created the web-like membranes sealing their lairs. That too crashed against the invisible walls, making it sparkle as it quickly damaged the wards. With so severe an onslaught, my protections wouldn't last long before they were overwhelmed.

Invoking my Blood Magic, I reached out to the blood darts my wards had automatically launched at the creatures. I could feel them dissolve inside their bloodstream, giving me an anchor to seize control of their organs. There were too many creatures to manage them all at once, but I could tackle at least half a dozen simultaneously. I could only pray that my wards would hold long enough for me to significantly dwindle their numbers.

But before I could cast the first spell, Pharos inhaled sharply, and his eyes shot open. I gasped when a blast of Death Magic emanated from him, spreading over a wide radius to the edges of the outer platforms. It passed through me like an icy wind. While it left me unscathed, every Skarach clawing at my wards disintegrated into piles of ashes.

"You cheat!" Grizelle screeched angrily.

Now fully detached from the wall, she flapped her bat wings to fly over us like a vulture circling its prey.

I stared in disbelief as Pharos's body exponentially regenerated, undoubtedly from having completely siphoned the life force of all the creatures that had come out. His desiccated limbs and flattened chest filled up as the muscles beneath swelled. His withered skin stretched, losing its leathery and wrinkled appearance to take on a smooth texture with a healthy grayish-brown tone.

"I do not cheat," Pharos replied.

He slurred his words a bit, likely from the disuse of his vocal cords and of him still being in the process of regenerating. Still, his voice was beautifully haunting, although it sounded a little strange to my ears now that it no longer had that disembodied echo.

"I'm weakened by centuries of you draining me. I'm allowed to feed off lower forms of life to heal. It's only fair that your minions should replenish what you've stolen from me for so long," he continued.

Grizelle angrily hissed. That she didn't challenge his words confirmed the validity of his arguments. My heart soared that Pharos had found a clever approach to protect me. Now that I no longer hosted any part of him, I understood the extent of the power enhancement he had procured for me. Without his magic, I felt as weak as a novice.

However, my relief at having the threat so swiftly wiped out gave way to another wave of worry as the eyes inside the skulls dangling from her hair grew back. The malicious grin that stretched her lips, despite her anger still visible, sent a chill down my spine.

"It is a long way out of the crypt, Reaper. That excuse will only last so long before your reserves are fully replenished. And I have plenty of friends wanting to play with your pet!" Grizelle said in an evil sing-song voice.

My insides twisted upon hearing her speak the exact fear gnawing at me.

"Don't you have a battlefield to scavenge?" Pharos replied in a glacial tone.

His voice was already a lot clearer and his body a lot more defined, but still resembling that of someone a little emaciated.

"Of course," she retorted in an indulgent tone. "And I will… once I've eaten your pet for stealing my endless feast."

I half tuned them out and glanced around the room and out the wide hallway beyond the still open doors of the chamber. During the brief time I held all of Pharos, I'd been able to locate the potential threats and tools at my disposal. My mind raced as I strategized on the battle that awaited me.

Thanks to Pharos feeding off the Skarachs that came out of the alcoves, most of my blood darts remained intact by the wards. I knew far more Skarachs remained inside their lairs, ready to come after me as soon as their mistress gave them the signal. I wanted to believe my companion would devour them as well to finish healing himself. Although he was still regenerating, the pace had significantly reduced now that he had nothing else in range to feed from. Therefore, I summoned my blood darts back to me and returned them to the pouch hanging on my belt.

Even as she continued to provoke Pharos, Grizelle gave me a triumphant smile. The foul demon probably assumed I'd grown overconfident. Her face took on a taunting expression as the freshly regrown eyes in her skull hair also scurried out towards the dark depths of the alcoves on both sides of the room.

I dismissed her again. My wards would help hold off the creatures long enough for me to make a dash towards the exit. But as they were extremely fast and could spit that wretched phlegm with a poisonous and acidic coating, I needed something to further stall and ideally destroy them. Had there been fewer of them, I could have used my Bone or Blood Magic to take control of their skeleton or organs to achieve that goal.

Extending my senses down the hallway, I assessed the countless bones and partial skeletons beyond. Most were inert and with extremely low magic remaining. I discreetly cast a series of spells, reshaping some of the loose bones into spikes, and assembling the partial skeletons into walking constructs so that they could run interference to cover my retreat.

Unfortunately, there was no way for me to hide from the Keres what I was up to. Surprisingly, she didn't attempt to sabotage it. I presumed it was part of the restrictions she fell under. With dark magic, you could almost always find a workaround by playing on technicalities. Although she was the one summoning the abominations that would hunt me down, there was no law preventing a sorcerer from awakening their pets. Even though Grizelle knew they would attack me, so long as she wasn't giving them the order to do so, she didn't break her covenant. It wasn't *her fault* that fiendish creatures naturally displayed predatory behavior.

However, a powerful blast of energy rippled through the room to propagate outwards and throughout the crypt. My stomach dropped as another wave of fear rose within me. Grizelle had sent out a call, like a silent horn blast, for all to hear. In seconds, malevolent energy surged all around us. The bloody pool bubbled, and fleshy mutants started crawling out of it, their twisted hands clawing at the edges of the island to hoist themselves onto it. Simultaneously, even more Skarachs crawled out of the countless openings in the walls.

Like the first time, Death Magic radiated out of Pharos, wiping out all the visible creatures. His entire body almost appeared to glow as his regeneration once more went into overdrive.

By the Gods, he was breathtaking!

Pharos looked nothing like the bone knight I had feared. Yes, he possessed some exposed bones around his eyes, and a few ribs on his upper chest and sides. But they didn't look like the result of a decaying corpse. They blended harmoniously with the flawless skin around it, giving him a fierce yet elegant look. His lips were plump and sensuous, made to be kissed and devoured.

His Roman nose gave him an air of nobility. And the three bone spikes jutting out of his chin, their rounded tips making them smooth, added to his otherworldly beauty. The hood attached to his pauldrons lay flat against his back, leaving his luscious, shoulder-length, wavy black hair streaked with silver to softly frame his fascinating features.

He suddenly sat up from his lying position. With a single flap of his majestic black, feathery wings, he hopped off the altar, hovering for a couple of seconds above the floor before landing next to me. He towered over me by a good head. But his mere presence, seeing Pharos whole with insane magic radiating from him, made me feel both fragile and protected.

He waved his hand towards the head of the altar, and the summoning circle I had created vanished. I flinched inwardly realizing I would have completely forgotten about it. Who knew how someone else might have used it against him in the future?

"Let's go!" Pharos ordered before running off the island.

The sensuous rumbling of his voice sent a delicious shiver down my spine. Without a word, I followed in his wake. Unfazed, Grizelle summoned more of her mutants and Skarachs. My initial excitement at seeing my companion effortlessly devour them even as they came out of their respective lairs vanished moments later when only a third of the latest wave of abominations turned into ashes.

The others kept coming at us… Or rather, at me. While my wards held off the Skarachs as I had hoped, the mutants were crawling onto the island and crossing the bridge to give chase. My only blessing in their case was that they were shambling, deformed things not really meant to walk, but more to swim or crawl. None of them looked alike. They seemed to be the result of random fleshy parts fusing together with the occasional misplaced bone here and there. I suspected they had formed out of the remains of sacrificed creatures and people discarded in the pool.

"Time to play!" Grizelle shouted before bursting into a diabolical—if not maniacal—laugh.

She flew overhead past us and blasted her silent summons again. She disappeared into the next room, and a long, rumbling groan resonated loudly in my ears. It seemed to come from everywhere at once, inside the large hallway we were now running through, from the sacrificial chamber we'd just left, and even ahead towards the lowest level of the stairs maze. It was as if the entire crypt had stirred to life and was expressing its discontent to have thus been disturbed.

My blood turned to ice as the dark silhouettes of dozens of Skarachs appeared in the distance, rushing from the stairs maze towards the hallway we were crossing. Without slowing down, I grabbed a handful of blood darts from my pouch, brought them to my lips to whisper an incantation, then threw them at the incoming swarm with all my strength. As if drawn by a magnet, each dart headed straight for its individual mark and buried itself deep into their flesh. I repeated the gesture twice before having to summon a blood shield to block the stream of phlegm the closest Skarach spat at me.

With some of them crawling on the wall, others on the ceiling, and even more rushing straight at me, I couldn't face them all at once. Pharos dashed forward, deliberately placing himself in the path of the swarm to force them into a voluntary or accidental attack against him.

I felt the congealed darts spreading inside my targets, granting me the hold I needed. I fisted my hands and violently spread my arms as if to fling something sideways while uttering a word of power. Nine Skarachs screeched as they were sent crashing against the side walls. With another spell, I snapped the bones of their articulations, forcing them into a crawl. I repeated the process with another group of creatures infused with my blood darts.

But as too many of them now invaded the room, not to

mention the abominations closing in on us from behind, I summoned a blood shield around me and then launched the bone spikes I had set up around the room. They shot out in every direction, some flying wide, but most impaling themselves into the monsters' flesh. Their deafening screeches filled the room. Many of them fell or lost their footing. The most unfortunate ones knocked into Pharos, who happily dispatched them. The others scrambled to get back on their feet, giving me a small amount of breathing room to raise the bone constructs I had briefly assembled. They stumbled about mindlessly, clawing, stabbing, and biting the Skarachs.

In the mayhem that ensued, Pharos and I burst out of the hallway into the wide-open space of the stairs maze. My heart sank as I watched Grizelle flying around, the thick tentacles of her hair flowing around her nightmarish face. But gone were the skulls at their tips. To my horror, I spotted a few of them running at dizzying speed on crab-like legs that had protruded from the side of the skulls. They were racing towards what I had mistakenly assumed to be random bone piles. But they were the bodies of Bone Fiends.

I felt petrified as a first head jumped onto the jutting part protruding at the end of a Bone Fiend's spine. It immediately came to life, its skeletal body filling up with an odd layer of thin skin while vicious bone spikes grew on its back. They would be able to fire those like arrows over an insane distance.

They were located on some of the lower and upper platforms of the maze, making sure there would be no way for me to avoid them. But more Skarachs continued to pour out of the alcoves along the walls of the maze. Seeing some of them straightening on two legs instead felt even more terrifying than when they crawled like spiders. They were a frightening sight to behold, with their impossibly long and spindly limbs raised menacingly like so many demonic swords ready to stab and impale.

In that instant, I realized how foolish it had been of me to ever think I could make it out of here alive. There was a reason people said the journey into Hemdell Crypt was a one-way ticket. Tears pricked my eyes as I braced myself for the inevitable. But I wouldn't go down passively. I would take as many of these abominations with me as possible.

I threw all the blood darts I still had and raised what inert skeletons I could to impede the advance of the monsters. Between a flurry of Blood Magic spells to repel their attacks or shield myself from theirs, and Bone Magic to dislocate joints and break limbs and spines, I frantically tried to keep up with Pharos who was desperately trying to open a path for me. But climbing out of the depths of hell was far more trying than descending into it.

My legs were burning from running up the stairs while dodging the vicious assaults of my would-be assassins. My lungs were on fire as I tried to catch my breath between incantations.

And we were only halfway up the second platform.

A scream of pain escaped me as a boned dart pierced through the fleshy part of my upper arm and flew right through. I instinctively slapped my hand over it and whispered a healing spell. From the way it burned, the thrice damned thing had been poisoned. I could only cast a blood spell to keep it from spreading until I hopefully had a chance to properly cure myself.

Pharos looked at me over his shoulder. The fear on his face wrecked me. It wasn't fear for himself, but for me. He knew I wasn't going to make it. He spread his wings wide so that another volley of bone spikes from the Fiends would strike him instead of me, allowing him to slay the creatures that had launched them.

But he couldn't cover me from every angle.

On the upper levels, the Bone Fiends were lining the edges of the platforms, pressing their foreheads to the floor so their spiked backs would face towards me before launching their deadly weapons at me. Between the Skarachs, mutants, and Bone

Fiends, it felt like a swarm of locusts closing in on all sides, blotting out the light, and choking the very air out of the room.

With my blood shield too weak to withstand the brute force of the bone spikes, I summoned the Shield of Azriel instead. It was powerful against both physical and magical attacks, but it was meant to be used while stationary. Walking around with the shield active weakened it. But it would still be more powerful than the other one. And it proved useful until we reached the next landing.

However, a Skarach crawling on the wall suddenly launched itself at me, striking me violently on the right side. Too busy trying to shield me from the darts of the Bone Fiends on the other levels, Pharos didn't notice until I screamed from the force of the impact. It sent me flying across the narrow platform. In slow motion, I felt myself lose my footing and fall over the edge.

"KALI!" Pharos yelled.

Time froze as I prepared to plummet to my death and for my body to shatter on the dark stones of the staircase below. The surface of the somber pool of murky water rippled as the massive silhouette of the creature that lurked in its depths stirred. If I survived the fall, it would undoubtedly devour me.

But Pharos dove down, caught my wrist, and all but threw me back onto the platform. I landed so hard, it knocked the wind out of me. In the distance, I heard Pharos cry out. I wanted to glance his way to see what had caused him pain, but the Skarach that had nearly sent me to my death rose on to its two feet. Towering over me at an impossible height, he raised his remaining six limbs to stab me. I barely had time to restore my Shield of Azriel before he repeatedly pummeled it with the dagger-like tips of his limbs.

I scrambled back onto my feet as the shield flickered under the brutal assault from both the Skarach and the other darts being fired at me. Using my Bone Magic, I shattered both his legs, but as he collapsed, he viciously swiped two of his upper limbs at me, sending me crashing against the wall. I crumbled to the floor, dazed. My teeth rattled in my head, and the room spun.

Pharos once more yelling my name was buried by my own strident scream of agony as a heavy weight settled on my right leg, followed by a sizzling sound as the acid of a Skarach's phlegm began eating through the leather of my pants and then my flesh. I cast a repulsion spell to throw it off me. It felt as if it was tearing half of my skin off as it flew away.

As too many shadows closed in on me, I cast the bone bomb spell in one last desperate effort. It caused every bone in range to shatter and detonate like an explosive device, sending fragments flying in every direction, shredding everything in its path. The room blurred in a shower of bones and semi-mummified flesh. Feeling drained, I attempted to cast another repulsion spell on the imposing silhouette that appeared before me only to realize it was Pharos.

Guilt fleetingly coursed through me as I realized my spell could have seriously damaged him. However, he looked unscathed but for a huge gash across his palm and disappearing under the bracer on his forearm to reappear at the other end and taper off below his elbow. I didn't have time to dwell on it as he grabbed my upper arm and dragged me after him to one of the semi-hidden passages along the platform. He didn't continue straight ahead but slapped his hand against what I had assumed to be a textured section of the wall. To my shock, a red light glowed around the edges of a huge set of doors, which parted open before us.

I blindly cast another repulsion spell behind me as Pharos pulled me inside a huge, empty room. My spell had been too weak, and three Skarachs managed to lunge behind us. One of them crawled up the ceiling before leaping at me. I screamed, knowing I'd never have time to dodge. It vanished in a rain of ashes, as did the other two that had squeezed their way in before Pharos could slam the doors shut.

He roared in pain and fell to his knees. Resting his palms on the dust covered floor, his wings hanging limply on the sides of his broad shoulders, Pharos was shaking, head bowed, as if on the verge of going into shock.

Despite the excruciating pain radiating from my wounded leg, I limped to his side, ignoring the pounding sounds of the monsters trying to break into the room.

"Pharos! Are you okay?!" I shouted, falling to my knees next to him.

Teeth clenched, he lifted his face to look at me. I covered my mouth with my palm, horrified to see deep cuts, similar to the one I'd previously noticed on his hand and wrist. This time, they sliced his face from the forehead, across his right eye, and through the base of his jaw. Other similar gaping wounds lacerated his chest and arms. Although wet with blood, they didn't drip thanks to his accelerated regeneration. But they were closing at a snail's pace.

And then it dawned on me.

Those wounds were his punishment for breaking the covenant… for killing without being attacked.

For protecting me…

Without a word, he painfully got back on his feet. I imitated him, grinding my teeth through the pain ravaging my leg, ignoring the throbbing bruising in my side, and the burning in my upper arm.

The look on Pharos's face tore me apart. It was a devastating mix of sorrow, anger, resignation, and defeat. He straightened and cupped my face between his hands.

"You will not survive this, my Kali. I cannot protect you. Please, give me your soul. I don't want to lose you," he pleaded, his voice raw from the pain he visibly still felt.

My lips quivered, and my throat constricted as a wave of despair crashed over me. There was no arguing against the truth of his words. By rights, I should already be dead. The minute the doors opened, it would be all over for me.

I don't want to die. But am I willing to give away my soul?

The visceral terror that prospect systematically awakened in me twisted my insides as images of Jasper flashed in my mind. I'd seen firsthand what happened when the person who owned your soul decided to turn on you. Pharos's intentions towards me might be good *now*, but what if I angered him in the future? I barely knew him. What if centuries of Cornelius's foul influence lay dormant in him and triggered at some point when I least expected it? Pictures of me rotting on my feet, my mind fading as my soul wasted away, replaced those of my brother. If the Reaper cursed me, no one would come to my rescue.

Accepting death now guarantees such a horrible fate can never befall me.

Such a monumental decision couldn't be rushed. I would have needed much more time to get to know him better before committing to something so extreme and irreversible. But the clock was ticking against me.

Pharos was free. He would see to it that Cornélius got his comeuppance. I had lived a decent life. If I died now, a pleasant afterlife would await me.

An afterlife without Pharos and without having saved Jasper.

Tears of rage pricked my eyes at the unfairness of it all.

"Your stupid rules don't make sense," I said angrily in a teary voice. "Why can't you protect me? I get that you can't interfere with Fate, but every living being is allowed to look after those they love. It's illogical that you should be expected to stand by idly while your mate or children are getting slaughtered!"

He stiffened, and a strange expression fleeted over his features. The gaping wound still slowly closing made reading him a bit more difficult.

"I would be allowed to protect my mate or offspring," he corrected in a soft voice.

"Then why the fuck can't you protect me? Am I not your bride?" I challenged.

"No, Kali. You are not," he said in a factual tone.

That cut me deep. I recoiled and pulled away from him, making no effort to hide my shock and disbelief.

"So you've been lying all along?" I whispered, my voice filled with pain. "You were playing me all those times you called me your bride?"

"I was not. I want you to be mine, Kali," he said with a conviction that left me confused. "I meant it every time I called you my bride, but you rejected me."

"What? I did not!" I argued, even more baffled. "Did I not welcome you every night?"

"You yielded to me for the sake of this mission. But every time I called you my bride, you rejected my claim," he insisted.

In that instant, the memory of all the times he gave me that title came back to the fore. And I indeed had systematically told him that I wasn't his bride.

"Right… But… I didn't really mean it. Like… You know…"

A savage roar and the right door whining on its hinges reminded me that we were running out of time.

"I accept your claim," I blurted out. "I am your bride… willingly."

My heart sank when he gave me a sad look.

"It's not that simple, my Kali. For it to work, the bond has to be genuine. You cannot simply consent to earn my protection. This is not a commercial transaction or a trade. You must want us. You must truly want *me*."

"But I do want you!" I countered. "Over those three days while you were away, I didn't stop thinking how broken-hearted I was at the prospect of potentially never seeing you again. I was wondering if you would want to pursue a relationship with me after this or if our coupling had merely been a means to an end for you."

"It wasn't!" Pharos said forcefully. "I want you, Kali. I want all of you, including your heart and your soul. But if your heart is all you can give me for now, I will take it to save you, if you truly want me."

"I do, Pharos. I sincerely care about you and want us to be together."

His eyes flicked between mine with great intensity. I held his gaze unwaveringly, confident in the sincerity of my feelings. Although he still seemed uncertain, Pharos leaned forward and captured my lips in a tender kiss laced with a hint of despair. I instantly melted against him, the warmth of his body and of his soul wrapping around me like a blanket. The entire world faded, including the feral screams and savage banging on the doors.

The softness of his lips and the hardness of his muscular body messed with my brain. He was the same lover I had been giving myself to over the past few days and yet, in the flesh, it felt different, in its own wonderful way. A tingling sensation spread from my mouth, down my throat, and throughout my chest. Before I could analyze it, a soft swishing sound followed by a wave of malice put an end to the kiss.

We both jerked our heads to look at the left side of the room. The nightmarish silhouette of Grizelle appeared to glide through the wall as she entered our temporary refuge.

"Come out, come out, wherever you are. It is quite rude of you to leave in the middle of the game," she said in a tauntingly chastising tone. "More of my little friends have come out to play. The door is about to break. Time to say your farewells. Tic-toc, tic-toc, little human."

"Fuck you," I hissed.

"Wow! So mean," Grizelle said in an overly dramatic fashion. "Clearly, you were not taught proper manners. But that matters not. However impolite you may be, I'll still enjoy feasting slowly on you."

"You will not," Pharos said harshly, his voice dripping with contempt. "We're done playing your little game. I'm taking my bride home."

Grizelle recoiled, shock and a sliver of fear sparking in her eyes. "She's not your bride! You still bear the scars of breaking the covenant!" she added, pointing an angry finger at the open wounds that still hadn't fully closed.

"She wasn't then, but she is now," he replied smugly.

"You lie!!" she shouted.

"What?!" I whispered, my head jerking back towards him. "It worked?"

The most wondrous smile softened his features, and his eyes glowed with a possessiveness that made my stomach flutter. "Yes, my Kali. I told you you'd be my bride. We are linked."

He kissed me, and the burning pain in both my upper arm and leg immediately dampened as the tingling sensation further spread.

His regeneration! He's using his powers to heal me!

Healing was too strong a term. I didn't know that he could use his powers to truly remove poison, mend injuries, or cure illnesses in someone else. But I welcomed this notable reduction of the increasingly debilitating pain from my wounds.

Grizelle's enraged scream broke the magic. With a wave of her hand, she flung the doors wide open. The nightmarish horde that had been attempting to break in tumbled inside as if the floodgates of a dam had broken. They barely even got a couple of steps inside before Pharos blasted his death aura on a ten-meter radius. Every single creature that made it into the room and a short distance outside just crumbled into ashes.

But that didn't stop the swarm behind them from trying to rush in. Pushing me behind him, Pharos turned to face the incoming threat, and flung his hands out sideways, as if trying to throw something sticky. Instead, a luminous pair of ghostly scythes appeared in each of his hands. A chain made of bones connected the two shorter weapons.

"No! You can't use that!" Grizelle shouted, true terror descending over her nightmarish features.

Ignoring her, Pharos surged forward, swiping and slashing with both hands at the creatures. Every single one touched by the ghostly blades shattered into pieces, their bones piling up haphazardly where their owner previously stood.

By the ear-splitting, shrill sound the Keres emitted, I first assumed she'd also been wounded somehow, even though she was nowhere near where Pharos was battling. But then I saw the tentacles of her hair bleeding at the tips where the skulls previously dangled. I realized then that the scythe was inflicting permanent death to whatever it touched. I'd seen her regrow the eyes and skulls in her hair after the Skarachs and Bone Fiends they'd previously animated were destroyed.

But this was truly harming her. Except, thanks to yet another loophole of the covenant, Pharos was not attacking Grizelle, but merely defending his mate—me—from the monsters threatening me. It wasn't his fault that doing so also maimed her.

She pleaded and begged him to stop, her voice drowned in the cacophony of dying screams of her minions. To my shock, Pharos stretched both his scythes apart, pulling taut the bone chain connecting them. Its glow intensified for half a beat before turning into a staff with a bladed scythe at each end. He flung it like a boomerang through the open space of the stair maze outside, and the blade just flew around slicing through countless creatures.

Grizelle fell to her knees, gaping wounds appearing all over her shriveled body. Only then did I notice multiple creatures outside crumbling on their own. The Bone Fiend's heads ran away, abandoning the bodies to which they were previously attached. A couple of them raced directly to their mistress to reattach to her hair. Similarly, the spider eyeballs scurried out of the cyclops orbit in the forehead of the Skarachs. Half stumbling, half running, Grizelle stormed out of the room before taking flight. From where I stood, she appeared to be rushing back to her sacrificial chamber, where the spider eyeballs and walking skulls were also headed, undoubtedly to seek refuge from the Reaper's wrath.

With their mistress fleeing, the remaining horde also scattered, most of them taking cover inside the many alcoves pockmarking the walls of the vast chamber.

I stood transfixed as Pharos turned back to face me. The deep wound he'd sustained for breaking the covenant to protect me earlier had completely vanished. He glowed with an almost divine aura and insane power that made my skin tingle. He smiled and extended a hand towards me. Without hesitation, I rushed out of the room and took it. He drew me against his body. For a brief instant, I thought he would kiss me. Instead, he took flight.

I gasped and threw my arms around his neck to hang on—not that I needed to, considering his phenomenal strength. As we flew towards the next platform, a savage roar resonated below us accompanied by the loud splash of water. I turned my head to look down at what it could be, but Pharos's massive black wings blocked my view. A single flick of his wrist sufficed to draw a loud shriek out of whatever had meant to mess with us. Another big splash seemed to indicate the beast had realized the error of its ways and backed off.

While it had taken me approximately forty minutes to reach the sacrificial chamber on my way in, Pharos completed the journey back in less than five. He didn't even slow down when we reached that narrow passage with the bone shelves on each side. He merely dashed forward and flattened his wings against his body at the entrance, shooting right through like an arrow, only deploying his wings again on the other side.

Undoubtedly lured by the previous ruckus, a few fiendish creatures poked their heads out from wherever they'd been lurking. But a glimpse at the Reaper sufficed for them to cower and return from whence they came.

Despite how quickly Pharos got us out, it was still far too long for me. Although his regeneration powers had initially dampened my pain, it was returning with savage intensity. My stomach roiled, and my head swam.

When we exited the mausoleum that served as entrance to the crypt, I was shocked to be greeted by the mid-afternoon sun. It had been so dark and somber below, I had lost all sense of time. In my mind, we were in the dead of night.

But the daylight lit a fire under the poison spreading through me. My skin burned and seemed on the verge of combusting. The dull throbbing in my leg was now feeling like a thousand needles stabbing repeatedly at the muscles all the way down to the bones. Even the wind blowing past us as he flew at great speed failed to cool the heat engulfing me. It took me a moment to realize the pained moans filling my ears were actually mine. Through the fever setting me ablaze, I felt the tingling of Pharos's regeneration, but it did little this time. I needed more than just an antidote. Only magic could heal me at this stage.

"Hang on, my mate. I will take you home and tend to your injuries. Your thread does not end today," Pharos said in a reassuring tone.

A neighing sound startled me. Through my growing confusion, I realized he had taken me to my horse. I wanted to feel ashamed for having forgotten all about the poor animal. Pharos settled me on top before sitting behind me. That confused me. Flying would be much faster. I doubted I could last through the long ride back home.

My head spinning, I attempted to cast a healing spell on myself but failed miserably.

"Rest, my Kali. We will be home in a second," Pharos said softly.

The wind blew around us as if we'd been caught in a vortex. My entire body tingled, and a queasy falling sensation swept through me before settling. I blinked through my blurred vision to make sense of what resembled tall columns framing the entrance of an imposing mansion in an environment I'd never seen before.

"W-what…?"

"We're home, my Kali. My home. Yours is not safe for now. Rest, my bride. I will take care of your wounds."

I opened my mouth to ask another question… not even sure what. But my eyelids felt too heavy and my mind too foggy. A veil of darkness fell before my eyes, taking away my pain and confusion.

CHAPTER 10
PHAROS

I tightened my hold around the unconscious form of my mate as I crossed the large terrace of my domain. Even though she hadn't given me her soul, I could feel her pain. I hated that she should have suffered because of that damn covenant. As I approached the tall doors into the living area, my eyes widened when they parted open on the frail silhouette of Myress.

"Welcome home, Master," she said in a breathy voice. "It has been a long time."

"I told you not to call me master," I gently chastised her.

As was her wont, she shrugged but didn't otherwise comment. It bothered me that she perceived me that way, even though I understood it was genetically impossible for her to see it otherwise.

"I'm surprised you're still here," I said, marching with determined steps towards the bathroom.

"Where else would I go, Master?" she asked, seeming genuinely baffled.

"You could have explored the realms, found a mate, or crossed the Veil," I said gently.

"That world is not for me," she replied with a shudder. "Here is home. Here is safe. Here, I am happy."

I nodded, my chest constricted for the Cambion. Born of the frolicking of a human male and a succubus, Myress had gotten the short stick of the DNA lottery. Physically, she'd inherited enough demonic traits to look unnatural to humans, but too few of her mother's offensive and survival powers to be welcomed among her peers.

"Such a pretty soul," she said wistfully while peering at my mate. "She's dying. Are you going to reap her?"

"No. I'm going to heal her. And I can use your help. Please, bring me healing herbs for Skarach and Bone Fiend poison."

Her oversized, golden eyes widened in surprise, and confusion settled on her face before giving way to a sliver of worry. Before I could question her as to what prompted that reaction, my servant hurried out of the bathroom, her flowy white dress making her look even more skinny and fragile.

I filled the huge, recessed tub with warm water, then proceeded to remove Kali's clothes. A wave of anger surged within me upon seeing the extent of the injuries she had sustained. Angry welts puckered around the edges of the wounds where her skin had been flat out peeled off by the acid of the Skarach's phlegm. Where the Bone Fiend's darts had pierced her upper arm, a network of dark tendrils spread outwards around the puncture wound, indicating where infection and necrosis was spreading.

Myress returned just as I was finishing to undress her.

"I will help with the poison," she said in a muted voice while setting the couple of flasks and jar she had returned with down on the bathroom counter.

"Thank you," I said with genuine gratitude.

Her presence was truly a blessing. I never hoped she would still be here after my unexpected absence for half a millennium. But what she lacked in offensive skills she more than compensated for with defensive ones. And right this instant, her ability to extract and assimilate poison couldn't have been more welcome.

I held Kali, partially sitting at the edge of the counter, and partially leaning against me. Myress leaned her unnaturally narrow and long face towards my mate's leg, which had sustained the most grievous injury from the Skarach's phlegm wrapping around it. She slightly parted her lips, then her narrow tongue shot out, stabbing into the wound. It vaguely resembled the hooked tongue of a fly, but with a straight dart at the tip instead of recurved.

Magic radiated from her, and the narrow funnel of her appendage discreetly undulated as she drained the poison from Kali. After a few moments, she pulled her tongue out to stab at an unscathed part of my mate's upper thigh and repeated the process. She eventually moved to the wound on her upper arm before straightening.

I couldn't deny that the satisfaction with which Myress licked her lips—like one does after a delicious meal—unnerved me. It was a good thing my bride had been unconscious through it. There was no question in my mind she would have been creeped out.

I hope they will get along.

"It is done. But by the Gods, there was a lot," Myress mused aloud, looking surprised. "As a human, she should be dead already. You circumvented the covenant."

"She's my bride," I said, the pride I felt audible in my voice.

"So I see," she replied pensively, the narrow slit of her vertical pupils widening as she studied Kali's features. "You will have to tell me the story of how that came to pass and of your whereabouts during all those centuries."

"At some point," I said in a non-committal fashion.

She nodded, content with that response. Myress then held her hands a few centimeters from my woman's body, moving them up and down as she whispered a few healing incantations. By the time she was done, Kali had stopped trembling, and her skin no longer felt feverish.

Myress picked up the flasks and jar she brought and poured a small amount from each into the bath. After setting the containers down, she waved her hand over the warm water with another spell. I could have performed that part myself but welcomed her assistance.

"I will go air your room for you," the Cambion said as she turned to leave.

"Thank you, Myress. But please prepare a guest room for Kali, as well as a nightgown and fresh clothes for when she wakes," I requested.

She recoiled, baffled that I wouldn't just take Kali to my room. By the way she pursed her very thin lips, she was itching to question me about it, but thankfully thought better of it. She gave me a stiff nod before exiting the room.

Obviously, I wanted nothing more than to share a room with my mate. But I wouldn't be so bold as to assume her consent. After all, I took her to my home without asking first. However, I didn't doubt for a second that Cornelius was currently tracking down where she resided and likely already knew. He would never stop seeking to punish her in the most atrocious way for 'stealing' from him.

I stripped out of my clothes, which proved a little awkward while still supporting my woman, then carried her into the tub. I settled inside it first and held her against me. Although my regeneration powers had already fully restored me, the healing magic in the water seeped deep into me, relaxing and soothing every cell of my being. I could feel it coursing through my mate. Through the clear water—which had taken a slightly purple tinge due to the herbs and oils Myress poured into it—I watched Kali's wounds slowly mend.

Simultaneously, I shared my regeneration aura with her. I

couldn't heal another person with it the way I healed myself, but it helped accelerate the process, enhancing both her body's natural abilities and the magic in the water.

By the Gods, this felt so right! Her body aligned perfectly with mine. Her soul sang the most enthralling melody, harmonizing flawlessly with my own. I could stay like this, embracing my soulmate for eternity.

To think I nearly lost her...

The memory of those dire last few minutes before I managed to drag her into that safe room had my anger instantly flaring. A part of me wanted to spank Kali for her stubbornness. It hurt me that she genuinely considered death over giving me her soul. She should trust me. Granted, we'd only met a few days ago. Kali barely knew me, and after the mess between her brother Jasper and Cornelius, she had every reason to be wary of what could befall her should she ever allow another to take over the most precious thing anyone possessed.

And yet, I had to acknowledge that after I'd spent centuries being enslaved, sharing the mind and vessel of a narcissistic psychopath, my mate couldn't be sure that I hadn't somehow been corrupted by him. Frankly, I couldn't swear to it either.

Nevertheless, Kali was almost fully mine now. I still couldn't believe she felt strong and genuine enough affection for me to enable the mate bond. Had I even remotely suspected that possibility, I would have brought it up to her.

But she likes me. She genuinely likes me.

The joy that swelled in my heart came crashing down moments later as a dreadful thought popped into my head. Yes, Kali was almost fully mine, but I was not fully free. Until I was made whole again, I couldn't plan a future with her.

The clock was ticking, and I needed answers.

I remained in the water with my woman for a while longer until the magic concluded its work. I stepped out of the tub, dried my mate, then took her to the guest room. A nice fire was burning in the fireplace, and an elegant flowy nightgown was neatly folded on top of the fresh blankets. I swiftly dressed Kali before tucking her in bed. She would remain unconscious for a few hours, giving me the time I needed to handle my business.

I brushed my lips against hers, then headed back to the terrace. I took flight even as I opened a rift through the Veil and teleported a hundred meters outside of the Weaver's domain. Contrary to widespread belief, Reapers couldn't simply teleport at will anywhere we pleased. We could do so near a dying person assigned to us for reaping, or near people or places with whom we shared a powerful bond...

As was my case with the Weaver…

Flapping my wings—which were still a bit wet from the bath —I carefully approached the imposing gates of her domain. The guardian imps didn't stir, and the gates didn't open for me. Although a more official welcome would have been appreciated, I simply flew over the closed entrance, unimpeded. Had I been trespassing, the Weaver's powerful magic would have taught me the error of my ways.

The door of the ridiculous little thatched-roof witch hut illusion she gave her mansion opened as soon as I landed in front of the house. I walked in to find the Weaver sitting next to her spinning wheel, as always.

"My son," she said, her eyes still glued to the glowing thread between her fingers.

"Mother," I replied in greeting, my chest filling with warmth as I admired her timeless beauty. "It's been too long."

She nodded and stopped the wheel. "Too long, indeed."

She rose to her feet and circled around the large table a short distance from where she sat at her wheel, and which faced the door like a reception desk. I stood still as she slowly examined me from head to toe. She caressed my right cheek, her soft hand gliding down to my chest before her index finger traced one of the exposed bones of my rib cage.

"By the Gods, I do make beautiful offspring," she said wistfully before caressing my wing.

I snorted, and shook my head at her, having no word to respond.

"You regenerated well," she added approvingly.

"I have. The Keres in the crypt provided me with quite a few of her minions to feed on," I said mockingly.

My mother snorted. "Grizelle is most displeased. She's roaming over every battlefield to try and compensate for your loss."

"I was never meant to be her meal," I ground through my teeth.

She looked at me with an unreadable expression before slowly nodding. "You are correct. But you kept her eternal hunger at bay for centuries. People never take kindly to losing a privilege they've come to consider their due."

"Like Cornelius," I replied grimly, understanding her underlying meaning.

She dropped her hand from my wing and nodded with a serious expression. "This isn't done yet, my son."

"I know," I said with a sigh. "But the first and most crucial step is finally done. Thank you."

She waved a dismissive hand. "You knew I would eventually get you out."

I tilted my head to the side while giving her an assessing look. "Yes. I figured you would. But why now?"

"I needed to find the person able to help you," she said with a shrug.

"It took you five hundred years?" I asked with disbelief devoid of any anger.

"The potential candidates were much too likely to keep you for themselves. And none of them were your soulmate," Mother said matter-of-factly.

"So she *is* my soulmate!" I exclaimed, my heart soaring.

"Of course, she is. You know that," she replied as if I'd said something silly and obvious.

"I suspected," I replied in a slightly defensive tone. "I felt it the very first time I met her. Kali has such a beautiful soul. It's mesmerizing."

"A soul that you don't own," she countered in a disapproving tone while running a hand over her endless, silver-white braid.

I stiffened, worry immediately swelling within me. My mother never said anything just to make small talk. If you were wise, you noted every single thing she alluded to. It usually was the difference between life and death.

But what more does she want with my mate?

"I eventually will," I retorted sternly. "Kali needs more time."

"You don't have it," she snapped, her sudden mood swing taking me aback.

"What do you mean?" I asked. "I have taken her to the Shadow Realms. She's safe from Cornelius."

"*She* may be, for now. But *you* are not."

I heaved a sigh again, frustrated that even now the necromancer continued to poison my life. "Yes, I know. I need my scythe back. I have a few days to plan—"

"Two days, Pharos," my mother said in a tone that brooked no argument, interrupting me. "You only have two days."

"What?! Why?" I exclaimed. "It will take him more time to gather all the reagents to compensate for my magic and to set things up for the inevitable battle he knows I will bring to him."

"No, my son," she said with a conviction that twisted my insides. "You only have two days because of the manticore heart you helped him acquire. There's a reason Cornelius has been hiding things from you. The manticore was the final ingredient he needed to permanently bind you to him. If he succeeds, not only will you never be free again, you will in fact cease to exist while he will retain all your powers."

I took an involuntary step back, shock and horror swelling through me.

"This cannot be allowed, Pharos," she said, her face expressing the closest thing I'd ever seen to distress from her.

My mother never showed her softer emotions. She would shower you with sarcasm, disdain, and anger, but would express her affection and tenderness in very subtle ways. That she would allow herself to display any type of vulnerability had all my senses go into high alert.

"The fact that he'd been able to use your powers for so long has already significantly upset the balance," my mother explained. "The manticore should have lived. His thread was not meant to be severed like this. That in turn has had a domino effect on many other threads that will now no longer be woven, that got cut short, or completely derailed. To make matters worse, Cornelius intends to try to harness Charon, the same way he harnessed you."

"Charon?! The Ferryman of the dead?!" I shouted.

She nodded with a somber expression. "Cornelius needed at the very least manticore bones to perform the binding ritual. But the heart is even more potent. With it, he will be able to ensnare both you and Charon. Once the ritual is complete, you will make him nearly immortal. And this time, he will enjoy the full spectrum of your Death and Regeneration Magic, without being bound by the covenant against killing."

"Harnessing me, I understand. But why Charon?" I asked, confused.

"Because the Ferryman will provide him with an endless supply of souls," my mother explained grimly. "Instead of ferrying the deceased to their appropriate realm of the afterlife, Cornelius will funnel them into his constructs. He will amass an immense army of enslaved souls, trapped in the powerful creations that he will build."

"By the Gods…!" I whispered, horrified.

"By the gods, indeed. The Gods, the Ancients, and the netherworld as a whole is in uproar. My son, Cornelius's fate is sealed. In two days, on All Souls' Day, he intends to perform the ritual while the Veil is the thinnest. He must be stopped before it is complete. You must defeat him. If you fail, if he ensnares you, all will be lost. Therefore, we will have no choice but to finish the task."

The intensity in her eyes made her underlying meaning clear. If Cornelius won and managed to bind me again, they would have no choice but to kill him, which also meant me in the process.

I gave her a stiff nod. "I understand. This gives me less time than I thought, but very well. I will be ready."

"You cannot do this alone, Pharos," she warned in a soft voice.

I immediately stiffened. "Not Kali. She wouldn't survive."

"She will if you claim her," she replied dismissively.

"It must be her choice," I said in an obvious tone.

"Then make her choose to go through with it," she retorted with a hint of irritation. "Do you really think your female will sit on the sidelines while you confront Cornelius after what he has done to her brother? If she's not tethered to you, she will die."

"I won't let her come unless she's bound to me," I said firmly.

"You cannot shackle her, you fool. You should know by now she has her own mind," Mother said, rolling her eyes.

She then waved at the large wall on the left side of the room next to her spinning wheel. An intricate network of threads came into focus. Most people couldn't see it, even if they tried, unless she deliberately showed it as she was now. As a Reaper, I could always see people's life threads. Out of respect, I never peered at my mother's wall by altering my vision when I used to visit her before. But this time, I greedily studied it only to feel my blood drain from my face.

Two threads shone brighter among the complex web that very few sentient beings could even begin to guess how to interpret. They belonged to Kali and me. They branched out, showing the possible outcomes of our future. Normally, a person's life thread was like a tree, its limbs spreading in various directions, some branching out further, and others cutting short quickly.

While my own thread was a source of concern, it was Kali's that retained my attention. There were only six branches, four of which indicated her death either in the next couple of days or within the year. Of the remaining two where she lived, only one matched my own exceptionally long thread of near immortality.

"She only lives in two scenarios?!" I exclaimed with disbelief. "And they're both the palest options?! Why just these two?"

The thickness and intensity of the glow of a thread indicated the likelihood that it would come to pass. The paler it was, the less probable it would be the path taken by the person concerned. Various choices they made along the way could shift the focus from a different path making the desirable one become stronger. I needed to make this happen for my mate.

"Because she's your soulmate. If she doesn't die by your side in two days, she will wither away without you if you fall alongside Cornelius. Guilt and sorrow will eat away at her. Kali will only live and thrive if you do. So you must convince her."

"Don't you think I want to?" I asked, my anger not aimed at her but at the situation. "In the end, she doesn't owe me her soul or to sacrifice herself for me. Surely there is another path where I keep her safe even should the worst happen, and I fall?"

She snorted and shook her head with a mix of affection, amusement, and discouragement.

"Oh, Pharos, you are always so angelic. You would get along with Asheron. You are both too sweet for your own good. Did you not get any of my ruthlessness?"

"You can't blame us for that," I teased affectionately. "You chose to have us with angels."

She made an unimpressed face while waving a dismissive hand. "For your father, I'll grant you that. But Asheron's sire is a true fallen. And an obnoxious one at that."

She muttered that last sentence under her breath, making me chuckle.

"Alderan is of the divine, nonetheless, even though he's more chaotic," I said gently. "I'm assuming it was your hand that helped free my brother?"

She lifted her chin defiantly. "No one messes with my children and gets away with it. It doesn't matter how long it takes. Bind her, Pharos. I'm not losing you now. You do not understand how many loopholes I had to exploit to get your mate to act now before it was too late. This is the best outcome for the both of you. But you only have two days."

"She cannot be coerced into this, Mother," I said with frustration as I began pacing around the room. "And telling her any of this feels like blackmail and manipulation."

My mother huffed and rolled her eyes at me. "Truth beats deception any day. Kali wants you. She wants a future with you. The mate bond never would have worked otherwise, and she would have died in the crypt. Stop overthinking everything. By keeping quiet, you're not protecting her. All you're doing is taking away her free choice."

That gave me pause.

I turned back to face her and shifted my wings to loosen some of the tension knotting my back. She was making a fair point. Were our roles reversed, I would want Kali to be honest with me and allow me to make an enlightened decision.

"Understood. I will speak with her," I said with a sigh, surprised to find it felt like a weight had been lifted off my shoulders. "I must go back to her now. She will awaken soon."

I smiled and turned to leave.

"Pharos!" my mother called out.

She closed the distance between us and plucked two strands

of her extremely long, silver-white hair from her head. Despite it being plaited into a single long braid, the strands came out effortlessly without breaking. I watched in fascination as she tied each one around my bracers. They fused with the metal, giving it a silver glow.

"I thought you couldn't intervene?" I challenged as I felt the potent magic radiating from it.

She shrugged. "A mother is allowed to offer her son a gift from time to time."

I snorted. "You know all the workarounds, don't you?"

"I've lived since the dawn of time, Pharos. I've seen it all," she said, her face taking on a serious expression. "Death Magic wielded by a Blood Mage is a powerful thing. People wrongly assume that Flesh Magic is best to control constructs. But what binds the various parts that shape them is blood and the fluids in their tissue."

With these cryptic words, my mother drew me into her arms and hugged me. Too stunned by this highly unusual display of affection, I just froze. Before I could snap out of it and return her embrace, mother kissed my cheek then pulled away from me. Without another word, she returned to her spinning wheel, indicating this meeting was over.

My heart ached at the sudden realization that this maternal embrace was in case we may never meet again. As much as it saddened me, it also whipped me into being even more determined that it would not be. I had not been a prisoner all this time to only enjoy freedom for a couple of days before my final death. I would prevail, and I would live happily ever after with my soulmate.

"Thank you, Mother," I said.

Although she didn't glance back at me, the pleased smile that stretched her lips confirmed she had sensed my reaction. I smiled in return, understanding it had been her intention all along. She was constantly playing the most advanced game of chess, always five moves ahead of everyone.

I walked out of her house and took flight before opening a rift in the Veil to teleport back home. As soon as I appeared above my terrace, my blood turned to ice.

A Grim Reaper was in my house.

CHAPTER 11
KALI

I stirred, gradually emerging from the most amazing rest. My entire body felt languid, my skin tingling in a delicious fashion. Even as memories of the terrible ordeal we'd just been through flooded back to the surface, I couldn't feel the slightest pain or discomfort.

But I could feel a presence nearby observing me.

My eyes snapped open. I was lying in an amazingly comfortable bed, a thick duvet agreeably weighing me down. The first thing I saw was the insanely high ceilings with intricate crown molding. The pale stones of the walls gave me the impression of ancient Roman architecture.

I jerked my head to the left from whence that impression of being observed emanated, expecting to see Pharos. Instead, a dark figure sat on the windowsill of one of the massive windows adorning the walls of the immense bedroom.

A frightened gasp escaped me as I shot to a sitting position, instinctively backing away, ready to cast a defensive or offensive spell. Judging by the broadness of the shoulders, I presumed the intruder to be a male. But he was exactly how I had initially assumed Pharos looked like in person: a skeletal knight covered in a dark hooded robe. He was lazily spinning the long staff of his single-bladed scythe.

For half a beat, I wondered if it was one of Pharos's alternate appearances. But a quick shift of my vision confirmed that Reaper did not possess the same mesmerizing aura I had become so enthralled with. In a flash of lucidity, I also remembered Pharos wielding a pair of shorter scythes, one in each hand, connected by a bone chain. They'd been ghostly, not made of physical material like his. And when he joined them into a single staff, it had been double-bladed.

The stranger tilted his head to the side before rising to his feet. Despite his slow, non-threatening movements, I once more scrambled backwards, panicked.

"You can't reap me! I didn't die!" I blurted out.

Despite the absence of skin over his skeletal face, his features still moved in an uncanny fashion as his mouth stretched into a smile.

"You didn't die… *yet*," he conceded.

"It is not my time!" I said forcefully as I jumped out of the bed on the opposite side from him. "Pharos healed me. He marked me so that no one else could reap me!"

A rumbling chuckle escaped him. He rested the base of his scythe on the darker stone floors and stared at me with an amused expression. The red glow of his eyes felt ominous.

"I am not here to reap you, little human," he said mockingly.

I released a shuddering breath of relief. But that didn't alleviate any of my concerns.

"Then why are you here watching me? Where's Pharos? Who are you?"

He emitted that insufferable chuckle again before grabbing his staff with the other hand, slightly leaning it against his chest as he gave me an assessing once over.

"So many questions… My name is Haroth, and I am here to see both of you."

"Both of us?! Why? What's wrong?"

He didn't answer right away, his eyes glowing as he studied me. That only freaked me out further.

"You have a beautiful soul, Kali Jenkins. I can see why my brother is so taken by you," he pensively said at last.

"Your brother?!" I echoed, flabbergasted.

My cheeks burned with embarrassment when I caught myself eyeing him from head to toe. Granted, they were both Reapers and shared some skeletal traits. He didn't appear to have much skin at all. Or rather, it seemed to be a very thin layer over an even thinner amount of muscle beneath. It wasn't wrinkled or sunken in like a mummy, but it also wasn't the normal proportion of a human, unlike Pharos.

His mouth stretched in that odd smile again, having guessed the thoughts coursing through my mind.

"Where is Pharos?" I asked, glancing around the immense and elegant room I had awakened in.

"He went to see his mother. He will return soon."

"*His* mother? Not *yours*, too?"

He shook his head and casually started walking around the room. I eyed him warily, although relieved that he didn't try to approach me.

"We only share a father, hence why our appearances differ so much," he added teasingly, while admiring an adorned vase on the large dresser between two of the tall windows.

"I was wondering about that," I admitted sheepishly.

He peered at me over his shoulder and gave me that amused smirk again. "I noticed. For the difference isn't so much that we have different mothers, but the fact that I'm a Grim Reaper whereas he's an Angel of Death."

"I suspected as much," I said pensively. "But I'm not quite certain what the difference is between the two."

He turned back to face me and casually leaned against the dresser. "I can kill at will, even if my target's thread hasn't technically reached its end, much like humans can. Obviously, such actions could have unpleasant repercussions for me if done so in a reckless and gratuitous fashion, just like murder is punished among your people. But angels like him are bound by a different covenant. They can only kill someone already doomed out of mercy, near their end of life, or in order to defend themselves or the restricted number of people that can fall under his protection."

"Like his mate and offspring," I replied.

He nodded. "It was wise of you to become his mate. But why have you not given him your soul?"

I instantly bristled at that. Crossing my arms over my chest, I narrowed my eyes at him. "Did Pharos send you to convince me?"

He snorted and shook his head. "Most certainly not. He doesn't even know I'm here. But you haven't answered my question."

"Because that's none of your business," I retorted in a clipped tone. "And what's with you folks and your obsession with appropriating other people's souls? No one just hands over the very essence of who they are to some stranger."

"Pharos is not a stranger," Haroth replied in a much cooler voice. "Giving him your soul merely creates a unique and unbreakable bond between the two of you. You'll remain in your body, still go about your life as usual, with your own free will. And on top of that, you will be nearly immortal."

"But he could still choose to abuse that power. I barely know him. We just met a few days ago!" I exclaimed.

"And yet, he gave you his, did he not?" he countered. "Pharos had a lot more to lose than you do. You felt his power during the short time you hosted him. Had you so wished, you could have simply walked away without transferring him back into his own vessel. There would have been nothing he could have done to stop you."

"I never would have done that!" I exclaimed, feeling offended. "Anyway, I'm sure he would have fought back."

"There wouldn't be much he could have done about it, had you gone that route. Unlike with Cornelius, Pharos willingly gave himself to you. That bond was even greater than the one forced upon him by the necromancer. You would have been more powerful than Cornelius ever was. And I'm sure the thought crossed your mind, did it not?" he challenged.

My cheeks heated at the memory of the jealous anger that had indeed surged within me for the briefest moment at the thought of letting him go. Sure, the immense power had been alluring. But it had been the wondrous feeling of his soul inside me, of being in perfect harmony that had been intoxicating. *That*, not his power, had been the real source of temptation.

"What person wouldn't be tempted by such a gift?" I retorted defensively. "But it's not because a thought popped into my head that I would be okay with acting on it. And clearly, I wasn't."

"You were not. However, most people would not only have considered it, but also acted on it. Why do you think his mother left him trapped for so long? All the people who would have wanted to go after Cornelius either didn't have the right skill to see the mission through or the moral fortitude not to become the new prison for my brother so that they could appropriate his powers. She searched long and hard for you."

"What? His mother searched for...? By the Gods, who is his mother?" I whispered, shocked by what I guessed his answer would be.

"The Weaver, of course," he replied, amused.

Stunned, I let myself drop at the edge of the bed, my mind racing as I replayed my meeting with her in my head.

"She didn't search for me," I argued feebly. "I went to her looking for help."

Haroth snorted. "You went to her because she made sure you would. In all these years, you never once thought of approaching the Weaver, until recently, am I right? Didn't you find it strange how everywhere you went, random people would suddenly mention the topic of the Weaver within earshot of you? Did that not plant the seed that set you on the path to seek her?"

My jaw dropped. He was correct. Over the past three months, I'd started hearing a lot about the Weaver, and how she could help solve the most improbable challenges. It even haunted my dreams with growing urgency over the past few weeks, only relenting once I set my journey here in motion.

"But why? Why me? Surely, I couldn't be the only person with the ability and morality to see this through?" I asked, floored.

"Because she recognized you as his soulmate. She knew you could be trusted with his soul, and that in turn, you would be able to trust him with yours, even in such a short time."

I instantly felt myself closing off again, which irritated him.

"Look, I believe you have the best of intentions, but I have no desire to give my soul away to anyone, especially after what happened to Jasper. That's the only reason I got involved in this entire mess to begin with. I never want to put myself in a position where I could be this helpless. I genuinely care about Pharos. From what little I've learned of him, I could see a long-term future with him, if he wishes for one with me. But I need time to get to know him."

"My dear Kali, you already know my brother better than anyone else on any plane of existence, even more than Cornelius who hosted him for the past five hundred years."

I blinked, completely taken aback by that comment.

Haroth gave me an indulgent smile. "You shared with him a more intimate bond than most beings ever will. The whole time he was Cornelius's prisoner, my brother shielded himself as much as possible from his corruption. But today, you held his soul within you. As he freely gave himself to you, you felt and shared everything that he is. Did any of it make you cringe? Did any part of him set your senses on high alert and scream danger or deception to you?"

I froze. No, holding Pharos inside me had been like being filled by the divine lights of the Gods themselves. It had been blissful, glorious, the closest thing to feeling whole I had ever felt in my life. I didn't speak, but the expression on his face told me that my own revealed the thoughts crossing my mind.

"You are a fledgling Soul Mage. Granted, your powers are on the weaker side, but they are strong enough for you to see when a soul is slimy or shady. Has a soul ever made you feel happier or more fulfilled than his?"

I shook my head and hugged my waist, more troubled by his words than I would ever admit.

"Exactly, and that's because you are soulmates. Pharos felt the same when he was with you. That's why he loves you, and why he deliberately broke the covenant to try and protect you."

"Why do you care so much?" I suddenly asked, baffled by it all. "Yes, I'll admit that I absolutely loved the feel of his soul for the brief moment I held him. It does move me deeply that he trusted me enough to do this. I'm not sure that I will ever want to part with mine. But we have the rest of our lives to decide on that. Pharos is free. Once we've taken care of Cornelius—"

"Pharos is *not* free yet," Haroth countered forcefully.

"What?!" I exclaimed, my stomach knotting with an automatic sense of doom.

To my surprise, Haroth thrust his scythe towards me, not in a menacing fashion, but angled in a way to show me the base of the blade, right below where it attached to the staff.

"Notice anything different than my brother's scythe?" he asked.

I frowned and licked my lips nervously before answering as I searched my memory. "Yours is solid whereas his was ethereal. He also had two blades connected by a bone chain. But I'm assuming it's the difference between a Grim Reaper and an Angel of Death?"

He shook his head. "A ghost scythe is the weaker, temporary version. If you see a Reaper using one, it's because he no longer has his real weapon. My brother's scythe is currently in the necromancer's possession."

"No!" I breathed out, horrified.

"Yes. And without it, Pharos is incomplete," Haroth said in a somber tone before pointing at what I first assumed to be bone-shaped decorations at the base of the blade. "This is my spinal vertebrae. To be more specific, every Reaper grows a couple of extra cervical vertebrae that naturally come off once we reach maturity. We use them to forge our scythe. It is how Cornelius was able to trap Pharos."

"By stealing his scythe?!" I exclaimed.

He nodded. "As part of the binding ritual, yes."

I jumped to my feet, shock and denial swelling through me. "Does that mean that he can bind him again since he still has his scythe?"

"That's exactly what I'm saying, and what Cornelius intends to do."

"Like hell he will!" I hissed, my hands fisting with anger. "We are going to kill him anyway to make him pay and to free my brother."

"You cannot help him as a mortal," Haroth said with a finality that took my breath away.

"As his mate—his bride as he calls me—"

"You *will* die," the Grim Reaper interrupted sharply. "You have two choices, stay behind or bond with him. I can see the threads of life. There is no question that you will die if you help him confront Cornelius without having given him your soul."

I shuddered and hugged my waist, my eyes flicking from side to side as I assessed his words.

"And what of Pharos? What does his thread look like? Do

Reapers even have one?" I asked, still struggling to come to terms with his words.

"He will likely die," Haroth said in a factual manner.

"What?! How?"

"If Cornelius didn't have his scythe, Pharos would easily crush him. But without it, and the other rituals the necromancer is plotting, it will be extremely challenging for him, and nearly impossible on his own."

"You have your scythe. Can't you help him?" I asked, my voice pleading.

"Unfortunately, I cannot," he said in an apologetic tone.

I recoiled, anger instantly surging within me. "Why the hell not?! And don't give me that covenant nonsense. Of your own admission, you're a Grim Reaper, not an Angel of Death, which means you can kill at will. Plus Pharos is your blood brother. What greater bond to justify helping him?"

"Your statements are correct, but your interpretation is not. You will recall that I said that Grims can kill at will, but there is a cost like when a human commits a murder. Gods, Ancients, and most demigods like me are not allowed to interfere in the affairs of mortals. We can only step in if the outcome of an action performed by a mortal threatens the balance."

"But there is a direct threat against your brother! How is that the affairs of mortals?" I argued, baffled.

"Because the entire situation was created by a human seeking to elevate himself. Throughout your history, practitioners of the dark arts have devised clever ways to harness the powers of the netherworld or enslave beings from beyond the Veil for their own benefit. As upset as this makes us, we never interfere, as it is part of the path the mortals have chosen for themselves. It is unfortunate for those who got trapped, like my brother, but it is part of their own journey to fight their way back out of it."

"Humans screw over demigods, angels, and demons, and a

lot of you just sit back beating your chests and sending thoughts and prayers?!" I snapped angrily.

"While I wouldn't have quite put it that way, that description is fairly accurate minus the beating our chest part," he replied in a slightly mocking fashion before sobering. "We can help tip the scale, like I'm doing right now by trying to nudge you into assisting him. But I cannot interfere directly."

"If that's true, why didn't Pharos tell me about any of this?" I challenged.

"First, probably because he didn't have a chance to do so, thanks to the impromptu trip Cornelius took them on. Second, because he probably wanted to see if you both would even make it out of this first mission in one piece. And last, but not least, because he's finding out just now from his mother about the diabolical plan the necromancer has in store for him."

I opened my mouth to ask a question, but a ripple in the Veil stopped me. I jerked my head to the right, towards the large doors leading to a private terrace.

"Speaking of the little Angel..." Haroth said teasingly.

He made his way towards the patio doors. They parted open before him in response to a flick of his hand. Only then did I hear the flapping sound of wings. I instinctively hastened after him. I no sooner emerged on the impressively large balcony than Pharos entered my line of sight, flying from another balcony located near the main entrance.

The look of panic on his handsome face upon seeing his brother knotted my insides. Had Haroth lied to me? Was he in fact an enemy? I perceived no deception from him, and his words had all been aimed at benefiting Pharos.

But my man diving and landing in front of me in a protective stance put an end to my musings.

"What the fuck are you doing here?" Pharos demanded angrily at his brother, his wings spread as a protective wall to shield me from him.

"Peace, Brother," Haroth said in that same insufferable mocking tone.

"Her time is not now!" Pharos continued, his voice still as harsh, seeming oblivious to the Grim Reaper's comment. "I've seen her thread. And I marked her."

Hoisting myself on my tippy toes, I stretched my neck to peer at his brother over the broad span of my man's black wings. He had that smug and amused look I was already starting to grow used to.

"I said peace, Pharos. I didn't come here to reap your mate, but to warn the both of you. Except Myress informed me that you spoke with the Weaver."

"I have," Pharos replied stiffly, anger and tension bleeding out of him.

"So you understand what's coming?" Haroth insisted, all amusement fading from his voice.

"Yes, I do. In two days, Cornelius will die, whether by my hand or someone else's," he replied.

With all signs of potential danger lifted, I gently touched Pharos's left wing as I started circling around it. He glanced at me over his shoulder before folding his wings and drawing me against him. I went willingly and leaned into him.

Haroth's gaze flicked towards me. It lingered for a moment, his expression unreadable before he returned his attention to his brother.

"That's correct. Cornelius will die, even if that means you must die, too."

"What?!" I exclaimed.

Pharos flinched but didn't argue. Seeing him respond with a stiff nod freaked me out.

"Why would you have to die, too?" I asked, worry making my voice pitch higher.

"Cornelius threatens the balance," Pharos replied in a tired voice. "His crazy plans jeopardize the world order, which cannot be allowed. In two days, he will perform a ritual to bind me permanently as well as another demigod. If he succeeds, he will become an unstoppable menace."

"A menace that only my brothers and I, our father, the Gods and the Ancients would be able to stop," Haroth said. "The only way to do that will be to kill Cornelius. But if he manages to reclaim Pharos, then we will have to kill him as well in the process."

"No!" I exclaimed, jerking my head in turn between the two males in disbelief. "Surely we can free him again first, like I just did!"

He shook his head. "No, my bride. This time would be different. My mother explained to me what his plans are. If he succeeds, I will cease to exist as an individual. I will become an intrinsic part of him—or rather my powers will. Killing him—and therefore what's left of me—will be the only option. I just never thought you would be the executioner," Pharos added, glancing at his brother.

"A few of us will be there to intervene if needed. Believe me, we all pray you will prevail. We have waited a long time, allowed atrocities we normally never would have out of love for you. But this is going too far," Haroth said apologetically.

"I understand, and I truly appreciate it," Pharos said with genuine gratitude.

"But why don't you just stop him now?" I argued, still struggling to comprehend the subtleties of that stupid covenant. "You already know he needs to be put down in two days. Why not just take him out now instead of allowing Pharos to get in harm's way?"

"Because the crime that warrants his execution has not been committed yet. You cannot punish someone for their thoughts or aspirations. There is still a path where Cornelius sees reason. It is extremely dim and unlikely, but so long as it exists, it must be given a chance."

I shook my head, disgusted and frustrated. Sure, I understood his logic but totally disagreed with it. We all knew Cornelius would stop at nothing to satisfy his lust for power.

"Settle it, my brother," Haroth said firmly. "Please don't make us do this."

"I have every reason not to fail," Pharos said calmly, before casting a meaningful glance my way.

That wrecked me. I gave him a sad smile that he returned, my chest constricting from the strength of the emotions I felt for this male I'd only met a few days ago.

He turned back to look at Haroth with a serious expression. "However, should I fall, Kali's brother—"

"Will be handled," Haroth interrupted in a way that sounded like a pledge. "He has suffered enough for his foolishness. Severing his thread will not affect the balance."

Tears pricked my eyes as I gazed at the Grim Reaper. "Thank you," I said with a shaky voice.

"Yes, Brother, thank you," Pharos echoed.

"There's no need to thank me. But if you insist, you can do so by prevailing. You *can* do it, but you will need *her*." He turned towards me, his eyes glowing with great intensity. "Do not fail him, Kali… or yourself."

"Haroth!" Pharos said in a warning tone.

"Farewell, you two. Do not waste the next couple of days," Haroth said, ignoring his brother's warning.

The space around him blurred as he opened a doorway through the Veil. He stepped forward and vanished from view. The blurring faded, and I turned my gaze towards Pharos, still shaken by this encounter.

"How are you faring?" he asked, studying my features.

"I'm fine," I said in a slightly distracted tone. "Actually, I feel great. Whatever magic you used to heal me is amazing. But I'm more concerned about this thing with Cornelius. Did you know about this?"

"What exactly did my brother tell you?"

Although annoyed that he didn't immediately answer my question, I answered his by giving him a quick summary of our discussion. Pharos pinched his lips, visibly displeased by some of the things Haroth told me.

"I didn't know about Cornelius's master plan. I knew he would want to get me back and intended to tell you after we had completed the first mission. I just wish my brother wouldn't have interfered the way he did."

"Why not?" I asked, feeling somewhat offended. "I needed to know this. How am I to make an enlightened decision about how to manage the situation if I don't have the full picture?"

"I know. Sadly, I have this insane urge to protect you. I'm damned if I do and damned if I don't. You only have two days to decide. It feels like an unfair amount of pressure. You cannot come without giving me your soul. If you do, we are both guaranteed to die. So how do I tell you that without you thinking that I'm trying to coerce you into giving in to me?"

A horrible thought suddenly hit me as he spoke those words.

"Is that why you've been asking for my soul this whole time? Because you can't succeed without owning me?"

I felt guilty as soon as I blurted out those words. Seeing him recoil and a hurt expression descending over his features only heightened my guilt.

"No, Kali. Long before I even knew you would be my salvation, I wanted you. I've hungered for your soul from the very first time I saw you. You were standing by the entrance of Cornelius's mansion with your brother. The whole time he was making his case about why Cornelius should take you both as apprentices, I was just transfixed by you. When I gave you my soul in the crypt, it was like being hugged by the Gods themselves. For the first time since this whole nightmare began, I actually wanted to be fully owned by someone. I could have remained a part of you forever."

My throat constricted, and I slipped my arms around his waist. He drew me against him and wrapped his wings around me.

"I have seen and felt your soul, Kali. We were one, in perfect unison. So long as I draw breath, I can never want anyone else more than I want you."

"I felt you, too, Pharos. It was… perfect harmony. I also remember thinking it was like the light of the Gods had filled me."

"It's because we are soulmates, my bride."

"I think you're right. I think we *are* soulmates," I said, the truth of that statement settling deeply in my heart.

Pharos leaned forward and claimed my lips in a kiss filled with such tenderness I felt myself melting from the inside out. My hands glided up his broad chest, over his shoulders, and sank into the soft locks of his black hair streaked with silver.

He immediately deepened the kiss, the flame of passion sparking low in my belly in response. He picked me up, and I wrapped my legs around his waist, our tongues still mingling as he carried me back inside my room.

CHAPTER 12
KALI

My stomach fluttered with anticipation as Pharos stopped right in front of the bed. He didn't put me down right away, as reluctant as I was to end the kiss. Just like when he had been in his Wraith form during our couplings prior to his rebirth, his body was warm, but his breath cool. He tasted fresh, like anise and mint with a hint of honey. The texture of his tongue had lost that sponginess to be more like the one of a human although a bit rougher.

He finally loosened his hold around me, letting me slide along his muscular body until I was back on my feet. However, he pulled up the flowy, white nightgown I hadn't even noticed I was wearing. By the fresh and slightly fruity scent emanating from my skin, I realized that my man had bathed me before putting that gown on me.

I'd been too frazzled by finding Haroth in my room when I woke up to really pay attention to such a detail. But the silkiness of the fabric against my skin as he pulled it off me screamed its luxury. He tossed it aside before reclaiming my lips. The heat of his body against mine sent a shiver down my spine. But the hard-

176

ness of his pauldrons, and the skirted belt that covered his tight pants annoyed me to no end.

I wanted to explore and feel all of him… the *real* him.

Even as our tongues warred, I let my hands roam down his sides, lingering for the briefest moment on the exposed bones of his ribcage that peeked between the skin. It could have been creepy, but in his case, it was not only sexy, but it also gave him a dangerous and otherworldly edge that I found quite the turn on.

Pursuing their journey south, my hands settled on the large metallic belt adorned with a skull. I blindly fiddled with it until I successfully unclasped it. I let it fall off him. It landed on the floor with the soft rustling sound of fabric followed by the muffled thump of the belt. I immediately went on to loosen the lace holding up his pants. Pharos didn't resist, but broke the kiss, his right hand fisting my hair on my nape as he began to cover my jaw and neck with kisses.

Another shiver coursed through me when he nibbled on that sensitive spot right in the crook of my neck. During our previous nights together, Pharos had been extremely attentive to my responses to his touch. His generosity as a lover had taken me by surprise. It had been difficult for me to fully assess his own reactions to my caresses. As a Wraith, his facial features had been too undefined to properly convey his emotions. His partially ethereal body had also made it impossible to know for certain what his responses would be to real physical contact. And I wanted to discover everything about him.

Starting with that mysterious cock of his…

As soon as I detached the lace, I tugged down the leathery fabric of his trousers. Pulling away from his lips still roaming over my neck and the curve of my shoulders, I started reciprocating with kisses along his neck and chest. The way he initially stiffened hinted that he wasn't necessarily keen on relinquishing control. To my delight, he gradually relaxed, his hand still cupping the back of my head, but without restraining my movements.

The texture of his skin on my lips wouldn't quite qualify as human. It was unnaturally soft and warm, the pigmentation so subtle you barely felt it. His scent was hard to define: an intoxicating mix of woodsy and smoky.

I brushed my lips over the exposed bones on his chest before kissing my way to his left nipple. His body slightly jerked when my mouth closed around it. I sucked on the little nub for a few seconds, then poked my tongue out to tease the areola. Once again, I couldn't define the taste, which combined a hint of spice and salt. But it was the way his breath hitched that retained my attention. I wanted to know all his secrets, all the ways I could make him fall apart for me like he repeatedly made me scream for him.

Impatient to discover my prize further down, I abandoned his chest to pepper kisses down the chiseled curves of his abs. While my left hand continued to lower his pants, the right one circled around to caress his back, and especially that area at the base of his wings covered in small down feathers.

It had been an innocent touch, but his strong response and the deep, rumbling growl that emanated from him confirmed his approval. I gently raked my nails over that sensitive spot, making him take a hissing breath that resonated directly between my thighs.

However, as I knelt in front of him, all thoughts of the erogenous spot around his wings faded away. My man was huge. Even only partially erect, Pharos had plenty to boast about. Just like the rest of his body, his pelvic area was smooth, devoid of any pilosity. His shaft—generally human in shape with two testicles —mesmerized me. I could now see in its full glory the source of the odd and wondrous sensation I'd felt when coupling with him.

I had felt some kind of ridges along his shaft when he was taking me in his Wraith form. Now, in the flesh, he appeared to have a network of subcutaneous implants. But upon closer inspection, I realized they were small bones, right below the skin. Fascinated, I ran my fingers along the ridges. Those on the front half of the upper side almost looked like a spine, running from the base of his shaft to the edge of the head. On the upper half, arched ridges emulated a ribcage, which continued on the underside. For a reason I couldn't explain, my mouth immediately watered.

Without thinking, I leaned forward and licked the vertical slit of the head. Pharos hissed again, his abdominal muscles contracting while his hand on my nape tightened around my hair. Still, he didn't attempt to control my movements, allowing me to continue to freely explore him.

Wrapping my hand around his cock, I slowly began stroking him, reveling in the unusual sensation of his ridges beneath my palm. Despite the hardness of the bones, the many joints kept them pliable as I squeezed my hand around them. My inner walls constricted spasmodically in anticipation. I felt hollow, eager to finally get the full experience of him.

Leaning forward again, I licked and teased the head with my tongue, before taking him inside my mouth. The strangled moan that escaped him made my nipples instantly hard and achy. I began to bob in front of him, stretching my mouth wide and relaxing my throat to try and take as much of him as possible. Sadly, his girth prevented me from taking half as much as I would have liked. I compensated by stroking the rest of his length with my hand moving in counterpoint to my mouth.

Judging by the voluptuous sounds emanating from my man, he more than approved of my ministrations. His breath quickly grew shorter and louder as I accelerated the pace. I could feel him struggling to keep himself from thrusting forward into my mouth. That didn't stop him from swaying, spasms contracting the muscles of his thighs and abdomen. By the way his legs were shaking, Pharos would soon find his release.

That spurred me on.

Just when I thought he would topple over, Pharos emitted a sharp cry and yanked my head back, but not before a few drops of precum spilled onto my tongue. Although feeling cheated to have him rob me of taking him to completion, I marveled at the wondrous taste of him. It was smooth and sweet, with a hint of anise, notes of creamy vanilla, and the nutty elements of whiskey without the burn.

I wanted more.

But the wretched man yanked me up effortlessly, and all but tossed me onto the bed. His head buried between my thighs silenced any protest I might have had. His expert tongue went to work on me with a deftness that had me cresting in no time. Pharos knew exactly where and how to focus his attention to make me squirm. The contrast between the warmth of his lips on my clit and the coolness of his tongue and breath as he licked and sucked my little nub was fanning the inferno raging inside me.

A series of needy moans tumbled out of me as two of his thick fingers slipped inside me, moving in deeper and faster, driving me insane. He would alternate between crooking his fingers to rub against my sensitive spot, sending sparks of pleasure through me, and scissoring them with each motion, stretching me to receive his considerable girth.

Chasing after my own release, I ground my pelvis against his hand. He accelerated the movement of his tongue on my clit until my body seized. I cried out as pleasure swept me away. With his mouth still devouring me, Pharos tilted his head up to look at me.

The red glow of his eyes illuminated the exposed bones around them, giving him an intimidating look that made my stomach perform a couple of somersaults.

It was sexy as hell.

As my orgasm receded, Pharos pulled his fingers out of me, licking my essence off them in a lascivious fashion that had me throbbing again. An almost evil smile stretched his lips before he started kissing a path back up my body. He carefully climbed on top of me and claimed my mouth with a burning passion and possessiveness.

I spread my legs wide to welcome him. Although he settled more comfortably between them, he didn't try to push himself in right away. For the next eternity, we kissed and caressed each other. I would never tire of the insanely smooth texture of his skin. It finally dawned on me that its flawlessness came from his constant regeneration. As pleasant as the feel of a man's calloused hands could be, the silkiness of Pharos's palms had something magical to them.

A thrill coursed through me when, at last, he rubbed his length against me. The slight friction of his bony ridges on my clit sent electric sparks throughout my nether region. He positioned himself but paused to lock eyes with me. That made me melt from the inside out. I smiled to confirm my consent, my chest warming with affection for him. I lifted my pelvis and squeezed the plump curve of his behind to squash any lingering doubt he might have.

"My bride," Pharos whispered tenderly before carefully starting to push himself in.

Unsurprisingly, my body quickly resisted his invasion. Considering how wild and unbridled our couplings had been over the past few days, I had expected to adapt more quickly to his non-negligible girth. However, he had been in his wraith form with a spongier and more flexible ethereal cock.

Having anticipated this, my lover didn't rush through any of it, showing admirable restraint as he slowly and methodically gained centimeter by centimeter with shallow thrusts. Through it all, he kissed and caressed me, whispering sweet words of devotion and encouragement that made me forget the slight discomfort.

And then my body yielded.

I barely even noticed the burn as he suddenly found himself buried to the hilt. My body was too focused on the insane sensation of his bone ridges inside me. A strangled moan rose in my throat as he slowly started moving. However wondrous he had felt in his Wraith form, this was multiplied by a thousandfold. Electric sparks went off inside me with each stroke, the ridges rubbing against my sweet spot both on the way in and out.

An inferno was raging in my loins as Pharos gradually accelerated the movement, taking me deeper and harder. The weight of his physical body pinned me down, making me feel helpless in a way that whipped my arousal into a frenzy. Still, I writhed beneath him as waves upon waves of pleasure swept through me. I felt on the verge of combusting from the liquid flames racing through my veins, the lava swirling in the pit of my stomach, threatening to erupt at any moment, and the searing heat of my lover's muscular body wrapped around me.

Our moans mingled, his chest occasionally vibrating with a low growl that made my toes curl. The slapping sound of our flesh colliding resonated throughout the room as Pharos pounded into me. He was so big, his cock stretched me to my limits and filled me to the brim in a blissful maelstrom of pleasure and pain.

My orgasm slammed into me, and I threw my head back with a shout, which Pharos echoed. For a brief instant of lucidity before being swept away, I thought he had found his release as well. But my man tightened his grip in a bruising fashion on my waist, his left hand slipping under my right leg to open me even wider for him.

Then he let loose.

I was flying high while he was destroying me, fucking me senseless with near savagery. His entire body seemed to glow from a magical halo. With every other thrust, his wings would spread as if he were fighting the urge to take flight. It would slightly lift me off the mattress only to slam me back down into the soft cushion as he rammed himself back in. I never got a chance to fully come back down before a third orgasm crashed into me.

My back arched, and my body seized. This time, Pharos roared as my inner walls clamped down on his cock. He slammed himself in deep, and threw his head back, wings spread wide as his seed shot into me. Nothing prepared me for the searing heat swirling with magic that flooded my battered insides.

It was nothing like our previous couplings where he'd shared a small part of his soul with me. And yet, the familiar tingling spread through my body. His soul wrapped around mine, soaring with me to endless heights. Lost in an ocean of bliss, it took me too long to realize he'd slowly resumed rocking in and out of me, his movement gentler until he was fully spent.

He collapsed on top of me. With his cock still buried deep, my inner walls contracting spasmodically with a will of their own around his length, Pharos turned us around. I rested my head on his chest, between the two halves of his exposed bones and listened to the thundering of his heart.

Utterly wrecked, I melted against him as he tightened his arms around me and closed his wings over us.

"You're mine, my Kali. My bride. I'm never letting you go."

After a couple more naughty rounds, Pharos and I finally surrendered to oblivion. Despite sleeping like the dead, my mind didn't rest at all. It was said that humans solved many of their problems during their sleep, and that definitely applied to me that night. I'd gone to sleep feeling like the weight of the world rested on my shoulders with impossible choices to make. But today, I felt at peace.

Things were only ever as complicated as we made them.

That morning, we got out of bed and took a shower together —which led to some more sexy times. To my surprise, upon returning to my room, the bed had been done and a beautiful dress was laid out on it for me with fresh underwear.

"What in the world…?" I whispered.

"Don't worry. Myress did this. You will meet her shortly. Technically, she would be deemed my servant."

"Technically?" I echoed.

He nodded and took my hand to lead me out of the room. I almost commented on the fact that he was still naked, but he seemed unfazed by it.

"I consider her more as a helper, but she insists on calling me Master."

We stepped into a large hallway of pale stone and majestic columns. It felt as if we had traveled back in time and entered an ancient Roman temple to some deity. We crossed into a large bedroom a few meters from mine. I realized then that it was his own room. A part of me was glad that he hadn't simply assumed I would share his bed, but another felt a little stung that he hadn't shown more possessiveness, even though it would have been a bit disrespectful.

But then, I never claimed that all my feelings were logical or rational.

Just like my room, his was massive, with huge windows and patio doors leading to a private balcony. The scarcity of furniture inside surprised me. It didn't look empty, just restrained, peaceful, and unencumbered. Considering the black hood, skirted belt, and somber leather pants and boots he had previously worn, I expected his personal space to reflect that edgier style, with sharp angles and an overall dark color scheme.

But the same lighter palette welcomed me. Soft, pastel colors in the earthier tones made the room warm and inviting. Above all, it screamed peace and serenity. My gaze lingered on the head of the immense bed propped against the back wall. It was carved either in stone or a very pale wood and represented a stylized sculpture of angel wings. Gold, burnished orange, and dark green pillows provided the right splash of color against the beige bedding. A Roman chaise lounge framed the fancy sitting area with a large fireplace and a shaggy white carpet in front.

"Myress is a Cambion," Pharos continued while opening the door to a huge walk-in closet.

Seeing the number of togas, skirts, and pants hanging from poles on the right wall took me aback. The vast majority of them were white or a very pale shade of cream or pastel. Once again, for the oddest reason I had expected to see mostly the same type of leather pants and dark clothes as what had been on his body on that altar.

The left wall had skirted belts, pauldrons, and bracers. On the back wall, a variety of boots, shoes, and sandals were artfully arranged on shoe racks. They framed a central display clearly meant to hold one main weapon. I instinctively knew this was where his scythe would have been.

My chest constricted at the reminder of the challenge that awaited us.

He picked up one of the toga skirts and put it on—no underwear.

"Myress looks too inhuman to live amongst your people, but her demonic powers are too weak to live with her kin in this realm," Pharos said while reaching for a pair of sandals that laced around the ankles. "She was shunned and bullied, which forced her to flee. I found her weak and starving in a nearby forest during a leisure flight. I took her in, and she has served me ever since."

"An Angel of Death with a half-demon servant. It sounds like an unexpected pairing," I said teasingly.

He chuckled. "Nothing is too weird or impossible here in the Shadow Realms," he said indulgently before taking my hand and leading me out of the room.

"The Shadow Realms? Is that where we are?" I asked with genuine curiosity.

Based on the lore, the Shadow Realms was the other side of the Veil, the parallel universe to the mortal plane.

Pharos nodded. "We are more specifically in the Nephilim Valley."

"Nephilim?" I repeated, stunned. "I would have expected them to be part of the Elysium, or Heaven."

He smiled while showing me the living area in this brief tour of the mansion. "Some of them live there now. Initially, the majority of the human-angel hybrid children were raised in the valley below. As most of them couldn't fly, coming up to a mansion like mine was too impractical. I have many angels, fallen and otherwise, living nearby. This house is carved directly inside one of the highest peaks of the mountain range surrounding the valley."

"So what happened?" I asked with curiosity as he continued the tour. "Did they die off?"

"Over the centuries, they naturally passed. But along the way, more order-aligned hybrids moved here. Those with flight abilities settled in aeries like I did."

"So this entire valley has no evil," I mused aloud, feeling a little relieved that I wouldn't have to constantly look over my shoulder in this space.

To my surprise, Pharos pursed his lips pensively as we walked through the impressive kitchen with a small adjoining dinette. Past the arched walls delimiting the room, I could see a formal dining room on the other side.

"Evil is a debatable concept," he said carefully. "What many perceive as evil is often just chaos. True evil would be someone like Cornelius. He has no compassion or empathy. He revels in the misery of others, not out of an instinctive response beyond his control, but because he's a psychopath. He understands the difference between right and wrong but doesn't care. His pleasure and satisfaction are all that matters."

I nodded grimly and opened my mouth to comment, but the sudden growling of my stomach had me gasping instead.

Pharos chuckled. "Perfect timing. Myress just finished laying a meal for us on the terrace. The view is too breathtaking here as the sun sets not to enjoy it. This way, my bride."

He didn't have to say it twice. A part of me wondered how his servant was always so on top of everything. I doubted she was spying on us. Did he telepathically communicate our needs to her?

As we emerged onto the terrace, the view indeed took my breath away. I'd had a glimpse through the tall windows, but the sheer white curtains in front of them had kept me from fully appreciating the uniqueness of the landscape. Even though I'd been on my bedroom balcony earlier when Haroth dropped by, I had been too distressed by the situation to truly pay attention to my surroundings.

Now, I could fully marvel at it. We were at least two hundred meters above the valley below. A series of dwellings were scattered at a reasonable distance from each other, forming a charming village that seemed to belong to a different era. Countless statues and fountains adorned the common areas with extensive gardens. The valley extended over a large distance before gradually turning into a thick forest. The mountain range surrounded half of it like a bay. They had carved a few other dwellings at different heights of the mountain face, but each of them angled in a way to ensure privacy.

The sky shimmered with the similar orange, purples, and magentas as the sunset on the mortal plane, but they danced in the sky like the Northern Lights.

However, it was the exotic female putting the finishing touches to a table laden with mouthwatering food that retained my attention. I immediately understood why she couldn't live among humans. Her face was overly long, with a chin too narrow, a skull too big, a mouth too wide and nearly non-existent lips, and her general body too skinny. And yet, she didn't seem starved or miserable, and in fact possessed an odd otherworldly beauty. Huge, golden eyes with narrow, vertical pupils peered at me with curiosity.

She flicked her long, straight black hair, which fell to her knees, with an extremely graceful movement. I immediately thought of a ballet dancer. Her simple black, sleeveless dress entirely covered her feet and even had a short train. It contrasted sharply with the pale color of her skin, which had a subtle hint of light gray or purple.

"Kali, this is Myress. She helped me heal you earlier today," Pharos said in a gentle voice while gesturing at the Cambion.

"Hello, Myress," I said in a friendly tone. "It is a pleasure to meet you. And thank you for your help. Whatever the two of you did, it was perfect. I feel wonderful."

"I am glad, Mistress," she said in a submissive voice. "Please enjoy your meal."

She gestured at the table then gave us a polite nod before quietly walking back inside the house. I couldn't tell if it was just an illusion caused by her long dress, but she appeared to glide rather than naturally walk.

I cast a slightly confused look at Pharos. Although I perceived no hostility from her, her behavior felt odd and distant.

Pharos smiled. "She's not very social and struggles interacting with people, especially ones she doesn't know yet. Do not be distraught by it. Myress is on the lower edge of chaotic, but she is extremely loyal. I trust her with my life. However, Grizelle is true chaos."

"WHAT?!" I exclaimed, staring at him in disbelief. "That female was pure evil, at the same level as Cornelius!"

Pharos snorted and shook his head. "She's nothing like him. But come, let's eat."

CHAPTER 13
PHAROS

I couldn't help another smile when my woman didn't hesitate to start piling a generous serving of the various dishes onto her plate. As guilty as I felt about exhausting her so thoroughly on an empty stomach earlier, I loved seeing my Kali have such a healthy appetite and especially enjoying Myress's cuisine.

My bride probably hadn't noticed, but I knew the Cambion well enough to have sensed her worry that Kali would ask her to leave. The poor Myress was so used to people rejecting her merely for what she was or her unusual appearance that she had come to expect it from anyone in some sort of position of power over her. Thankfully, I perceived no such sentiment from my female, only genuine curiosity.

"So please tell me in what world Grizelle is not evil," Kali demanded between two bites.

I chuckled while filling our respective glasses with wine. "Like all other Keres, Grizelle is a slave to her genetic nature which demands for her to constantly hunt and feed. It's nothing personal against you or anyone else. In many ways, she's like a wild beast."

"But she's sentient and able to hold a rational conversation. She was clearly mad at me for taking you from her," I argued.

"She was furious with you. You took away her greatest prize. Grizelle—like all Keres—is cursed by an insatiable hunger. In other words, no matter how much she eats, she will constantly feel hollow. I was an endless source of food for her. Losing me sets her to starving again. Instead of being able to rest in her temple while draining me, she will have to hunt every minute of every day. Today was a devastating blow for her after centuries of comfort," I said softly.

"Okay, I can see how that would be terrible for her. But that doesn't make it less evil that she would condemn you to this life of slavery," Kali challenged.

I smiled. "That would be true of a human or some of the more evolved species of the netherworld. But do not be fooled by her ability to hold a conversation. It's not a reflection of higher thinking. Have you ever spoken with a gnome? They can converse with you, but they're dumb as a rock. There is a reason many of the lesser demons and lower tier species never achieved the type of evolution humans have. They live in primitive conditions, only chasing after their next meal or a safe place to sleep, despite the powers that could have helped them advance. Their thinking capabilities and mental range are basic. They do not have the analytical minds to weigh things such as right and wrong, ethics, and morality in general."

Kali frowned and pursed her lips while reflecting on my words. "I see what you mean. But I still struggle with seeing her as something other than evil."

"Evil requires an intent to cause harm for the sake of cruelty or for entertainment. It is understanding right and wrong and choosing to go on the darker side. Creatures like Grizelle are literally unable to feel emotions such as empathy and compassion. They are purely driven by their instincts and will mindlessly pursue whatever can ensure their survival. To her, killing you or trapping me are logical actions that anyone in their right mind would do in her shoes."

"Right. I can see that," Kali conceded with a hint of reluctance.

I took a sip of my wine while reminiscing on how this entire mess took place to begin with.

"Creatures like her are easy to manipulate because their driving force is obvious, allowing to smoothly cater to it," I said pensively. "That's how Cornelius was able to recruit her into enslaving me."

"I wondered about that! But frankly, I thought it had been the other way around, and that Grizelle sweet-talked Cornelius into it."

I snorted and shook my head. "She's not intelligent enough for that. As I understand it, Cornelius brought her victims to feed her blood pool in exchange for information about Reapers."

"Information like what?" Kali asked while cutting a piece of meat, her eyes sparkling with curiosity.

I hesitated as to how to best answer the question. "Mortals are distributed among Reapers in order for us to harvest their souls upon death. Most of them are randomly assigned as they draw nearer to the end of their thread. But they are weak marks that could be overwritten by one of us if we wished to claim them as ours to escort."

"Like you did with me!" Kali said, her beautiful face lighting up with understanding.

I nodded. "Death creatures like Reapers and Keres—among others—can see that mark. It is like having our names branded on that person. Grizelle mostly haunts battlefields where she can get large feasts from all the fighters dying. She would roam around noting those marked by an Angel of Death instead of a Grim Reaper."

Her eyes widened with surprise. "Why specifically an Angel?"

"Because we are more compassionate. Cornelius needed one of us to increase his chances of achieving his plan. Grims usually teleport in, snatch the soul of the dying, and leave. We Angels tend to linger, comfort the dying, and ease them into departing."

"So she identified a few potential targets, and you just ended up being the unlucky one," my mate said pensively.

"Exactly," I said, bitterness seeping into my voice.

"But how? I always wondered how a much weaker necromancer could have ensnared a demigod," she asked sheepishly.

"It was part of the deal he made with Grizelle. Remember how the blood pool only had partial limbs and random organs floating inside?" I asked.

She nodded.

"The agreement was that Cornelius would bring humans for her to feed off their blood and life force, but he got to keep some of their parts for his constructs. It took a while, but he eventually managed to kidnap one of the humans marked by an Angel of Death who she had identified for him."

"Eventually managed?"

I nodded. "As most of the targets were on battlefields, too many died before he could get to them. It isn't easy to abduct someone surrounded by the other members of their units."

"Right, not to mention him getting to wherever the battle was taking place in time," she said.

"Exactly. But once he got the *almathar*, Cornelius set up the trap to lure me in. *Almathar* is the name we give a person about to die who we will escort shortly to the afterlife," I explained when she gave me a confused look. "As his magic wasn't powerful enough, Cornelius needed Grizelle's help to boost his own skills and achieve his goal."

"Wow, he really planned this out!"

"That's one thing I must grant him. Cornelius is extremely calculated and thorough. No challenge is too great when it can help further his ambitions."

"So I see," Kali replied with a shudder. "So what happened?"

"As soon as their life thread is about to end, we receive a call. It's a tug similar to what you felt when Cornelius was trying to pull me back as you were transferring me into my body."

She nodded.

"Normally, as soon as we receive the call, we can directly teleport to the location of our *almathar*. Unfortunately, certain places present an obstacle that requires us to appear a bit farther away, as is the case with the Hemdell Crypt. The place is cursed. Too much magic prevents us from materializing inside. The closest we can manifest is right outside the entrance in the burial grounds."

"That's why after we bonded you had to fly outside instead of just teleporting out?" Kali asked.

I smiled. "Correct. So that's what I did. I appeared outside the crypt and flew all the way down to the sacrificial chamber. By the time I arrived, my *almathar* was screaming while Cornelius was severing his limbs, cauterizing them as he went to keep him from bleeding to death. Grizelle was feeding on his life force and fear. Such cruelty infuriated me. A Grim should have been assigned to this man. They could have ended his pain immediately."

"But as an Angel of Death, you were forced to let it follow its course until he died," my bride said with empathy.

I nodded with a somber expression. "We're usually not assigned gruesome deaths. I could see that his thread had shifted from the original path. But as per the covenant, I could not end his life until his fate was 100% sealed. In this instance, Cornelius wasn't just sacrificing the human, he was turning him into a sentient construct. Therefore, there was still a slim possibility that the *almathar* would survive the ritual. The only thing I could do was to sever the soul from his body to end his pain."

"Wait, I'm confused. Wouldn't that kill him?"

I shook my head. "The soul can remain inside a body without

being directly connected to it for a maximum of twenty-four hours. During that time, while that soul still animates that body, it will not feel any of the pain that vessel endures. It is something we often do for extremely sick people in the last few hours of their lives. That's why you will sometimes hear of terminally ill patients who suddenly regain their lucidity and almost seem normal, hours before their passing."

"Oh wow! I didn't realize that," Kali said, impressed. "But how did Cornelius use that kindness against you?"

"He had already set up a ritual meant to trigger the moment I performed that specific act," I said, the old anger swelling again inside me. "To sever the link, we only use the tip of our scythe on the thin thread which connects to the spine right below the skull. It is a very precise procedure which requires great care. But the moment my scythe touched my *almathar's* soul, it felt as if I had been struck by lightning with such strength that I instinctively yanked my hand back. Unfortunately, with that gesture, I ended up involuntarily severing his head, killing him instantly."

"No!" Kali breathed out, before pressing her fingers over her mouth with a horrified expression.

"The worst pain I'd ever felt struck me to my knees. Remember the wounds I sustained for killing the Skarachs that attacked you in the crypt? The ones I received for killing that man before his time—a man whose thread still indicated he might survive—was a hundred times worse. Before I could recover, Grizelle swooped in and sucked me dry."

"By the Gods, you never stood a chance," Kali said, compassion and anger on my behalf filling her voice.

"None, and it was my own fault," I concurred with a dejected expression.

She recoiled. "How was that your fault? You were trapped!"

"I was," I conceded. "However, I felt something was off the moment I stepped onto the island. But that entire place is permeated with so much evil that I didn't really spare it much thought.

Since Cornelius was performing a ritual right there on my *almathar*, I just assumed what I felt was directed at him. But it was aimed at me."

"You still had no reason to suspect a trap. Who in their right mind would have expected a human to be so crazy as to go after a Reaper?" she challenged, as if I'd said something silly.

"Fair. But I should have listened to my instincts when they told me something was amiss. But Cornelius perfectly planned this whole thing. As is often the case with dark blood magic, a human sacrifice was required. For this specific one, it needed to be performed by an Angel. Therefore, he found a clever way to get me to do just that as I never would have consented to it otherwise."

Kali uttered a series of swear words under her breath. The self-righteous anger she felt on my behalf touched me deeply.

"So between the punishment of the covenant, and Grizelle leeching me, Cornelius was able to easily take my scythe from me and perform the binding ritual. And so, for the past five hundred years, I've been helplessly watching his power grow as he used me. The most painful part was witnessing him leverage my powers to doom my own brother and steal his tail," I said bitterly.

"Asheron?" she asked with sudden understanding.

I nodded.

"Jasper was obsessed with him," Kali said with a dejected expression. "During his apprenticeship with Cornelius, my brother kept talking about the Wraith. The fool thought he would be the one to find the way to ensnare him for Cornelius."

I bit back the urge to say that Jasper had always been an idiot who greatly overestimated his abilities. But she didn't need me to bring him down further. As Haroth said, her brother had suffered enough for his foolishness.

"I involuntarily caused so much suffering over the centuries. The way Cornelius used my powers allowed him to do things he never should have, and which increasingly affected the balance. To this day, I'm shocked that the Ancients didn't get us both executed sooner."

"You're not going to die, Pharos," Kali said with a conviction that took me aback. "You didn't survive this long and get this far only to fail now. Cornelius is going to pay for all the wrong he has done."

"This last part, I take great comfort in knowing it is now nearly inevitable," I said softly. "But the ultimate outcome for me isn't guaranteed. Still, whatever happens, I'm just grateful that I met you and got to spend these moments with you."

"And I feel the same about you. Tomorrow, Cornelius will proceed with his plan to bind you and Charon. We need to go there as soon as possible to stop him before he can get too far setting up his ritual," she said.

"Kali," I said in a chastising tone. "You know that—"

"Stop, Pharos. I know what you're going to say," she interrupted in a gentle but firm tone. "Look, I'm scared. Actually, terrified would be a more appropriate word. I've seen what happens to people who allow their souls to be taken over or stolen. I've spent the past few years watching my brother gradually degrade. He suffers, trapped in a decaying body, his mind still there but mostly faded. Once we free him, he will be a mindless, wandering soul."

"There are peaceful places in Erebus for souls such as his. Erebus is the region where we take our *almathars* until Charon takes them to the region of the afterlife best suited for them. It isn't limbo or purgatory. Haroth will make sure he's taken to a good place. With time, Jasper might become whole again and even be reborn as a human. But if he doesn't, he will never know pain or despair. He will be happy."

My chest constricted at the sight of the grateful tears welling in her eyes.

"I can never thank all of you enough for this," she said, her voice thick with emotion. "It is the best that I could have hoped for Jasper. But seeing what happened to him and recent events have taught me that I cannot allow fear to dictate my life. In fact, your brother really helped open my eyes."

"Haroth?!" I asked, surprised.

She nodded, a frown marring her forehead. "He reminded me of what it felt like when you gave your soul to me. For the first time in my life, I felt whole, at peace, and truly happy. But more importantly, I felt all of you. I may first and foremost be a Bone and Blood Mage, but I'm also a respectable Soul Mage. And when I held you, I perceived no malice, no evil, or underhanded intent from you towards me. Your feelings for me were pure and loving. We vibrated in perfect harmony."

My heart skipped a beat as her underlying meaning started making its way into my mind.

"What are you saying?"

She took a deep and fortifying breath before answering. "I'm saying that I am scared, but I believe in you. Therefore, the same way you trusted me with your soul in the crypt, I will trust you with mine."

I stiffened, joy, confusion, and worry battling inside me for dominance.

"You want to give me your soul?" I asked, wanting to make sure there was no misunderstanding.

Kali swallowed hard but nodded.

"You understand that it is not reversible?" I insisted.

"I do," she said firmly.

Still flabbergasted, considering how adamantly against it she had been not even twenty-four hours ago, I studied her features as if they could reveal the answer to this mystery.

"You have no obligation to make this sacrifice simply to save my life," I said carefully. "You have no debt towards me."

She waved a dismissive hand. "I know that. It is not guilt or a sense of obligation that made me come to that conclusion. To be honest, I would have preferred a lot more time to come to terms with such a monumental decision. But holding your soul convinced me that we are meant to be. We may not be in love with each other yet, but there is no doubt in my mind that it will come. I just know that I cannot contemplate a life without you. And I know you will not abuse this gift."

"But—"

"Stop arguing, Pharos," Kali said sternly. "I have made my decision, and you will not discourage me. I had the entire night to sleep on it, and I already knew that I would go through with this the moment I woke up this morning. I'm not doing this out of a sense of guilt, but because it's what I want. You took me out of hell yesterday. Tomorrow, you and I will send Cornelius to its darkest pit. And then, you will get to show me what it's like to be your bride for the rest of our lives."

"My Kali," I whispered, my heart filling to bursting.

Rising to my feet, I went over to her chair and pulled her into my embrace. As I claimed her lips, I thanked all the powers that be for sending my soulmate my way. Whatever future awaited us, this moment would have made it all worthwhile.

She was mine, and I wouldn't let anything or anyone stand in the way of the future I wanted for us.

CHAPTER 14
KALI

My pulse picked up when he broke the kiss. Eyes locked with mine, Pharos summoned his ghostly scythes by flicking his hands open on each side of his body. Memories of how things went sideways with his *almathar* flashed in my head. Obviously, that tragedy only occurred because Cornelius had trapped him. But I couldn't help the sliver of nervousness that coursed through me.

"Do you trust me, Kali?" Pharos asked in a gentle voice devoid of any accusation or suspicion.

In spite of the slight anxiety I felt at the prospect of what was about to take place, I didn't hesitate as I nodded firmly. "Yes, Pharos. I do."

And I meant it, too.

"Are you sure you want to go through with this?" he insisted.

That, more than anything else he might have said or done, put to rest the lingering uncertainty that gnawed at me.

"I would lie by saying I'm not feeling a little worried and unsettled by this whole thing. But yes, I am certain I want to go through with this. I truly trust you, and it would only be delaying the inevitable and needlessly putting both of us in danger," I replied calmly.

My stomach flip-flopped in response to the infinite tenderness with which he gazed upon me. Yeah, I was falling hard for my Reaper. Whatever misgivings I may have had, this felt right, like it had been ordained from the beginning of time.

"It will feel strange, but it will not cause you any pain," Pharos warned in a reassuring tone.

"Okay," I breathed out.

I rolled my shoulders and stretched my neck to release some of the tension building there. After shaking my hands to further loosen up, I gave him a stiff nod indicating for him to proceed.

He smiled again, then raised his blades in front of me. Very carefully, he poked the tips of each scythe in my chest, or more specifically into my lungs. I expected the sharp sting of a piercing wound, but it only provoked a cool sensation followed by a tingling. I stared in fascination as the ethereal blades sank deeper into me, the coolness of the tips reaching the base of my spine.

With the blades halfway in, Pharos stopped, and his eyes began to glow an intense red. Simultaneously, I felt a powerful tug, like when Cornelius was trying to pull Pharos back to him during the transfer I gasped, and my hands latched on to his waist, my nails digging into his skin.

I hadn't meant to do that. Startling Pharos might cause him to involuntarily harm me. To my relief, he remained stoic, his eyes locked with his scythes, entirely focused on his task. The pulling sensation intensified. Like he had warned, it didn't hurt, but it certainly wouldn't qualify as pleasant either.

To my shock, the bones at the base of the blades of each scythe—and which gradually turned into the staff—began to fill with a bright and mesmerizing light. I didn't need him to tell me that it was my essence infusing his primal blades. His ghostly scythes were an integral part of him, just like I was now.

For the briefest second, the nagging voice of doubt attempted to rear its head again, whispering that this might have been a mistake. But I immediately shut it down. It was done. And even if I could turn back time, I would still make the same decision.

A few moments later, Pharos pulled out his scythes. The cold sensation waned with their removal. A quick assessment of myself didn't indicate any perceptible change. If not for him telling me this process had resulted in him now owning my soul, I'd have no way of knowing.

The affection, gratitude, and wonder shining bright in his eyes as he gazed upon me had me weak in the knees.

"My Kali…" he whispered with something akin to awe. "Thank you for trusting me. You are mine forever. And now, I will be yours forever as well."

I blinked, confused as to what he meant. Before I could question him, he leaned forward and claimed my mouth. My lips voluntarily parted when he demanded entry. However, instead of the passionate, deep kiss I expected, I was shocked to receive instead a blast of energy similar to when he had transferred his soul to me in the crypt. It lasted no more than a few seconds, but even as he pulled back and straightened, I could feel his essence inside of me.

I pressed two fingers to my lips and stared at him wide-eyed.

He tenderly caressed my cheek as he studied my features with that same deep affection.

"I cannot give you my soul the way you gave me yours. But I can give you a part of me to always keep with you," he softly explained. "I cannot take it back. Only you can return it should you no longer wish to have me—which I hope will never happen."

Tears of joy pricked my eyes. I never would have demanded or even expected him to reciprocate in any way. But this cemented my conviction that I had made the right choice.

"My Pharos," I whispered before melting against him.

We kissed again, this time for real, each of us expressing the depth of the feelings bubbling inside us and steadily growing for each other. He truly was my soulmate. Whatever the future held for us, we would surmount it together.

With much reluctance, we parted. I silenced the part of me that wanted him to carry me back to either one of our rooms and further seal our new bond in all kinds of naughty ways. But we had a serious matter to resolve before we could indulge in building our future together.

"We need to deal with Cornelius now," I said with a frown.

He nodded, his expression hardening at the thought of his nemesis. "We do, but not now. Cornelius just arrived in Sageville," he explained at my surprised expression.

"Sageville? How do you know?" I asked.

"I can feel him. I can teleport to people with whom I have formed a close bond. A simple thought suffices for me to know exactly where they are, and how to get to them."

"That's perfect!" I exclaimed. "Then we should go right away and take him out before he's ready to perform his ritual."

He shook his head and gave me an apologetic look. "We can't. I need him to release my scythe from the secure location he currently holds it in. There are too many wards and protections on it. Cornelius is no fool. He will not make things easy for me. But even if I was willing to risk that, he has locked himself inside the Glocker Manor. There is no direct path to him. He stacked every possible banishment ward he could so that he could prepare. Only once he's ready will he open them."

"So you can't teleport directly inside?" I asked, my shoulders slouching in advance as I already guessed what his answer would be.

"Correct. It is very much like with the crypt," he explained. "Too much magic bars my ability to teleport within its walls. I can do so outside, but I would rather not. Cornelius knows the extent of my powers and limitations. There's no question he will have set a trap to ensnare me should I be so foolish."

"So what do we do? Ride there? It's at least four or five hours," I said pensively.

"We will fly," Pharos replied. "You weigh next to nothing, and it will take me less than an hour to get us there. Then we can scout the perimeter and figure out the best way in."

I nodded, my eyes flicking from side to side as I ran a variety of scenarios in my head.

"Is there any chance you could ask your brother Asheron to help?" I asked, hope audible in my voice. "He was seriously wronged by Cornelius as well."

Pharos heaved a sigh as he shook his head. "My brother doesn't know of my existence. He was born shortly after I was enslaved. Still, I doubt that would have stopped him from assisting me. And I even considered it, but he can't. When Asheron came to recover his tail from Cornelius, my brother pledged not to harm him so long as he left his mate Ronika alone. Cornelius may be a vile snake, but he is no fool. He has not broken their agreement."

"Damn it!" I muttered. "So what now?"

He smiled, the mischievous glimmer in his eyes piquing my curiosity.

"Now, we train you."

I recoiled, more confused than ever. "Train me to do what?"

"We are bonded, my bride. That automatically gives you access to my regeneration powers. But now that you also have a part of me in you, it grants you additional access to most of my Death Magic," he said smugly.

"Oh!" I whispered, my eyes widening with excitement. "By all means, train me!"

He chuckled then grabbed my arm before giving me a serious look. "Sorry about this. It's going to sting," he warned.

I nodded and watched with curiosity as the nail of his index finger extended into a sharp claw. He carefully raked it over the fleshy part of my forearm, making a one-inch incision. I barely winced and watched a few pearls of blood bead around the wound.

"Now pay attention," he said. "Inside your chest, near your heart, you will feel some kind of spark. Normally it's like a soft heat—although for some it's a bit more like static or electricity."

"Heat," I replied instantly. "It's not very strong, but I clearly feel it, and it's rather pleasant."

"Perfect. That's your regeneration well. It is weak and small because your wound is as well. Try to push that little heat into your arm. Will it to go to your wound."

I complied. Seconds later, my jaw dropped as the blood appeared to resorb into the cut, which sealed itself seamlessly, leaving flawless skin behind.

"Nine hells!" I whispered, flabbergasted. "Again!"

He burst out laughing, happiness and pride softening his beautiful features. He did it once more, but this time with a much longer gash. As he had stated, the spark in my chest felt stronger and bigger, proportional to the injury that needed to be mended. I repeated the process with the same amazing result.

"This is wonderful!" I said, my voice bubbling with excitement.

"It is. You cannot begin to understand how relieved I feel knowing that you now possess this ability," Pharos said with a seriousness that made me melt from the inside out.

This man truly cared about me and my welfare.

"For the rest of the evening, you will need to practice that among other things so that it becomes instinctive, a reflex for you. During battle, you cannot pause to focus on healing while attacks are still launched against you. It must come to you as naturally as breathing," he warned.

I licked my lips and nodded. During my apprenticeship as a Blood Mage, casting defensive spells on the fly had been one focus of our training. It had to become second nature to keep us from grievous harm. Your enemy wouldn't pause to give you time to sort yourself out.

"But now, I want to show you how to deal with poison and toxins. Be warned that this will be far more unpleasant as I will infect you with the plague. Only a tiny amount in a localized area," he added quickly when I took an involuntary step back. "It is slow acting, so you will not sustain any real harm. I just want to explain how you will counter it first so that you are ready."

"Right," I said nervously before rolling my shoulders to relax them.

"Whenever you are poisoned, you will feel the regeneration spark, but you will also feel the cleansing spark. To me, it glows red instead of white. But it also feels different, colder—which is counterintuitive with its color," he said with a sheepish expression.

I snorted, finding him ridiculously adorable. "Okay, a red glow that feels cold. Got it," I replied teasingly. "Go ahead, poison your soulmate. I'm ready."

He scrunched his face at me, not in the least amused by my teasing. Although he was doing it to further protect me, he clearly hated causing me pain in any way. That just made me melt even more for him.

He stuck the tip of the claw of his index finger at that same spot in my forearm. He didn't slice, simply kept it there half a centimeter in. I felt the Death Magic emanating from him a split second before he infected me with it. It instantly burned, as if a drop of acid had dropped there.

I hissed through my clenched teeth and fought the instinctive urge to yank my arm away from him. The skin around the infection spot immediately darkened. It didn't spread at a terrifying speed, but quickly enough to have my insides in a knot. Black tendrils slowly spread outwards like spilled ink.

"Focus, my Kali," Pharos gently said as he removed his finger.

I took a deep breath and looked inside me for that spark. Like him, it felt cold to me but also pulsated. It didn't look red in my mind's eye, but green. Following the previous lesson, I pushed it towards the infection site. While the regeneration spark had felt like heat gliding along my arm, this felt like an army of ants crawling all over it, but right below the surface of the skin.

Calling it unpleasant would be quite the understatement, but once again it worked wonders. A shadowy smoke rose out of the wound even as the dark tendrils receded and faded. It was as if the toxin was being burnt out at the same time the spark was pushing it out. The cleansing spark vanished as soon as the last of the toxin was removed. Without thinking, I pushed my regeneration spark in there, and it instantly sealed the remaining wound.

"Well done, my mate," Pharos said approvingly. "You will need to practice this one more as poison and toxins can cause debilitating pain that makes it harder to focus. If you receive copious amounts of poison, trying to push it out might be too slow and could allow it to spread too far before you can tackle it. Do not try to heal while you are poisoned. It will only seal it inside. If there is too much, trap the poison in a container shield."

He burst out laughing at my gaping expression. I could only imagine what I looked like. But what in the world did he mean by 'container shield'?

"It is the same thing you just did," he explained in an amused tone. "The difference is that once your cleansing spark reaches the infected area, harden the glow so that it forms a wall that will prevent it from spreading further in. It will grant you a bit more time to focus on the battle before you can properly expel it and heal. We will need to practice that quite a bit," he added apologetically.

"No need to apologize. This is amazing. Poison away. We have the rest of the day!" I said excitedly.

"Not quite, my darling. I have a lot more to teach you after that," Pharos said in a smug and mysterious fashion.

"More? Do tell," I said with blatant curiosity.

"I did say that you have access to a lot of my Death Magic. I'm going to teach you how to use it all."

"Blast it to Hell! Why didn't you tell me I would get all these perks? I wouldn't have played hard to get as much as I did!" I said in a playful tone.

"I wanted you to choose us freely, not because of any incentives. Then again, those perks only came from me giving myself to you because I'm crazy about you."

The silliest grin settled on my face as I fought the urge to give him a bone crushing hug.

But train me, he most certainly did. We spent the rest of the afternoon practicing combining his Death Magic to my Bone and Blood Magic. I had never felt so powerful in my entire life. Showing off for him also made me tingle in all the right places. Pharos did not practice Blood Magic. However, as he had mentioned that his mother said there would be great power in combining them, I freely experimented, blowing both of us away by how potent it was.

That night, despite feeling properly exhausted from the intense training, we lost ourselves in each other. Our love making was passionate and borderline desperate. Tomorrow could be the end for one or both of us. I refused to accept that possibility, but my mind had a will of its own.

CHAPTER 15
PHAROS

Morning came too soon. A part of me rejoiced that this horrible chapter of my life would finally end, one way or another. But another part of me was terrified at the potential outcome. As much as I didn't want to die, it was my mate I worried about.

Her life thread glowed with greater intensity. It had steadily increased since she voluntarily gave me her soul. The seriousness with which she trained all day yesterday further strengthened it. Although it gave me hope, there was still too great a possibility that things would not work out the way I wanted.

It tore me to shreds knowing that bringing her with me put her in harm's way, but that going without her also guaranteed my demise. The thought of taking my chances alone popped into my head multiple times. I systematically cast it aside. Beyond the fact that it would be suicidal and stupid, my bride would never consent to be left behind.

It warmed my heart to see how sincerely she cared about me and my welfare.

My farewell to Myress proved quite awkward. I did so while

Kali was packing the handful of items she would use in battle. She didn't need to witness this.

"If I do not return, you are to seek out my mate and teach her how to cross the Veil so that she can come here at will," I said in a factual manner. "This home and everything I own will be hers for as long as she lives."

"Yes, Master," she replied obediently. "Will she cast me out?"

I recoiled. "No, of course not. This is your home as well. She may be the mistress, but she will never leave you homeless. In fact, she will likely need your support to get through the first few months."

"I understand. But it will not be necessary. You will return. You always do. That mortal will never be allowed to slay the son of the Weaver and of the great Lord of Death Azrael. I didn't wait five hundred years for you to come home only to bury you. Make the necromancer suffer for all his wrongdoings. I will have your favorite meal ready when you return," she said with a conviction that oddly gave me a spark of hope.

Without waiting for my response, she just turned on her heels and went back to whatever duties called her. I snorted and shook my head before returning to my mate.

"Ready?" I asked softly.

Kali gave me a stiff nod. Pride filled my heart as she held my gaze with an undaunted determination that commanded respect. Most people would be quaking with fear.

After further consideration, instead of flying to Sageville, I decided to teleport us at a far enough distance from Glocker Manor to avoid landing in a trap. It would only have been an hour flight, but I preferred to save every ounce of energy I possessed on top of granting us additional time to survey the perimeter.

We ended up in the woods about half a mile from the mansion. To my delight, my mate withstood the teleportation without any discomfort. Humans sometimes felt queasy or disoriented for a while after it. The fact that we were bonded certainly played a part in making it easier on Kali.

She immediately went on the prowl, looking for a bird to ensnare. A raven would have been ideal, but there was none to be found in the vicinity. Luckily, she found a magpie. They weren't as powerfully aligned with magic as crows or ravens, but they served perfectly in this context.

With a swift possession spell, Kali took control of the bird and surveyed the land through its eyes. Under my guidance, she flew it to the mansion, describing what she saw along the way.

"The front gates are closed. A few lights are on inside the house, but I do not perceive the presence of anyone within the building. Casting Blood Magic through a thrall is quite difficult and limited," she added apologetically.

"There's no one there?" I asked, baffled.

I could clearly feel the pull of his presence at the Manor.

"Yes, there are people there, just not inside the house," she amended, her eyes still out of focus and gazing off into the distance. "I'm circling around the back now where I feel their presence."

My back stiffened when her facial expression changed to something akin to horror and disbelief.

"What the hell is going on?" she whispered, stunned.

"What do you see?" I asked, tension filling my voice.

"They're standing on the terrace outside," Kali said, her eyes flicking this way and that as she observed the scene through the eyes of the magpie. "Cornelius is near the wall to the left of the large patio doors. There's a huge altar in front of him. Your scythe is lying on it. There are all kinds of runes, polished bones, and blood surrounding it."

I cursed under my breath at this confirmation that he was indeed preparing the binding ritual that would bring about my ultimate demise. The mere thought of him desecrating my scythe had my blood bubbling with rage.

"Alva and Meri are standing to the left and right sides of the altar. They're reciting some kind of incantation. I cannot hear them, but I'm certain it has nothing to do with your scythe, and everything to do with Piers."

"Piers?" I echoed, taken aback. "What is he doing?"

"It looks like he's being sacrificed," Kali said with a frown. "He's lying on the ground, spread eagle, his wrists and ankles bound by blood shackles. He's screaming and... Oh Gods!"

"What?!" I exclaimed upon seeing blood draining from her face and her sudden air of panic.

"He knows we're here!" she whispered fearfully, tension stiffening her shoulders.

She breathed heavily for a few seconds, her eyes flicking from side to side while magical energy oozed out of her in droves. I wanted to pressure her into telling me what was happening but held my tongue, sensing that she needed her concentration. After thirty seconds that felt like hours, Kali's shoulders finally relaxed. She blinked then turned to look at me with a mix of worry and guilt.

"What is it?" I asked.

"I was flying over the courtyard when Cornelius looked up. He stared directly into the bird's eyes. He smiled and waved before resuming the ritual he was performing," she said with a shudder.

I cursed again. "You do not seem in pain or in distress. So I'm guessing you managed to escape?"

She hesitated. "I safely got the bird out of there and released it. But Cornelius didn't attack. He just wanted to make sure we knew he was aware of our presence. I don't understand why he didn't attack. For sure he knows that killing the bird while I controlled it would have harmed me."

"He's being cocky," I said, the hatred burning in my gut for him clearly audible in my voice. "He loves psychological warfare. This is simply his way of telling us that he's not bothered or afraid of our imminent attack. He's ready and welcomes it."

"But what's the deal with Piers?" she asked, a frown creasing her forehead. "He has been his loyal apprentice for quite a few years now."

"He has," I said pensively. "Cornelius always gave more importance to the two women. He enjoyed fucking Alva and admired her malicious personality. But he loved Meri's power. Piers had his purpose, but it did confuse me that he had not brought him when we went hunting the manticore. Now I wonder if it had been intentional to keep him in the dark as to the fate that awaited him."

"Is there any chance Piers submitted voluntarily to whatever is going on?" Kali asked.

I pursed my lips as I pondered the matter. "With those three, anything is possible. If Cornelius promised him a significant increase in power if he volunteered, I could see Piers consenting to it. But I also wouldn't put it past Cornelius to have conned or coerced him into whatever this is. Only time will tell. The question is—"

A sudden tug interrupted me. I inhaled sharply and jerked my head in the direction of the mansion.

"What is it?" Kali asked warily.

"The path is open," I said, my stomach knotting with apprehension. "Cornelius lifted the banishment wards. I can feel him pulling at me, baiting me."

"Should we go or delay then?" Kali asked, the same tension I felt audible in her voice.

"We must go," I ground through my teeth. "As much as I hate playing by his rules, delaying further will serve nothing. I will go in first in my wraith form. The women cannot see me unless they shift their vision. And even then, I can fade a bit more to be fully invisible. And unless he uses my scythe, Cornelius won't be able to either."

"No," Kali said firmly while shaking her head. "There's no question that he has set up a trap for you over there. Cornelius has hosted you for the past five centuries. He knows you well enough to expect you will come in using your invisibility powers. I should be the one to go first."

"WHAT?! Are you insane?" I exclaimed. "They will all be able to see you!"

"Yes," she conceded calmly. "But the women and Cornelius were using Blood Magic. I can read and interpret it. You can't. I'm certain there are traps on the ground that will trigger the moment you step into them. Why else would they have chosen such a large and open area with a flat terrain?"

"Even if that were true, it will still put you in harm's way," I argued.

"Any way you cut it, I am getting in harm's way today. But I will do so on my own terms. Cornelius doesn't want me, he wants you. I can create a distraction while remaining out of range of their spells and disrupt their ritual so that you can go in safely."

I clenched my teeth and involuntarily shook my head, further wanting to say no and argue.

Kali pressed a palm to my chest and gently caressed it in a soothing fashion. "Look, I know you're scared for me. But both your mother and brother said I needed to come to this fight. Trust them and trust me. I must go first. I can feel it in my bones."

I stared at her for a while in silence, too many conflicting emotions warring within me. I placed my palm on the back of her hand on my chest, my heart aching at the thought of losing her.

"Don't you dare get hurt," I snarled at last.

She chuckled and leaned against me. My right arm immediately closed around her, drawing her tightly in my embrace.

"I can regenerate now, remember? Someone made me near unkillable," she said teasingly.

"You had better remember your lessons," I growled before claiming her lips with a possessiveness laced with passion and desperation.

With much reluctance, I released her and let my gaze roam over the perfection of her features as if to memorize them. I shifted my vision to peer at her thread. Despite the worry twisting my insides, I couldn't help a smile of relief.

"What is it?" she asked.

"Your life's thread is even brighter and stronger now than it was this morning," I confessed. "It's not yet at the level I wish it would be, but most of the dire paths are gone. We are making the right choices."

"Of course we are," she said with conviction. "We *are* going to win. But what about yours?"

I gave her an apologetic look. "Sadly, I cannot see my own. But seeing yours thrive gives me hope."

"Then let's go get rid of the trash and settle the matter once and for all," Kali said.

I nodded and claimed her lips in one final kiss. Picking her up in my arms, I flew her closer to the mansion, circling around the outer gates into the backyard. Despite my earlier reluctance, I felt silently grateful to have her able to scan for the wards and traps that might have been laid out for me.

I dropped her at the edge of the thick garden that provided some shelter from view. We didn't say a word. Heart heavy, I let my eyes do all the talking for me as I caressed her cheek. She smiled, leaned into my touch, then turned her face to kiss my palm. As I dropped my hand, I realized that I was in love with that woman. No matter what it took, neither of us would die this day. I had waited too long to find the other half of me for it to end now.

I faded into my ethereal form and started invisibly roaming

around the perimeter my mate had deemed safe. My stomach twisted as Kali boldly started walking towards the courtyard. I couldn't tell if I was more impressed than worried by her assurance. I wanted to believe it wasn't a sign of reckless arrogance now that she had enhanced powers. Knowing it was the fear I felt for her making me paranoid, I cast those negative thoughts out.

Seconds later, my blood turned into ice when Piers emitted a soul wrenching scream. His naked body began to swell, his limbs twisting like one would a wet towel to drain the water out. It was grotesque and horrendous. His skin darkened as inky blotches appeared all over his overly bloated body.

"Pharos, I can feel you lurking in the shadows!" Cornelius suddenly shouted, his eyes flicking this way and that looking for me. "Come out, come out, little Angel. Let's play!"

"I think not!" Kali shouted back as she continued her approach.

Cornelius's head jerked in her direction. The instant hatred and malice that descended over his features sent my protective instincts into overdrive. I barely refrained from rushing over to him and tearing him limb from limb for harboring ill intentions towards my bride.

"Well, well. If it isn't the little thief!" Cornelius hissed. "What's going on? Is Pharos too scared to face me? Does he need his little bitch to fight his battles for him?"

"You are one to talk, you carrion feeder," Kali retorted with contempt as she continued her approach. "You need both of your bitches to fight your battle and to sacrifice that fool. Sounds pretty pathetic to me."

Under different circumstances, I would have laughed at Cornelius's outraged expression. That monster was insanely thin skinned. He could dish out the insults but couldn't withstand even the smallest slight.

"I'm going to have fun with you once I'm done with him.

You will be my obedient little bitch. I'll keep that foul mouth of yours too full of cocks to spew anymore disrespect at your betters," Cornelius shouted, his anger almost palpable.

But his words fanned my own.

Kali waved a dismissive hand. "Your threats are no more than a fart in the wind. You will not live past this night. I will enjoy watching you beg for mercy before none is granted."

"Thanks to that pathetic Reaper, I will live forever, you cunt. Forever! And when I'm done using you in every conceivable way, I'll make you the local town whore and even have you entertain what's left of your brother. After all, he hasn't had pussy in a while."

Blinded by fury, I began moving forward towards the inner courtyard.

"Pharos, stop!" Kali shouted.

Her voice pierced through the red haze that had descended before my eyes. I froze. For half a beat, I almost panicked, thinking I had come out of my Wraith form in my anger. How else could she see me? And then it struck me that as my bonded mate, she could always feel where I was within a certain radius.

Cornelius perked up, his head jerking this way and that, looking for me. Even altering his vision did not allow him to detect me.

That pleased me tremendously.

However, Kali slicing her palm open, then spreading her arms wide, hands facing up, reclaimed my attention. She began uttering an incantation. Within seconds, the largest magic ring I'd ever seen came into focus in the courtyard, the pale pink glow quickly intensifying into an angry shade of red.

My blood turned to ice as I recognized some of the patterns of the first circle he had trapped me with in Hemdell Crypt. It wasn't identical. That one was far more complex with a slew of symbols I'd never seen before. A series of lines, swirls, and runes had been etched in a pattern that seemed to point towards the altar. Although I didn't know much about Blood Magic, I recognized the section that served as a trap deeper into the circle.

This whole thing screamed of the type of ancient magic that very few people would dare to even attempt. And without my woman stopping me, I would have crossed the outer edge of the circle in only a couple more steps.

"Well, well," Kali said, echoing the necromancer in a taunting fashion. "Up to your good old dirty tricks again, Cornelius? Too bad they're not going to work this time."

An endless string of curses tumbled out of my nemesis' mouth to have his trap thus exposed.

Totally unfazed, my mate resumed speaking words of power. A wave of Death Magic emanated from her, laced with a hefty amount of Blood Magic. I couldn't even pretend to comprehend what kind of spell she was casting, but its effects quickly became obvious. I stared in awe as the edges of the circle began to unravel.

"You wretched cunt!" Cornelius screamed.

To my shock, he launched two dozen blood darts at her. I shifted out of my wraith form, becoming visible again and sucked the life force out of the darts. They faded into ashes blown away by this soft evening breeze long before they could reach my woman. Without missing a beat, I cast a death strike at Cornelius, knowing it wouldn't be that easy. Sure enough, the spell struck the blood shield they had erected to protect him and his two female apprentices.

Anyway, even without the shield, my death strike would have caused insignificant damage. The ring was dampening my magic as it traveled through it, weakening it further as it crossed the distance.

Cornelius burst out laughing, his eyes sparkling with malicious glee upon finally seeing me.

"There you are, my little pet. Now, the real fun begins.

Prepare to suffer like you've never suffered before," the necromancer shouted.

He pronounced a series of words of power. My stomach dropped when the blood shackles pinning Piers to the stone covered ground fell off and he shot to his feet—twisted though they were—in one swift movement. The handsome, lanky young man he had once been no longer existed. In his stead, a monstrous, bloated creature stared at me with bloodshot bulging eyes. He appeared much too big for his skin, which looked like excessively stretched fabric over whatever was wiggling beneath it, seeming like it was on the verge of bursting open.

Piers lumbered forward, his mouth opening impossibly wide to release an ear-splitting screech. Endless rows of teeth filled his mouth.

To my shock, instead of coming for me, he turned to look at Kali before spitting a stream of black, oily substance towards her. Like I had done with Cornelius's blood darts, I drained the energy from whatever that substance was. It once again dispelled in a shower of ashes. However, I could feel the acid and virulent toxin that had been in it.

"What have you done to him?!" I exclaimed, horror and disbelief filling my voice.

"I've made him incredibly lethal and immortal!" Cornelius boasted.

"I don't think so," I retorted, a challenge in my voice.

Invoking all my power, I cast a potent death strike on Piers. To my dismay, the abomination he had turned into didn't instantly die as he should have. He merely screamed and stumbled a few steps forward before regaining his bearings. However, his skin stretched further as he gained more mass. Somehow, the damage he sustained made him grow.

I repeated the attack a couple more times, frustrated not to be able to just charge in. But the wretched dampening effect of the circle kept thwarting my efforts. Kali was diligently unraveling it. However, it would take a while, considering its massive size and the power of the sorcerers who had cast it to begin with.

Aggravated by Piers's continued advance towards my female, I summoned my ghostly scythes, straightened the bone chain linking them to turn it into a double-bladed staff, then threw it like a boomerang at the lumbering abomination. As soon as my weapon left my hand, I realized I had made a mistake. Cornelius's triumphant expression terrified me. I extended my hand towards the blade to recall it to me, but it was too late.

It found its mark and cut through Piers.

The moment the blade made contact, the apprentice exploded into what I initially assumed to be a shower of the same blackish oil he had spit at Kali. But they turned out to be giant shadow tentacles with vicious spikes at the tips. They shot out in every direction, two of them racing straight at my woman. I barely had time to shove her aside with an elemental strike. She'd been too focused on unraveling the circle to properly react to the threat.

But a few more tentacles racing towards me forced me to dodge out of their path. Without pausing, I cast another death strike at the giant shadow creature Piers had turned into while catching my returning scythes. To my shock, the creature faded into dark shadows, my spell passing right through him and fizzling over the distance due to the circle's dampening effect.

In the back, the two female apprentices increased the intensity of their incantations. Simultaneously, Piers grew in size and mass, easily reaching a height of four meters, with his tentacles extending nearly three times that length. I couldn't give a name to what he had become. The beast slithered on the ground like a squid but possessed a humanoid upper torso. The head—which also had smaller tentacles as hair—had a mix of canine and reptilian to it, with half a dozen glowing red eyes and endless rows of dagger teeth filling its oversized mouth. Unlike a squid, no suction cups lined the tentacles of its lower body. Instead, spiked scales covered it with vicious hooked claws at the tips.

The beast attacked again. I flew out of the way and immediately blasted it with my necrosis on top of casting my death aura at it. Piers screeched as the end of his tentacles began to wither before they could reach either my mate or me. However, he faded back to his shadowy form, instantly shedding the necrosis.

Although I still couldn't enter the circle, Kali was making impressive progress wrecking it. She cleverly realized that combining necrosis to her Blood Magic acted like a virus that chipped away at the circle, unraveling it even faster. I only needed to keep her safe while she performed that task. I flew around the area directly in front of her, using my powers to destroy any tentacle rushing in our direction, slicing through others with my scythe, and forcing Piers to vanish into smoke with my death aura.

To my delight, the creature was quickly faltering as Alva and Meri struggled to counter my attacks. It was clear that they were the puppet masters fueling whatever monster they had turned Piers into. But for all their powers, they didn't know Death Magic or how to counter it.

The tide was turning in our favor, and soon I would be able to go tear them to shreds.

Focused on pushing back the beast and protecting my woman, I didn't notice that Piers was shooting his tentacles at a much shorter distance than before. In order to cut them off with my scythes, I needed to move forward. By the time I realized what was happening, I'd already crossed into the magic circle.

Before I could dash back out of it, Cornelius slapped his hand on the spinal bone of my scythe and shouted a word of power.

A debilitating pain ripped through my spine and tore at my soul. It was as if I had traveled back in time to that dreadful day in the crypt when I accidentally killed that human. I felt myself plummeting towards the ground from where I'd been flying in front of Kali. I tried to recover before I would crash, but three of the beast's tentacles speared right through me—two in my chest, and one in my right thigh.

I cried out as Piers yanked me like with a roped harpoon towards his gigantic mouth.

"PHAROS!" Kali screamed.

Through the haze of agony tearing me apart, I instinctively swiped my scythe at the creature. Half a beat before it would have connected with the side of his mouth, Piers turned back into smoke in an evasive maneuver. As he faded, so did the tentacles impaling me. I fell the short distance to the ground and landed heavily onto the hard stones paving it. My breath rushed out of me, and the gaping wounds left by the tentacles bled heavily.

Spilling my own blood inside a sacrificial circle was the last thing I needed.

As I tried to fly away while invoking my regeneration, what felt like a hundred giant needles speared me again from every side, as the beast materialized again but this time with much smaller tentacles. I shouted in agony, realizing he was going to put me through an endless cycle of pain to break me while he stole my powers. However, before I could cast another death aura or necrosis, Cornelius slammed the bone on my scythe lying on the altar before him again.

This time, I felt my spine shattering. My head spun, and I struggled to keep my eyes from rolling to the back of my head as another round of needles stabbed through me, piercing flesh and organs. Through blurred vision, I saw a flurry of red streaks flashing by. Only once I heard Meri scream did I realize that the red streaks had been blood darts launched by my woman. Dark spots of necrosis spread around the entry points of each dart that had found its mark on Meri. She clawed at herself while stumbling back.

Without her magic feeding it, the beast faltered, freeing me. I drained as much of the creature's life force as I could to regenerate before it turned into shadows. But just as Cornelius was going to wreck me again by bashing my scythe, another flurry of blood darts forced him to cast a protective spell to parry my mate's attack. It was the tiny opening I needed. Fighting through the pain, I threw my ghostly scythe at the necromancer. He barely managed to dodge and once more tried to smash my weapon only to be thwarted but another volley of darts.

I charged forward even as my ghostly scythe was returning to me. With a flick of my wrist, I redirected it towards Alva while casting my death aura to wither any new tentacles or needles Piers might want to shoot at me. But my ghostly scythe sliced through Alva from the back, cutting her in half. Her torso fell to the ground before her lower body did, her face frozen in a shocked expression.

Piers screeched as the last of his handlers perished and turned back into his solid form. Without hesitation, my Kali cast a far more potent blood necrosis on him than I thought her capable of. The beast began to rot from the inside out at a terrifying rate. Under different circumstances, I would have wanted to admire the macabre spectacle. But I had more important matters to handle.

The panicked and terrified expression on Cornelius's face as he watched me flying at dizzying speed towards him was literally orgasmic. He attempted to cast an offensive spell against me, but my death strike shattered his blood shield and made him stumble back.

Behind me, I could hear my mate running towards us. As I closed the distance with my nemesis, I felt a wave of magic fly past me and strike the blood on the altar surrounding my weapon. It instantly levitated and flew towards me. I said a quiet thank you to my mate as I caught it mid-air and swung it so that the blade would cut Cornelius in half from the top of his head down to his chest.

Half a second before my true scythe would connect with his skull, a glowing sword appeared in front of me, blocking might blow. Then a powerful blast of magic sent me flying a few meters back. Shock and anger surged through me at this deception.

I prepared to retaliate against that treacherous foe but froze in place when I realized who had intervened.

"Father!" I breathed out.

CHAPTER 16
KALI

The victorious shout vibrating in my chest died in my throat when a shining blade just appeared out of thin air, preventing Pharos from slaying the thrice damned son of a bitch who had made our lives a living hell. Before I could fully comprehend what had caused it, I immediately began casting an offensive spell to blast the intruder, only to freeze in complete and utter shock.

My jaw dropped as the Weaver, the divine Angel of Death Azrael himself, and the High Hell Lord Alderan appeared around the altar. Standing quite a few meters behind his father, near the edge of what remained of the circle, Haroth was staring at Cornelius with a savage grin that should have terrified me. My brain briefly registered that—this time—Haroth actually had proper flesh under his skin instead of his previous skeletal appearance. By rights, I shouldn't have been able to guess the identity of the stunning male he was now embodying with a complexion the color of desert sand. But at a visceral level, I recognized him… felt him in my bones.

However, the scene unraveling before me reclaimed my attention.

"Father!" Pharos whispered in disbelief.

But his sire didn't respond.

Saying he was stunning couldn't begin to do him justice. He towered over his son by at least a good head, and his wings looked almost too massive for him to carry. And yet they hung gracefully and effortlessly, partially open behind him. They were pristine white, the same color as the skirt hanging from the golden belt around his waist. Like Pharos, he wore pauldrons, bracers, and an adorned belt, but his were of the shiniest gold encrusted with precious gems. A white hood, the same luxurious fabric as his skirt partially hid his face. Despite the shadow it cast, the white glow of his eyes illuminated his features enough for me to see the noble nose, full lips, and square jaw of my man's sire. A few strands of black hair peeked around the edges of his hood.

At the same time he blocked Pharos's scythe with his sword, Azrael flicked his right wrist, sending Cornelius flying back. The necromancer slammed his back hard against the wall located a couple of meters behind him. The air rushed out of him from the impact. He would have face-planted as gravity worked its magic. But Alderan closed his fist before him, turning it as if in a gesture to turn a key. Cornelius shrieked as the bones in his joints snapped open like grappling hooks, nailing him to the wall, arms and legs spread like the Vitruvian man.

I watched in complete shock as the Bone Demon Lord Alderan tore off four of the bone spikes protruding from his own forearms and threw them like daggers at Cornelius. Each one found its mark, perfectly embedding themselves one in each of his shoulders and the other two in the fleshy part of his thighs, providing further support so that he wouldn't slide down the wall.

I swallowed hard, my eyes flicking towards the Weaver. Nine hells, she was terrifying. Not in a monstrous way, but because of the sheer power and rage exuding from her. When I first met her,

I had thought how ageless she looked, although clearly an older female, despite her mostly smooth and flawless skin.

Right now, her age was even more undefinable. At a first glance, she looked barely twenty-five. Her slightly tanned skin seemed surrounded by a soft glow, as did her insanely long silver white hair. In her witch hut, her hair somewhat gave the impression it was that color due to the graying that came with age. Here, it was clearly just the pristine ivory of her unusual color and flowing loosely behind her, freed of the previous single braid it had been plaited into. Her normally purple eyes seemed filled with lightning as she all but bared her teeth at him. Gone was the long, medieval-looking golden dress with a thick fur collar she had worn in her cabin. Right now, she reminded me of the Goddess Athena in her dark leather short Roman skirt and leather breastplate.

"You… you can't!" Cornelius cried out, his voice strained by the excruciating pain of being crucified against the wall. "The… the covenant—"

His words were abruptly cut short when Azrael made a grabbing gesture. My blood turned to ice as he quite literally tore Cornelius's soul right out of his body. It looked like a luminous silhouette of the necromancer. To my shock, it withered, its light fading into dark smoke, and his soul appearing deflated and shriveled. It only took seconds, filled with the disembodied screams of Cornelius. With the same nonchalance, Azrael tossed the necromancer's 'soul' back into his impaled corporal vessel.

Although Cornelius took a ragged breath as soon as he reintegrated his body, I could feel that there was no true life left in him. I couldn't even describe what he had become. He was dead and yet not.

His eyes remaining locked on the necromancer with a mix of hatred and something else I couldn't define, Pharos approached me. He blindly reached for my hand and drew me against him in a protective fashion.

"You can't do this!" Cornelius shouted. "You cannot inter-vene in mortal affairs!"

"We absolutely can, you worm," Cliona hissed, taking a few steps closer to the altar. "My Pharos ended your thread moments ago. Azrael merely ensured you're no longer alive by human rules. Now, *we* get to play. You never should have harmed my children!"

"What?!" Cornelius sputtered, terror mixing with the pain wrecking him.

"You wanted to be immortal?" Azrael asked, his booming voice almost sounding like crackling Thunder. "I have granted you that wish. Nothing and no one can ever end your life… such as it is now. You also wanted endless regeneration. Consider that wish also granted. Trust me, you will regret ever coveting what wasn't yours."

With that, four-inch-long claws protruded out of Azrael's fingertips before he stabbed them into the fool's heart. My hair stood on end from the powerful blast of magic that radiated from the Angel. Cornelius emitted an ear-splitting scream as a red glow began to pulse in his chest.

As soon as Azrael yanked his hand out, Cliona pulled out a few strands of her hair and whipped them towards the necro-mancer. She released them, and they split into five-inch-long needles as they flew like a volley of arrows at her target.

"This is for my Asheron," the Weaver said as the hair stabbed into his skin.

They immediately bent into hook shapes, pulling on the skin stretching it impossibly until it began to tear. But regeneration kicking in sent it into an endless loop.

"And this is for my Pharos," she continued while tossing an additional few strands of hair.

These did not split but embedded themselves inside his body like worms digging their way in. A shudder coursed through me as I could see the strands circling slowly around inside him, piercing organs along the way like a snake looking for a way out. I didn't need to alter my vision or invoke magic to know the regeneration was healing the damage right after it was caused.

This torture could last for eternity, and he would never die from it.

Not that he has any true life left that could be ended to grant him mercy.

Alderan came to stand in front of Cornelius. I had seen bone demons in various illustrations, including some of his. But nothing could have prepared me for how imposing and intimidating one of them would be in the flesh—one of the most powerful at that. Alderan was a Prince of Hell, the son of Astaroth, the Duke of Hell himself.

Well over seven feet tall, broad-shouldered, and with muscles for days, Alderan was a beast of a male. Small bone scales were scattered all over his grayish skin. A few bone spikes—some rounded, others recurved—lined the sides of his arms. A long black skirt made it impossible to get a good glimpse of his legs. Six heavy horns sat on his head like a crown amidst the undisciplined wavy locks of his below-the-shoulder-length black hair. Bone ridges and scales adorned his forehead, and more small, rounded bone spikes lined the sides of his neck, growing high around the curve of his shoulders. I suspected that, in battle, they would extrude into vicious spikes that could inflict grievous damage to anyone attempting to grab him. More spikes covered the length of his exoskeletal spine, which extended into an impressive bone tail with a sharp, dagger-like tip.

My brother Jasper had told me what he'd found out about Asheron's story. A little over three centuries ago, Cornelius had tricked him to harness his power on behalf of a powerful patron. The ritual had failed, turning Asheron into a Wraith instead, cursed to wander the Earth in endless pain and rage, spreading death and misery on his path. A young healer from Willow Grove, harassed by Cornelius, had managed to free Asheron from the madness controlling him, and dealt a major blow to the necromancer.

But never in a million years would I have guessed the Wraith was the offspring of the Weaver with a Prince of Hell.

"And this is for damning my son," Alderan said, his rumbling voice so deep I could have sworn the ground vibrated beneath my feet.

He didn't make a single gesture, and yet I felt the type of powerful Bone Magic I never would have thought possible. In a blink, every single one of Cornelius's bones snapped. With his legs broken, leaving only the demon bones in his shoulders nailing him to the wall as main support, he immediately began to suffocate.

"You were a talented necromancer," Alderan said with contempt in his voice. "You could have achieved greatness and been long lived. But your ambition had no measure. How dare you covet the powers of the gods? How dare you enslave one of our children for your own advancement? Did you really think we would allow it to go on? Well now, you shall reap what you sowed. You only lasted this long because my Cliona wanted her son Pharos freed first. Otherwise, I would have destroyed you centuries ago. You should have refused Isabella's request to help her enslave my son. But fear not, I will give her your regards while she continues to suffer in my playground."

I didn't know how much of his words Cornelius understood. An endless flow of screams and moans of agony tumbled out of him in between unintelligible pleading words, sobs, and strangled gasps for air. I watched the whole scene with morbid fascination as his wounds continuously attempted to heal and his bones to mend only for the damage to be inflicted again in an endless infernal loop.

This truly was hell.

"Five hundred years you have enslaved my Pharos, and you cursed my Asheron to three-hundred and fifty years of madness on top of robbing him of his angelic purity. For those offenses, you shall remain like this for the next eight hundred and fifty years. Only then will Death decide whether to grant you mercy," the Weaver said with malicious glee. "But if I have any say in the matter, you shall receive the same mercy you would have shown my sons and the Ferryman, had you gotten your way."

"P-plea-please," Cornelius sputtered between two screams.

Alderan uttered an incantation that had my skin erupting in goosebumps. A series of glowing runes appeared, forming a half-circle on the ground around Cornelius's feet, and another half-circle on the wall surrounding him. It was the type of ward that only a fool would try to break or lift. Anyone in their right mind would stay away from this accursed place.

Then, as one, the three powerful beings turned towards Pharos. My back immediately tensed. It made no sense as he had won his battle, and they were clearly here exacting revenge on his behalf. And yet, I felt tiny and insanely vulnerable in the presence of these god-like beings.

"My son," Azrael said as he placed both hands on Pharos's shoulders. "It pleases me to no end that you prevailed this day. Forgive me for stealing your righteous kill, but I couldn't allow him to enjoy the quick escape of death. He has caused too much wrong and must answer for it."

"I cannot begrudge you this outcome, Father. It couldn't be more fitting for all the crimes he has committed using me."

Azrael smiled, a world of affection illuminating his handsome features as he gazed lovingly at his son. I moved aside when he drew him into his arms. Pharos initially resisted my attempt to move away but caved in to return his embrace. It was mind boggling to see my man looking so small in comparison to his giant father, which only made me feel even tinier. My chest constricted with happy emotions when Pharos flattened his wings against his back allowing his father to wrap his own massive alabaster wings around him. A white halo glowed brightly around them, screaming of the divine nature.

After a moment, Azrael released his son and pressed his lips to his forehead before turning to look at me. I instantly straightened, back stiff, and eyes wide. I had not prepared for this. How was one supposed to react to one of the highest-ranking Angels?

"Thank you, Daughter, for freeing my Pharos," he said gently.

My toes curled, and my chest warmed as goosebumps erupted all over my body. Despite his beauty and mesmerizing voice, there was nothing sexual in my reaction to him. But the depth of kindness and holy love from him made me feel like the light of God himself was shining over me.

"You truly have a beautiful soul, as strong and kind as your heart. A fitting mate for my son. I can see that he has already enhanced you. But as his bride, and now my Daughter, you need more. I will not have you depend on his presence to keep you safe. Will you accept my gift?"

I gaped at him, stunned and robbed of words. Pharos slipping a protective arm around my waist snapped me out of my befuddled daze. I glanced at him to find him staring at his father with endless gratitude. Likely feeling my gaze on him, my man turned his eyes towards me. Reading the unspoken question on my face, he nodded with an encouraging smile.

I returned my attention to his father and gave him a timid nod. He smiled, a glimmer of amusement in his eyes before he raised his palm to my chest. My breath caught in my throat when he placed it against my solar plexus. An intense—but comfortable—heat emanated from his hand. It seeped deep inside me. To my pleasant surprise, he didn't use his claws to sink them into me as he had done with the necromancer. Instead, his palm seemed illuminated from the inside, the intensity of the luminosity growing steadily as the same wondrous warmth spread through every cell of my body. I almost felt as if I was levitating.

My skin tingled, the heat gradually dampening as he pulled his hand away from me.

I almost grabbed it to press it to my chest again, feeling oddly bereft.

"From this day forth, Kali, disease, poison, or any physical wounds shall never have hold over you," Azrael said gently.

I pressed my palm to my chest, realizing he had effectively made me immortal. While Pharos's gift of regeneration had previously allowed me to actively heal my wounds or expel poison, his father had made it so my body would passively manage it all on my behalf. With my soul in my man's safekeeping, nothing would ever succeed in killing me.

"Thank you," I whispered, my throat constricted by emotion.

He smiled, softly caressed my cheek then took a couple of steps back. Pharos gave his father a grateful smile. He appeared intent on saying something, but Alderan approaching us silenced him.

In the back, Cornelius continued to scream and moan. However, it suddenly seeped into my mind how dimmed the sound was, almost like background noise. I suspected one of them had used their incredible powers to quiet him down. But the Demon Prince stopping right in front of me chased all thought of the necromancer out of my mind.

I had to tilt my head all the way back to be able to look at that beast of a male standing in front of me. Where Azrael had made me feel like I was wrapped in a thick blanket of endless love and protection, Alderan felt like a stirring volcano ready to erupt. But instead of lava, it was lightning, and an overload of energy that seemed ready to burst out of him at any moment. Oddly, it didn't frighten me. It made me restless and whipped my blood into a type of pre-battle frenzy.

It felt both dangerous and exciting.

"Little Kali," Alderan said in a purring voice that would have had me running for the hills under different circumstances.

He sounded like a predator about to make mincemeat out of some prey who had foolishly ventured into his domain. Even as he spoke, the rounded bone spikes at the tip of each shoulder extruded into sharp shards. He snapped them off and held them like a pair of daggers. My breath caught in my throat as I remembered how he had used similar bone shards from his forearms to crucify Cornelius against the wall.

"You are not my daughter. But thanks to you, I have finally been able to avenge my Asheron. For this, I would grant you a boon. Will you accept it?"

I swallowed hard and glanced once more at Pharos. To my dismay, he didn't seem to notice as he was too busy staring with great intensity at the Bone Demon Lord. My eyes flicked towards the Weaver. She didn't speak a word, but the 'What the fuck are you waiting for?' look she gave me followed by an almost imperceptible 'go ahead' gesture with her head whipped me into responding.

"Yes, my Lord. I would be honored for your boon, though none is required," I said in a submissive tone.

Pharos's hold around my waist tightened in a reassuring fashion. I took a sharp breath when Alderan pressed the sharp tips of his bone shards right in the soft tissue behind the clavicle but in front of my trapezius muscles. The initial sting should have been followed by an intense stabbing pain. But the regeneration warmth I'd experienced since bonding with Pharos grew a thousandfold.

As suspected, Azrael's gift kicked in on its own, without requiring me to push the regeneration spark into the wounded area. The puncture locations tingled, and a cool sensation surrounded the area. It didn't stop me from feeling the bone shards sinking into my flesh, but it numbed what should have been debilitating discomfort. Pharos moved to stand behind me and wrapped both arms around my midsection. I closed my hands around his wrists, clinging to them as tension continued to rage within me, and pressed my back against his broad chest for further support.

I wished Alderan had told me what the 'gift' was prior to me accepting it. But when dealing with Gods, demigods, and Ancients, several unspoken rules needed to be followed. Here, these gifts were both a reward and a test. Did I trust them enough to take an engagement without having a clear contract and understanding first?

In the arcane world, you never entered into an agreement without a clear pledge from both sides. This was one of the rare exceptions. Under different circumstances, I would have told him to keep his gift rather than risk potential foul play. But this was Pharos's family, his parents, and the father of his half-brother.

I gasped when something suddenly shifted inside of me. My bones began to morph. Panic almost took over me as horrible images of skeletal abominations began to flash before my mind's eye. Had he cursed me or…

"Peace, my mate. All his well," Pharos whispered in my ear, his arms tightening around me as if to keep me in place.

He kissed my temple, and I squeezed his wrists more firmly to try and calm myself down a bit. I jerked my head down as my clavicles appeared to push forward. My eyes widened as my skin split open, revealing discreet, softly rounded vertical ridges the length of my clavicles, as if the bone had become ribbed. If not for the fact that they were actual bones, from a distance, one could have mistaken them for scarification tattoos. A similar phenomenon occurred along my radius and ulna—the bones of my forearms. However, my skin didn't split open there. The ridges merely formed an elegant pattern under the skin and the length of both forearms.

And with them came a tremendous amount of power. My jaw dropped, and my eyes widened as my senses expanded, and my fingers vibrated with the urge to cast Bone Magic. I could feel every being who possessed a skeleton, teeth, horns, or claws on a wide radius. Even without invoking my new powers, I knew beyond a doubt that I could effortlessly shift, break, or manipulate their bones like never before.

Alderan's face split into a smug grin, giving me a glimpse of his sharp pair of double fangs.

"Enjoy your new powers, young Kali. You will find them quite entertaining. Should you have questions about them, have your mate bring you to me. I will gladly assist."

"Thank you, my Lord," I said, my voice betraying my awe and how intimidated I felt.

"Alderan," he corrected firmly.

"Alderan," I repeated, docile, my cheeks heating for no reason.

He chuckled with that same smugness laced with a taunting edge then turned his gaze towards my mate.

"Pharos," he said as a farewell before glancing at Azrael. "Death."

To my surprise, Azrael gave him a nod in response then slightly lifted his chin with a hint of defiance. The taunting smirk —subtle though it was—that stretched the Demon Lord's lips screamed of a barely veiled rivalry. As if to confirm those suspicions, Alderan turned towards the Weaver. The way he strutted back to her, shifting his wings in a way that made him look bigger without flat out spreading them, and waving his tail in a slow and hypnotic fashion perfectly matched the way a wild beast would present for the prime female he coveted.

Although her expression remained mostly unreadable, I didn't miss the discreet way the vertical slits of her pupils widened briefly as she gave him a quick once over before they narrowed again.

The Weaver didn't hate what she was seeing.

I could see why. Everything about him screamed danger, and yet had an undeniable appeal. Many a woman would want to be caught by such a beast, knowing he could destroy her with a mere thought and tear her to shreds with his vicious claws and phenomenal strength. But also knowing he would treat her—*just her*—with the perfect mix of tenderness and savagery.

"You must let me visit you again soon, my Cliona. It's been too long," he said in a purring tone as he came to a stop in front of the Weaver. "Surely, you must miss me as much as I miss you."

Technically, he was much too close, invading her personal space. She held his gaze unwaveringly, merely lifting an eyebrow in a way that hinted his request was absurd.

"Miss you?" she echoed with disbelief. "Have you forgotten how insufferable and obnoxious you are?"

"It is part of my charm," he replied in that same purring tone while edging even closer to her. "You've always loved a bad boy. And you're long overdue for giving me a daughter."

She snorted and shook her head, looking almost flabber-gasted. Although clearly not intending to give in to any of his requests, the Weaver didn't back away or push him. She merely lifted her chin with an even greater air of defiance.

"First off, you never have daughters, only sons. Second, it will be at least another thousand years before I would even start missing your arrogant and overly entitled self."

Pharos shifted behind me. I bit the insides of my cheeks, imagining how uncomfortable it had to be to see a male openly coming on to his mother, and in front of his father no less.

"You wound me, my beloved," the Demon Lord said, sounding totally unfazed. "But very well. A thousand years it is. You are well worth the wait. But should you change your mind prior, you know where to find me."

Eyes locked with hers, Alderan grabbed a handful of her long, silver-white hair and let it glide through his fingers in a gentle caress. The sexual tension between them was almost palpable. Although she kept a neutral expression, he gave her that obnoxious smirk again before letting go of her hair. He took a step back, and the air around him blurred seconds before he vanished.

The Weaver lowered her eyes and pursed her lips. In that instant, my gut screamed at me that his smugness had been warranted. She had been tempted by his offer. I cast a sideways glance at Azrael to see how he was responding to seeing the mother of one of his children being openly flirted with by a more recent partner. His face was unreadable although it softened as Cliona approached us.

She came directly to me, an approving smile stretching her lips. "I searched a long time for you, Kali Jennings. And you did not disappoint. I leave my son in your care. Together, you will accomplish remarkable things. Do not underestimate the tremendous gifts that were bestowed upon you. Use them wisely but without fear. You have a beautiful soul. Such powers would not have been given were you likely to abuse them."

"Thank you for finding me and luring me here, to my soulmate," I said, my throat constricted by emotion.

I glanced at Pharos over my shoulder, who was still holding me from behind. He smiled tenderly and kissed my temple.

"Thank you for heeding the call, Daughter," Cliona simply replied.

She caressed my cheek, smiled at her son, then turned to face Azrael. I barely managed to repress my shock at the way she looked at him, mirrored on his own face. A deep affection—maybe even love—bound those two. And yet, I didn't perceive the same wild and barely repressed lust between them that had shone bright with Alderan.

"You said you would save our son, and against all odds, you did," Azrael said tenderly.

"No one harms my children in all impunity," she replied, her face hardening and hatred sparkling in her eyes as she turned her face towards Cornelius.

The necromancer was still writhing and screaming in agony as his bones went into an endless cycle of breaking and mending, while Cliona's hair hooks continued to stretch his skin until it tore and the longer strands wormed their way through the insides of his body, wrecking him from within.

"No, my darling," Azrael said in a gentle but softly chastising tone. "Cast the hatred out of your heart. He has received his punishment for his crimes and will serve his sentence. Do not waste your thoughts on him."

"Five hundred years, Azrael! He tortured him for five hundred years!" she exclaimed, outraged.

They said Hell hath no fury like a woman scorned. But in this instant, it became clear to me that a mother's wrath was an even more lethal threat.

"And he will serve an equal time for both your sons consecutively. Your Asheron is safe and happy, and you reunited our son with his soulmate. Do not let this foul necromancer tarnish your light. He's not worthy of any more of your attention, and your other children need you."

Her anger seemed to instantly melt, as she slowly nodded. She gave him a sheepish smile and raised her palm to settle it on his right cheek. He leaned into her touch, his halo bathing both of them in a soft glow. Like I had done earlier in the forest with Pharos, Azrael turned his face to kiss the inside of the Weaver's palm before straightening. Her smile broadened with that same air of deep affection. Yes, these two loved each other, but were not *in love*.

A pity…

"Until we meet again," she whispered.

"Until we meet again," he echoed.

She turned around, walked to the altar and picked up the manticore bones and heart. And then, just like that, she vanished. No air blurring around her, no portal… She was just gone.

To my surprise, Azrael looked at something in the distance

before making a subtle head gesture. I turned to the right to see what had caught his attention. My stomach did a somersault, and my chest constricted with emotion as I watched Haroth and a hooded figure I didn't know framing my brother. As I had not perceived his presence in the mansion when I first surveyed it through the eyes of the magpie, I assumed Cornelius had left Jasper back in Willow Grove. I couldn't tell whether some of the wards had kept me from detecting him, or if the Grim Reaper had gone to fetch him. Either way, I was elated.

"Jasper!" I called out.

Without thinking, I broke free of Pharos's embrace and ran to my brother. I all but collided with him, squeezing him in a bone crushing hug. To my shock, his body was no longer half decayed. Even though his soul was but a shadow of its former self, his corporal vessel had clearly benefited from magical regeneration. Even as I tightened my hold around him, I cast a grateful glance at Haroth. Tears of gratitude, relief, and sorrow that I could not have rescued my brother sooner blurred my vision.

This healing wouldn't allow Jasper to resume his former life here in the mortal plane. He was already a walking dead, his soul bound here through a curse. But it was a gift to me, to allow me to see him in his past glory in that final farewell. However, the absence of a heartbeat in his chest reminded me of our stark reality.

A choked sob rose in my throat, and tears freely fell down my cheeks when my brother hesitantly closed his arms around me. I had not expected any response from him, thinking him too far gone for that.

"Kali," he said, his voice uncertain, and his pronunciation slurred as if he'd forgotten how to speak after years of disuse.

"It's over, Jasper. You're free. I'm sorry it took so long," I said in a shaky voice, my cheek still pressed against his chest before I lifted my head to gaze upon his handsome face.

His eyes were glazed over. He stared at me with a slight frown as if struggling to recognize me. And yet, deep down, he knew me or at least understood who I was.

"Can we go home now?" he asked.

I swallowed back another sob and forced myself to smile while blinking away the tears still welling in my eyes.

"You are going to a different place, Jasper. It's going to be a nice and peaceful place where you can rest and find yourself. No one will ever hurt you again."

"Peace and rest," he repeated, his eyes going out of focus for a few seconds before locking with mine again. "That sounds nice. Are you coming with me?"

"That place is not meant for her," the hooded male to his right said in a firm but gentle tone. "But as she helped protect me against the necromancer's plans, I will bring her to see you whenever she wishes."

My breath hitched as I finally realized he was Charon, the Ferryman of the dead who Cornelius had sought to enslave as well.

"Thank you," I whispered, floored that this would even be a possibility.

"It is I who thanks you," Charon replied.

Although I couldn't see his features from the deep shadows cast by his hood, I could sense and hear the smile in his voice.

"But we must depart. Please say your farewells," the Ferryman said. "When you wish to visit, your mate will bring you to me."

I nodded and gave my brother one final bone crushing hug and gently kissed his cheek. "Be happy, Jas. I'll come see you soon."

"Okay," he said, his voice almost devoid of emotion. "See you soon."

With much reluctance, I released my brother and stepped back. To my surprise, it was Azrael who stepped forward. He gently reached towards Jasper's neck. His hand lost its opacity as it sank into him before gently pulling back out. With it, the ghostly silhouette of my brother's soul was plucked out. My chest constricted at how flimsy and translucid it looked, confirming it had been decaying for a long time. Without missing a beat, Haroth caught my brother's now soulless body. It unraveled, not into ashes like someone getting drained out of their lifeforce, but into a shadowy smoke that evaporated into thin air.

"Do not be saddened, Daughter," Azrael said in a comforting voice. "Jasper's soul is damaged, but in time, it will be mended. And you now have all the time in the world. One day, he will be whole again."

"Thank you," I said, feeling like an emotional wreck as I leaned against Pharos for support.

He smiled and wiped the wetness from my cheek with the back of two fingers. That simple touch had his divine light seeping through me. A wave of peace washed over me. I watched in silence as Charon placed this hand on my brother's upper arm. Azrael then released Jasper's nape. Seconds later, the Ferryman and my brother's soul vanished.

Although my chest was constricted, a sense of peace dominated. This wasn't farewell, but merely a temporary goodbye. Azrael smiled at Pharos and me in turn then gave his other son a gentle squeeze on the shoulder. With one powerful flap of his wings, he took flight before vanishing in a blast of light.

"Well done, Sister," Haroth said with an approving smile. "You made the right choice. I look forward to seeing the both of you often in the future."

"It was indeed the right choice. Thanks for helping me see reason," I said.

"Thanks for being open to reason," he replied with that taunting edge I was growing familiar with where he was concerned. "Go home and rest, brother. Your time off has come to an end. Your roster is already filling up with *almathars* to escort. Welcome back."

Pharos snorted and released me before pulling Haroth into his embrace. The Grim Reaper seemed stunned at first. It struck me then that this was either an unusual display of affection from my man or that Haroth himself wasn't much of the physical type.

My gut said it was the latter.

Still, he relaxed and hugged his brother back. After they released each other, Haroth opened a portal and teleported out.

"Let's go home, my mate. We have much to celebrate," Pharos said.

"Yes, let's go home," I said, my heart filling with joy.

He drew me against him. As the air blurred around us, I cast one last glance at the necromancer, trapped in the eternal hell he had brought upon himself. A part of me thought that I should feel a sliver of pity for him. But the memory of all those he had wronged, abused, tortured, and destroyed wiped out any such lingering thought from my mind.

As the world vanished around us, I smiled.

EPILOGUE
PHAROS

I teleported us outside my… *our* home. As soon as we appeared, I felt Myress's presence nearby. Even as I flew towards the balcony to my bedroom, I saw her poke her head out on the main terrace. Our eyes locked for a brief second. Although she was never one to display strong emotions, I felt her joy mixed with a sliver of smugness upon seeing our safe return. She had called it.

And I couldn't be happier for it.

As was her wont, she made herself scarce again and would redouble her efforts to prepare a celebration feast for us.

But, right this instant, I had a different type of feast in mind.

I landed on the balcony and marched boldly towards the tall doors leading to my room. Using my elemental magic, I flicked the doors open as I carried my mate to my immense bed. A single look at Kali's face sufficed for me to know she clearly understood my intentions…

…and she was fully on board.

The scent of her arousal whipped my blood into a frenzy. I'd gone through too many emotional extremes over the past few days. Now, for the first time in centuries, I was free, truly free, with the love of my life in my arms.

My Kali, my strong, bold, undaunted bride, who had faced impossible odds without faltering out of selfless love for her brother and for me. I would spend the rest of eternity reciprocating that love.

As I closed the distance with the bed, I claimed her lips in a voracious kiss. Kali responded in kind, her lips eagerly parting to welcome my invading tongue. My cock immediately strained against the confines of my trousers. It throbbed and ached with the need to bury itself deep in the searing heat of my woman's sheath.

Without breaking the kiss, I laid her on top of the mattress. Kali tried to draw me against her, but I resisted, my hands frantically working on ridding her of the pants she'd worn today for the mission. I made a mental note to forbid her from wearing such obnoxious garments in the future as it blocked my easy access to what I craved. In my aggravation, I nearly tore them to shreds.

Once her belt and buttons gave way, I forced myself to end the kiss in order to tug her pants off her. As I did so, my mate kicked her boots off, aiding me in my task of ridding her of the wretched piece of clothing. I didn't show her undergarment the same courtesy and summarily sliced right through it with my claws.

Kali's token protest morphed into a voluptuous moan when I buried my face between her thighs. By the Gods! Her taste on my tongue, her intoxicating musk filling my nose, and the fierce way she fisted my hair sent even more blood rushing into my groin. I almost climbed on top of her to ram myself in.

I wanted—*needed*—to be one with her. Silencing the burning urge twisting my insides, I licked and sucked on her little nub with the voracity of a starving man. My fingers dipped within her slit, quickly setting a fast pace as I impatiently stretched her to receive me. Her essence gushed all over my fingers, testifying to her own fierce arousal.

Her moans and the way her hips gyrated as I feasted on her heralded her imminent climax. As I needed her to fall apart soon before I lost control, I further accelerated the movement of my hand making love to her. Crooking my fingers, I frantically rubbed her sensitive bundle of nerves until she finally cried out, her legs shaking around my face.

Under normal circumstances, I would pursue my ministrations to keep her flying high longer, but my lust for her had me on the verge of losing my mind. I reluctantly pushed away, settling on my knees between her thighs.

Nine hells, she looked stunning!

Hair splayed around the mattress, her eyes darkened by lust, lips swollen by my kiss, she was looking at me, her gorgeous face dissolved in an air of pure bliss. Her leather vest was partially open from her trying to detach it while I had been devouring her. It made the portrait even more sexy to have her lower half completely bare, her legs spread wide and her petals glistening with her essence from the pleasure I'd given her.

I nearly ripped off my belt before tossing it aside. In my urgency, I didn't bother undoing the buttons of my trousers and simply tore them right off then lowered the waist enough to free my throbbing cock. Without delay, I pushed myself inside my Kali's welcoming heat and crushed her lips in a possessive kiss. Despite her body's initial resistance, I thrust forward with increasing force, spurred on by my woman clinging to me and lifting her pelvis to meet me.

A deep growl vibrated through my chest when her inner walls yielded at last. It had only taken a few seconds, but the rabid hunger clawing at me made it seem like an eternity.

I didn't give her time to adjust to me and immediately set a punishing pace. Kali's throaty moans in my ears as she writhed beneath me sent me over the edge. I pounded into her, an inferno raging in my loins as she squeezed my cock from all sides in a greedy caress that drove me insane with lust.

I couldn't get enough of her or get close enough to my woman. I wanted to touch, caress, kiss every inch of her even as I lost myself in her burning core. But the wretched clothes we still wore cheated me out of it. The distant sound of tearing fabric barely registered in my mind. It was only once I felt the searing heat of her feverish skin against mine that I realized I had shredded her top to pieces.

I took her hard and deep, my head spinning from a whirlwind of sensations overwhelming me. For so long I had ached for the true feel of her, of our bodies coming as one, not just the dimmed coupling in my ethereal form. Liquid flames coursed through my veins as she met me thrust for thrust, her nails raking the sensitive areas at the base of my wings, sending electric sparks to each of my nerve endings.

She was mine… all mine… for eternity.

My bride's second climax slammed into her unannounced. She cried out, her back arching, and her nails digging into my flesh in the small of my back. Her inner walls clamped down on my cock, and it was as if lightning struck my spine. A bright light exploded before my eyes, and I roared as I slammed myself deep inside my woman. My seed shot out of me in powerful spurts of liquid ecstasy. Violent spasms shook my body. My skin tingled, and the oddest sensation swelled deep inside me, engulfing my entire being in an ocean of love and adoration.

My mate's soul…

I embraced her, basking in the infinite love she bore me and reciprocating the one I felt for her. We hadn't spoken those words to each other yet, but we didn't need to. Our souls had done it on our behalf. There could be no secret when two beings achieved this perfect level of communion.

Once fully spent, I collapsed on top of her, then swiftly rolled onto my back, drawing her on my chest.

"My Kali, my bride…" I whispered, while brushing aside a lock of damp hair on her forehead. "You are my heart, my everything. I am yours, now and for eternity."

"As I am yours, now and always. I love you, Pharos."

"My love," I whispered, my throat too constricted to speak anymore.

After stripping out of my remaining clothes, we spent the next few hours basking in each other's love, expressing all that we felt for each other with our words, hands, mouths, bodies, and intertwined souls.

~

KALI

Saying that I was enjoying my new powers would be the understatement of the century. The regeneration gift Azrael had given me not only healed me in seconds but made me nearly immune to pain. Although it made me a little reckless, I didn't push my luck as far as my sometimes adventurous side needled me to try. Technically, I would survive a beheading since Pharos owning my soul would keep it from departing, therefore giving my body the time it needed to mend itself.

Still, on that front, I was content with assuming that it would theoretically be the case.

However, it allowed me to take on more challenging mandates than before. I used to make a living by ridding villages and random customers of smaller hauntings and demonic invasions. Now, I could take on far more lethal foes with little risk to myself.

That said, I'd also taken a liking to my new role as a bonesetter. Grievous fractures were quite common both among people and animals. Word of my ability to perfectly stitch back any bone, even help grow back those that had been chopped off or never properly developed during gestation spread far and wide, giving me no small amount of business.

In truth, I didn't really need to work anymore. As my brother's sole surviving relative, I received a considerable compensation from Cornelius's estate getting liquidated after his untimely 'passing.' I didn't quite understand the legalities on how they had pulled off getting official papers drawn up for him and his four apprentices. Although he'd been using Jasper as his zombie driver for the past few years, his official contract still had him labeled as one of four apprentices.

Obviously, when he failed to show up for more than two weeks without communicating with his servants, someone was sent to look for him at Glocker Manor. They found the mangled remains of his apprentices, and the even less decipherable corpse of whatever Piers had turned into. As some of Piers's facial features had been recognizable as he partially shifted back to his old self before he died, they were able to identify him. Since the servants confirmed that Jasper had traveled with the rest of them, they simply assumed his remains had been part of the monstrous fleshy remains they found in the courtyard, which were in fact just part of the tentacles Pharos had chopped off during the battle.

Seeing what remained of Cornelius trapped in that eternal torture had the investigators desperately eager to leave that accursed place. The wards themselves sufficed to keep them from coming too close to the necromancer. Countless powerful sorcerers, mages, and conjurers were asked to study the matter to determine if foul play had been involved. The swiftness with which all of them agreed that it was merely the result of an extremely powerful ritual backfiring told me they either feared to anger whatever being had been strong enough to cast such a spell

—or rather combination of them—or they hated him enough to protect the culprit.

I suspected it was a mix of both.

No one shed a tear over his demise. To the contrary, many heaved a sigh of relief as the debts or whatever other leverage he held over them like a sword of Damocles had been removed with his death. A few people tried to argue that he was in fact still alive since some kind of soul animated the tortured body crucified to the wall. But with multiple Soul Mages and Necromancers adamantly stating that no true life remained in that shadow of Cornelius, the authorities were more than happy to leave well enough alone.

And with that, Glocker Manor became even more of a cursed place feared and avoided by all, just like Hemdell Manor.

But I didn't care. My brother was free and thriving in the plains of Erebus. I was madly in love with a wonderful man who had made me essentially immortal, and I was living my best life.

"My Kali," Pharos said, startling me as I was gazing down at the Nephilim Valley from our main terrace. "I have an *almathar* to release. He is one of those cases to whom I will grant a choice. You were curious about it. Do you wish to bear witness?"

I nodded frantically. He grinned and took me by the hand to lead me to one of the comfortable couches by the sitting area so that I could settle down. As I had given him my soul, I could shadow him whenever he allowed it, my consciousness being a part of him, permitting me to see through his eyes the same way I had done with the magpie.

Once correctly propped in a position that I wouldn't fall from, I let my consciousness flow towards him as he tugged me in. The disembodied sensation was always odd, but I loved finding myself surrounded by the beauty of my man's soul.

The world blurred around us, and seconds later, we were standing inside a hospital room. An older man was moaning in excruciating pain. His emaciated face strained as he clenched his teeth, his hands shaking as he tried in vain to reach for the little cord that would ring the bell to call a nurse for assistance.

"Greetings, Paul," Pharos said in a gentle voice.

The old man's head jerked to the left, and his eyes widened as he recognized who had come to pay him a visit.

"Reaper!" he whispered in a trembling voice.

The sliver of fear that crossed his features was quickly replaced by one of relief mixed with resignation. To my shock, here inside Pharos, I could perceive so many things I normally never would, including seeing the tiny thread of Paul's life surrounded by the shimmering colors of his soul. Judging by their pleasant hue, I could only assume he had been a decent person.

"I am ready," Paul said. "I cannot keep fighting this body that has failed me. Just please tell me that where I'm going will not lead me to even more pain."

I felt Pharos's lips stretch into a smile. "No, my friend. There will be no pain where you are going. You have lived a good life and therefore will have plenty of choices for the afterlife."

"Thank the Gods," the old man said with a quiver in his voice.

"But before we go, you have one final choice to make," Pharos continued. "Your estranged daughter and her son have heard of your circumstances. Whatever disagreement tore you apart, she doesn't want you to leave before you can mend things. She's but twenty minutes away and hurrying here. If you wish to wait for her, we can delay your departure."

The old man's lips quivered as a powerful emotion filled his eyes. Longing, sadness, regrets, and pain fought for dominance within him.

"I want to see her. I was such a fool… such a stubborn and arrogant fool. But I don't think I can last this long. The pain…"

"If you wish to wait, I can take away your pain so that you can enjoy your last moments with your loved ones," Pharos said.

"You… you could really do that?!" Paul exclaimed, hope and disbelief lighting up his wizened features.

Outside, the muffled voices of two nurses reached us. As the door was closed, I suspected we could only hear them due to Pharos's enhanced hearing, but that Paul would be oblivious to them.

"Poor Mr. Lane is talking to himself," one of the nurses said. "The pain is likely making him delirious again. Do you think we can give him another sedative?"

"We have exceeded the dose already," a male voice said.

"He only has a few hours left," the woman argued. "Shouldn't we try to make him as comfortable as possible in these last few moments? He has no chance of recovering."

"Very well. One more dose won't make much of a difference anyway," the man conceded.

"Yes, Paul. I can really do that," Pharos replied. "The pain will go away for up to twenty-four hours. When you are ready to go, simply wish for me to return, and I will come back immediately to escort you."

"And if the twenty-four hours go by?" Paul asked.

"Then I will come in the following two hours," Pharos replied.

"So I have a maximum of twenty-six hours left," the older man said with sudden understanding.

Pharos nodded.

"Please take away my pain," Paul said. "I would hug my daughter one last time."

Pharos flicked his right hand, and his bone scythe appeared in it, not the ghostly one he previously had. It looked terrifying with its vicious blades at each end. Even the old man seemed intimidated by it. Understanding the fear coursing through him, Pharos extended his open palm towards him. Paul glanced at it, swallowed hard, then placed his wrinkled, bony hand in his with much effort. But as soon as Pharos closed his fingers around it, a sense of peace descended over the old man.

"All will be well," Pharos said gently before carefully approaching the sharp tip of his blade near his nape.

Although still a little tense, Paul remained still. Through Pharos's eyes, I could see the glowing outline of his soul trapped inside his dying body, and a slim silver thread binding it to his spine. With surgical precision, my mate severed the thread with a careful flick of his blade.

The effect was immediate. The man's jaw dropped, his eyes flicking from side to side as if in search of something…

His pain.

"It's gone! It's all gone!" he said, tears welling in his eyes. "Thank you! By the Gods, thank you!"

A knock on the door startled me.

"Mr. Lane?" the female nurse called out before entering. "Would you like another dose of painkiller?"

She held a syringe in one hand and a small flask in the other. She showed him the latter with an air of deep sympathy and commiseration. I instantly liked her.

"No, my dear. That won't be necessary," Paul said with a surprisingly steady voice. "I have guests coming. Would you help me make myself a bit more presentable?"

The nurse gaped at him in complete shock. Then a sliver of pity quickly hidden crossed her clear brown eyes. She likely assumed him to be once more delirious or delusional. To my relief, she smiled and nodded. My heart further warmed for the young woman. So many would have dismissed him and walked away. But she was a true nurturer. She went to fetch a washcloth to freshen his face and brushed the sparse strands of hair still clinging to his mostly bald head. She even helped him put on a nice robe.

Just as she was settling him back in his bed, another knock on the door startled her. She stared in shock as a young lady, barely a few years older than she was, walked inside the room with a young boy, maybe six years of age.

"Dad," the young woman said, her eyes misting.

"My baby," Paul said, his lips quivering.

The room faded around us. A falling sensation swept through me. I blinked and found myself back inside my body, sitting on the couch on the patio door. Pharos was crouching in front of me, his dark wings folded behind him like a long cape.

I cupped his beautiful face with both hands, my heart filling with love for him. I finally fully understood why Cornelius had targeted him, an Angel of Death. He used and abused his natural compassion and empathy to achieve his nefarious plans.

"Thank you for giving them this final peace. Thank you for not allowing that wretched Cornelius to dim your light and the kindness of your heart. I love you."

"*You*, my Kali, are the light of my heart. Thank you for freeing me, for bringing back joy and purpose to my life. I love you, my bride."

THE END.

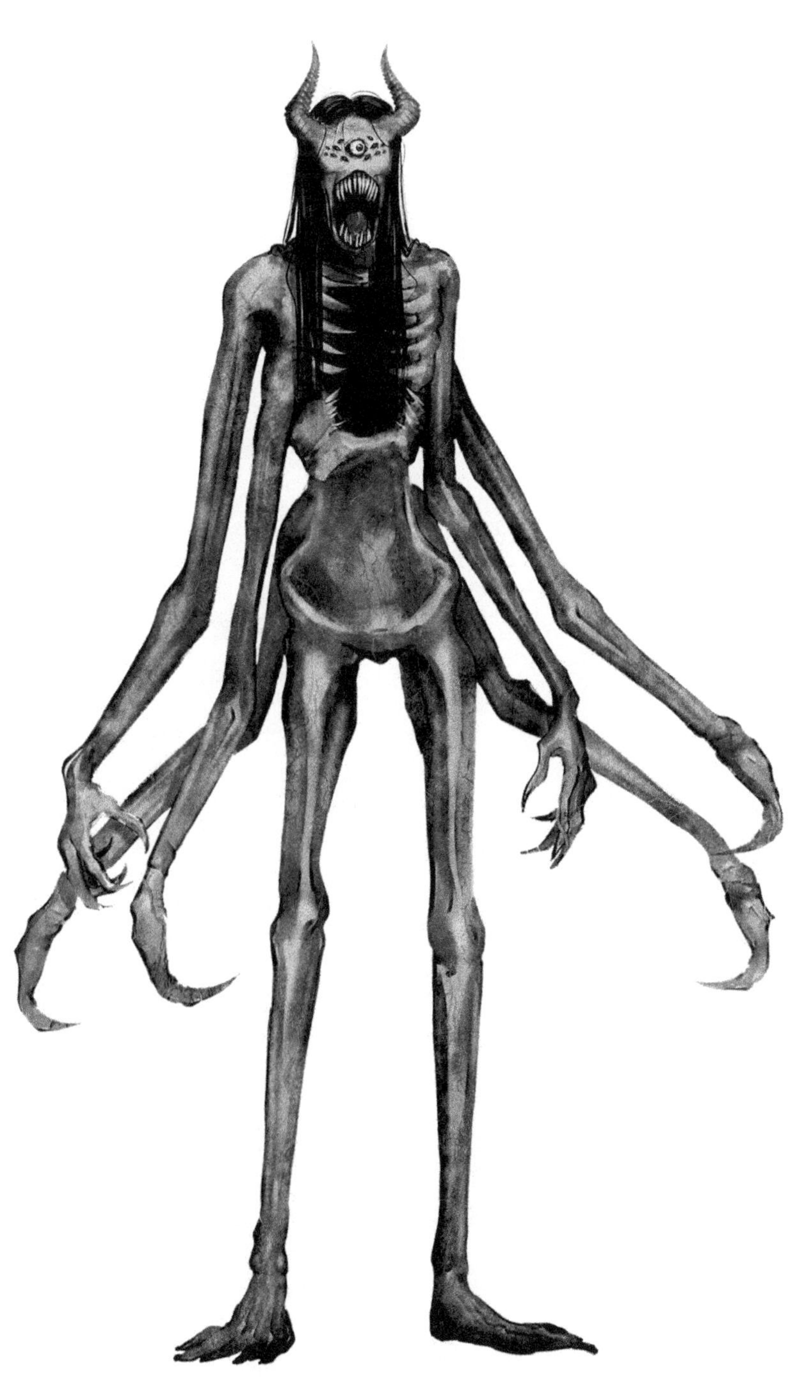

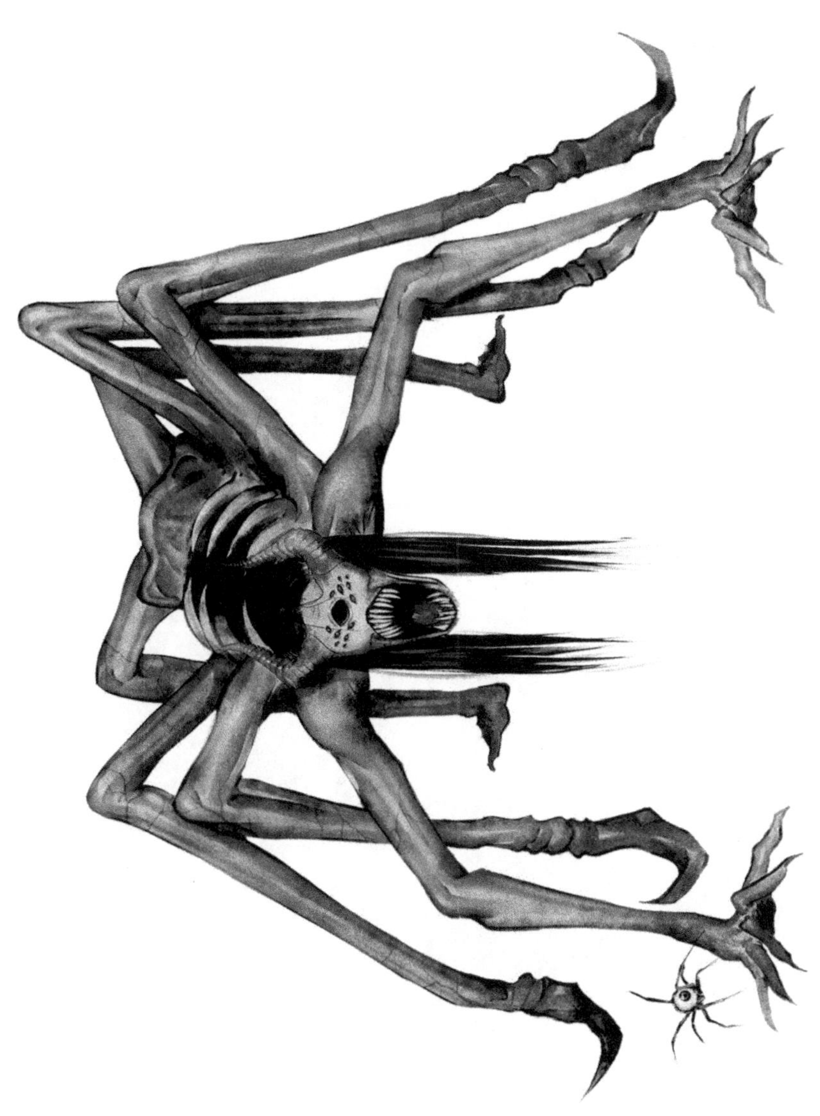

THE VEREDIAN CHRONICLES
Escaping Fate
Blind Fate
Raising Amalia
Twist of Fate
Hands of Fate
Defying Fate
Imperial Fate

BRAXIANS
Anton's Grace
Ravik's Mercy
Krygor's Hope
Keran's Dawn

XIAN WARRIORS
Doom
Legion
Raven
Bane
Chaos
Varnog
Reaper
Wrath
Xenon
Nevrik
Rogue

PRIME MATING AGENCY
I Married A Lizardman

ALSO BY REGINE ABEL

I Married A Naga
I Married A Birdman
I Married A Minotaur
I Married Wonjin
I Married A Merman
I Married A Dragon
I Married A Beast
I Married Krogal
I Married A Dryad
I Married An Incubus
I Married A Mothman
I Married A Catman

THE MIST
The Mistwalker
The Nightmare

DARK TALES
Bluebeard's Curse
The Hunchback

THE SHADOW REALMS
Destined to the Wraith
Destined to the Reaper

BLOOD MAIDENS OF KARTHIA
Claiming Thalia

VALOS OF SONHADRA
Unfrozen
Iced

EMPATHS OF LYRIA
An Alien For Christmas

OTHER

True As Steel
Alien Awakening
Heart of Stone

# ABOUT REGINE

USA Today bestselling author Regine Abel is a fantasy, paranormal and sci-fi junkie. Anything with a bit of magic, a touch of the unusual, and a lot of romance will have her jumping for joy. She loves creating hot alien warriors and no-nonsense, kick-ass heroines that evolve in fantastic new worlds while embarking on action-packed adventures filled with mystery and the twists you never saw coming.

Before devoting herself as a full-time writer, Regine had surrendered to her other passions: music and video games! After a decade working as a Sound Engineer in movie dubbing and live concerts, Regine became a professional Game Designer and Creative Director, a career that has led her from her home in Canada to the US and various countries in Europe and Asia.

Facebook

https://www.facebook.com/regine.abel.author/

Website

https://regineabel.com

Regine's Rebels Reader Group

https://www.facebook.com/groups/ReginesRebels/

Newsletter

http://smarturl.it/RA_Newsletter

Goodreads

http://smarturl.it/RA_Goodreads

Bookbub

https://www.bookbub.com/profile/regine-abel

Amazon

http://smarturl.it/AuthorAMS